W9-BMY-573

The Witches' Almanac

Spring 2019—Spring 2020

CONTAINING pictorial and explicit delineations of the
magical phases of the Moon together with information about astrological
portents of the year to come and various aspects of occult knowledge
enabling all who read to improve their lives in the old manner.

The Witches' Almanac, Ltd.

Publishers   Providence, Rhode Island
www.TheWitchesAlmanac.com

Address all inquiries and information to
THE WITCHES' ALMANAC, LTD.
P.O. Box 1292
Newport, RI   02840-9998

COPYRIGHT 2018 BY THE WITCHES' ALMANAC, LTD.
All rights reserved

10-ISBN: 1-881098-46-x

13-ISBN: 978-1-881098-46-1

E-Book 13-ISBN: 978-1-881098-47-8

ISSN: 1522-3184

First Printing July 2018

Printed in USA

Established 1971 by Elizabeth Pepper

HOW WELL do you know your familiar? Are you acquainted with that fraction of a moment before a cat chooses to strike? Can you see love in your dog's eyes? Have you appreciated a pet expressing compassion toward another? Have you seen a familiar just seem to know when you are not feeling well? When an unfriendly person enters the room, does your familiar suddenly become alert and place themselves at your side or between you and your opposer?

A Witch must always keep in mind that communication with a familiar isn't just a "common" exchange. Communicating with your familiar is not training it to obey commands or to heel at your side. The art of communication with an animal is a skill that many of us would do well to develop. You need to listen as well as articulate. Most pets do a better job of this than their human companions. Many understand a selection of human words, phrases and also body language. How many of your familiar's sounds do you understand? Do you listen as well as they do?

The relationship between a Witch and a familiar is customarily a very special one.

For the last nine years, we have noticed a closer relationship forming between Witches and their familiars. And, these animals are telling us something. They are telling us to "wake up" and to take control of our lives. Our familiars are more to us than just pets and we are more than just people. We have the power to shape our world. Take a lesson from our familiars—learn your surroundings, assess your options, then act in accordance with the natural laws and create the path that you want to walk. Do a good job and your familiar will be right there by your side.

Spring 2019 to Spring 2020

March 20 . . . . Vernal Equinox
April 1 . . . . All Fools' Day
April 30 . . . . Walpurgis Night
May 1 . . . . Beltane
May 8 . . . . White Lotus Day
May 18 . . . . Vesak Day
May 29 . . . . Oak Apple Day
June 5 . . . . Night of the Watchers
June 21 . . . . Summer Solstice
June 24 . . . . Midsummer
July 23 . . . . Ancient Egyptian New Year
July 31 . . . . Lughnassad Eve
August 1 . . . . Lammas
August 13 . . . . Diana's Day
August 16 . . . . Black Cat Appreciation Day
September 2 . . . . Ganesh Festival
September 23 . . . . Autumnal Equinox
October 31 . . . . Samhain Eve
November 1 . . . . Hallowmas
November 16 . . . . Hecate Night
December 16 . . . . Fairy Queen Eve
December 17 . . . . Saturnalia
December 21 . . . . Winter Solstice
January 9 . . . . Feast of Janus
January 25 . . . . Chinese New Year
February 1 . . . . Oimelc Eve
February 2 . . . . Candlemas
February 15 . . . . Lupercalia
March 1 . . . . Matronalia
March 19 . . . . Minerva's Day

Art Director . . . . Gwion Vran

Astrologer . . . . Dikki-Jo Mullen

Climatologist . . . . Tom C. Lang

Cover Art and Design . . . . Kathryn Sky-Peck

Sales . . . . Ellen Lynch

Shipping, Bookkeeping . . . . . D. Lamoureux

ANDREW THEITIC
Executive Editor

JEAN MARIE WALSH
Associate Editor

ANTHONY TETH
Copy Editor

Contents

Contents

土
豬

YEAR OF THE EARTH BOAR
February 5, 2019 – January 24, 2020

CHINESE ASTROLOGY is unique among the world's Zodiac calendars in that it follows a cycle of twelve years. Each year is associated with a different animal. This is the calendar followed throughout the Orient, from China to Japan, Vietnam, Cambodia, Sri Lanka, Korea, etc., and is probably familiar to a larger segment of the Earth's population than any other timetable. It began almost 5000 years ago with Buddha's legendary birthday party. All the animals were invited. The twelve who came were each gifted with a year along with the promise that they would be the animals to hide in the hearts of those born that year. Five elements (Fire, Water, Metal, Earth and Wood) distinguish the years. Every sixty years the cyclical pattern of element-animal pairs repeats.

The Boar or Pig was the last of the twelve animals to arrive at the gathering and to be rewarded by Buddha with a stewardship. Ever since the Boar has feared being late and has no patience with tardiness or those who waste valuable time. It doesn't do to wait until the last minute to complete projects this year. It will be worthwhile to arrive in plenty of time for appointments.

The Chinese New Year begins at the 2nd New Moon following the Winter Solstice. The date changes from year to year, occurring from late January to mid-February.

More information on the Elemental Animal can be found on our website at
http://TheWitchesAlmanac.com/almanac-extras/

Years of the Boar
1935, 1947, 1959, 1971, 1983, 1995, 2007, 2019, 2031

Illustration by Ogmios MacMerlin

Yesterday, Today and Tomorrow

by Timi Chasen

CITY BENEATH THE SAND The temples of Trapani, Sicily are familiar to archaeologists the world over, but more may be hiding beneath the ruined sanctuaries than originally thought. Situated on the island's picturesque West Coast, the Selinunte Archaeological Park, which claims to be the largest archaeological area in Europe, is comprised of nearly 700 acres of classical ruins. But geological researchers using a specially designed six-armed "hexicopter" drone with a thermal imaging attachment have been able to map what they believe to be a small city beneath the packed dirt and rock—far larger than their previous estimations.

Recently made famous among occult communities as the location of the oldest-known evidence of a cult to the mighty Goddess Hekate in the Greek-speaking ancient world, Selinunte now appears to possibly harbor the remains of a miniature Pompeii or Herculaneum beneath its already considerable treasures.

Destroyed by Carthaginians in 409 BCE and uninhabited since the First Punic War, archaeologists have been revealing troves of antiquities from the area, from statues and votive objects to a clever pipe system which fed running water to homes within the city. If the fancy cameras are correct, we can

expect plenty more wonders from this magical spot in the coming years.

CONJURE THIS Carleton University of Canada is looking for a new chair in the Study of the Conjuring Arts. Located in Ottawa, Ontario, the institution of higher learning (whose mascot is the Raven, no less) was recently searching for qualified individuals to fill the position dedicated to all things magical, allowing their scope to be rather broad in the process. Thus, the enviable position is open to any historian, anthropologist or other social scientist with an accredited PhD whose focus falls upon mystical, religious, occult or stage magical practices.

The chair itself was made available by a grant from the Slaight Family Foundation of two million dollars, later matched by the University itself. The foundation was established by philanthropist Allan Slaight, who made his fortune in mass media shortly after working as a travelling stage magician. With the money came a donated library of over 1600 magical books and essays, which will be overseen by the chair when the position is finally filled.

It appears plenty of applicants have been sending in their resumes since the job has been posted, and we here at the Witches' Almanac are willing to bet at least some of them are reading these words right now.

BAG LUNCH Leading researchers have been experimenting with certain types of caterpillars known colloquially as wax worms, believing they may have found a possible aid in the fight against the perpetual dilemma of plastics pollution. Discovered by accident when wax worm specimens for a different research project kept devouring portions of their tempo-

rary plastic bag containment units, scientists found the critters could not only eat but fully digest the polymers without any apparent discomfort.

The worms normally eat beeswax, which is a rather complex compound, described as a "natural plastic" by one researcher, and holds a strikingly similar chemical composition to polyethylene— one of the toughest and most commonly-used plastics. Currently, scientists are attempting to figure out precisely how the little wrigglers break down the substances in question, so they might find a way to safely synthesize the process down the road. Mandibles crossed.

SACRED STONE The Northern English city of Chester still contains an ancient shrine to the Roman Goddess Minerva, in a picturesque park along the river Dee. Built by the ancient workers who labored in a massive quarry that used to surround the venerable fain, the humble yet solid relic has stood carved into a mass of sand-stone for nearly 2000 years, in a green space later dedicated to King Edward the Peaceable.

Minerva was equivalent in many ways to the Greek Goddess Athena, divine matron of warriors, scholars and craftspeople. Though the years have been long and hard, her carved outline is still clearly visible in the rock face, with helmet, spear and owl upon her shoulder. To the right of the image, carved into the same huge stone, is a cave now barred from entry with iron, believed by many to be initially cut by the same laborers who constructed the shrine. It was renamed Edgar's Cave1 after the aforementioned monarch in the 10th century, but it is said some still make pilgrimages there in honor of its sacred genitrix.

REPAIRING MITHRAS Those fancying a more subterranean Roman Britain experience need look no further than the recently reopened Mithraeum in London's Victoria dis-

trict. Axis bombs destroyed sections of the City of Westminster during the Blitz, and an ancient, underground temple to the God Mithras was rediscovered nine years later during postwar reconstruction. After being moved from its original location, it has stood in various stages of disrepair until the property was purchased by the financial giant Bloomberg in 2012. Shortly after the plot was acquired, archaeologists were given the green light to investigate the area for more Roman artifacts which had been missed in the 1954 dig—and missed they were. Nearly three tons of animal bones were found on the property, along with ancient pairs of shoes, bits of clothing, and approximately 63,000 shards of Roman-era pottery. Now, an interactive museum with elegant walkways and dramatic lighting receives about 600 visitors per day.

Though the earliest written record of the God Mithras dates back to a treaty between the Hittites and Mitanni around 1400 BCE, the deity's story became far more complex over the centuries as both Hindu and Zoroastrian sources absorbed his worship into their pantheons. The Romans, themselves claiming to hail from Anatolian lands originally, reintroduced worship of the enigmatic immortal shortly after Pompey's war against a Mediterranean king whose name meant "gift of Mithra"—Mithridates VI of Pontus. By then, the deity had absorbed aspects of various Solar Gods, the hero Perseus, as well as a great deal of Stoic astro-mythology and came to Roman-controlled lands via a secretive, initiates-only mystery cult.

For more on the mysterious Mithras, feel free to check out TheWitchesAlmanac.com/mithras/

www.TheWitchesAlmanac.com

Shop Online

Author Bios

Meet New Contributors

Mat Auryn
Dolores Ashcroft-Nowicki
Breo
Debbie Chapnick
Sorita de Este

Lon Milo DuQuette
David Rankine
Alan Richardson
Oberon Zell

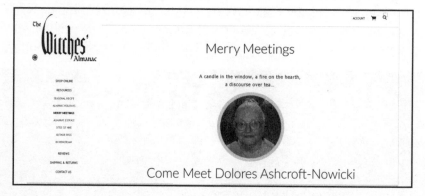

Merry Meetings

A candle in the window, a fire on the hearth,
a discourse over tea...

Come Meet Dolores Ashcroft-Nowicki

Come visit us at the Witches' Almanac website

News from The Witches' Almanac

Glad tidings from the staff

It has been a year since we have launched our overhaul to *The Witches' Almanac* site and cart—TheWitchesAlmanac.com. The response has been overwhelmingly positive. We've been busy uploading content and user experience awareness to each of the sections. We started the process by updating *In Memoriam*, our homage to some past elders who have graced this plane with their presence. It is unfortunate that we added Raymond Buckland to this list of elders—All Hail the Traveler! Also updated is *Merry Meetings*, putting up all the interviews we have conducted with various Witches, magicians and mages. And finally, where other updates are concerned, we have expanded *Almanac Extras!* capturing all of the Extras! going back to 2008. For navigation convenience, break out the three most recent years under their own headings, with the archive capturing the balance of *Extras!* articles.

Of course, there are other areas of *The Witches' Almanac* site worth checking on regularly such as *Author Bios*, *Seasonal Recipe* and *Sites of Awe*. The latter two are updated on a regular basis. If there is something we are not capturing that you think we should, shoot an email to info@TheWitchesAlmanac.com.

The Witches' Almanac is especially privileged to welcome new authors Mat Auryn, Debbie Chapnick, Sorita d'Este, Lon Milo DuQuette, Alan Richardson, David Rankine and Oberon Zell—each contributing incredible articles.

You might not have noticed that we added, as well as changed, several yearly features. John Michael Greer has given us a total rewrite of Moon Gardening. Lending his expertise to geomancy divination, each year John Michael will offer insight into one of the 16 classic signs. Of course, the Tarot and Celtic Tree features will continue to have their places in the Almanac.

The coming year promises to be yet another banner year for us here at The Witches' Almanac. We will be offering grimoires which promise to surprise and elevate the reader. This year will see the debut of The Witches' Almanac Wall Calendar. Our readers have told us time and again how much they enjoy the many insights provided in the Moon Calendar in each issue. We have heeded your advice: The standard Moon phases, channeled actions and an expanded version of the topic featured in the Moon Calendar will be available in a full-size wall calendar.

Finally, we are pleased to announce that The Witches' Almanac is now the exclusive distributor of Atramentous Press publications in America. Atramentous' offerings would be a remarkable addition to anyone's library. You can view Atramentous Press' publications at /TheWitchesAlmanac.com/Atramentous/

The Mari Lwyd

A Welsh Living Tradition of Death

DARK AND COLD. The night is still. You hold your breath as the clock ticks closer toward midnight. A knocking is heard. The heart stops. Death is at your door.

During the darkest part of the year, when spirits of the dead walk across the land of the living. When the living slam shut the doors and bar the window to the biting cold. When it feels like the lords of Winter will never lessen their grip. It is then that Mari Lwyd comes to chase away the darkness.

The snap of her teeth, the ring of her bell, the calls of her retinue herald her coming. She is instantly recognisable—a real horse's skull, teeth intact, glass bottle eyes, shrouded in white sheets, reined, adorned with ribbons, lace, maybe flowers and led by the ostler at the head of a party of revellers processing amongst communities in south Wales.

It is almost midnight. The new year tantalisingly close, yet out of grasp. The party rattle windows. A fear grows.

Midnight. Midnight. Midnight.
  Midnight.
Hark at the hands of the clock.
Now dead men rise in the frost
  of the stars
And fists on the coffins knock.

–Vernon Watkins
Ballad of the Mari Lwyd

As you crack the door ajar slightly and stare into the beer bottle eyes of the Mari you are transported. Carried from this world to hers. Taken into a place between places.

Juxtaposed against the sight of a skeletal horse's head draped in ghostly sheets are the hauntingly beautiful melodies of her carol. The voices and poetry wrap around you and carry you further into her clutches.

It is a striking experience, and one which is growing in popularity once again. Today the Mari Lwyd is a reconstruction, primarily an entertainment in most places, and it is doubtful that many taking part will be aware of its ancient origins.

But this is a ritual of liminality—a conversation between life and death. It is a chasing away of the old and the clearing of the dead ready for the new life of the New year.

First Encounters

One might meet the Mari for the first time in a small Welsh market town. Tucked away in the corner of an old-fashioned pub with roaring fire a commotion starts. Locals and strangers alike run to the windows to watch the Mari proceed down the street toward us. Hardcore old timers are wiser, using this moment of excitement to make it to the bar and order the next round of drinks.

Catching only glimpses of the strange party heading nearer, soon there's a rattling of the door and breaking somewhat with tradition, the party makes its way into the bar where the *Pwnco* begins.

The Pwnco is a sort of verbal contest, a poetic back and forth between the Mari Party and those inside. It can be rowdy, somewhat out of tune, but full of merriment. The Mari may be accompanied by a small troop—the

leader cracking his stick on the tables, a few singers with flat caps or blackened faces and a gent in a top hat. It is difficult to draw one's attention away from the skull. Logically one knows it is a person with a skull on a long stick, but in the midst of even the simplest of rituals, it is death herself—a still point in the midst of the merriment. Led from table to table the eyes pull one in—drawn to the mystical world of Welsh magical traditions.

Music

Once prepared the Mari is led from house to house, pub to pub, around the town seeking entry by means of a riddle and poetic battle. Almost all versions of the Mari maintain the traditional introductory verses, although the specifics of tune and wording may vary. As with all elements of the ritual, these could be made up on the spot, or are sometimes recorded and passed down through generations.

The verses generally announce the coming of the Mari Party, describe their journey and ask for food and refreshment to be prepared.

Once the people in the house have responded, the Pwnco begins. A back and forth, a battle of wits. A few good-humoured insults. If the Mari outsmarts the household then she can enter—so they must put up a good fight. The length of this section can vary enormously depending on the creativity and perseverance of each party.

Below is one example of Pwnco which remains popular across a number of communities. It was collected in a popular book on carolling traditions without its originating location being recorded. It is possible that it might have been introduced to many places in recent years by participants researching this less used element of the ritual rather than indicating a widespread traditional use of this format.

First Round
The Mari Lwyd party sing:

> *Open your doors,*
> *Let us come and play,*
> *It's cold here in the snow.*
> *At Christmastide.*
> The House-holders reply:
> *"Go away you old monkeys*
> *Your breath stinks*
> *And stop blathering.*
> *It's Christmastide."*

Second Round:
Outsiders:

> *Our mare is very pretty (The*
> *   Mari Lwyd),*
> *Let her come and play,*
> *Her hair is full of ribbons*
> *At Christmastide."*
> House-holders (Giving in):
> *Instead of freezing,*
> *We'll lead the Mari,*
> *Inside to amuse us*
> *Tonight is Christmastide."*
>   –Rev. Mark Lawton-Jones

Of course, eventually the Mari will be victorious, not least because of her hundreds of years of experience! Additionally her presence within the house is a blessing upon it and as such the inhabitants want her to enter.

After entering the house a party begins! The carols and songs performed by the company are an eclectic mix, once again different in each local area. In Llantrisant we find examples of carols which have their root in the mid-Wales plygain

tradition such as Ar Gyfer Heddiw'r Bore. Again, this points to an evolving and non-static tradition of the Mari, as well as a mingling of Christian and Pagan beliefs. It is likely these were introduced to the community in the heyday of the mining industry when significant population movements took place into the industrial areas of South Wales.

> *Ar gyfer heddiw'r bore*
> *'n faban bach, faban bach,*
> *Y ganwyd gwreiddyn Iesse*
> *'n faban bach;*
> *Y Cadarn ddaeth o Bosra,*
> *Y Deddfwr gynt ar Seina,*
> *Yr Iawn gaed ar Galfaria*
> *'n faban bach, faban bach,*
> *Yn sugno bron Maria*
> *'n faban bach.*
>
> *Am hyn, bechadur, brysia,*
> *fel yr wyt, fel yr wyt,*
> *I 'mofyn am dy Noddfa,*
> *fel yr wyt*
> *I ti'r agorwyd ffynnon*
> *A ylch dy glwyfau duon*

Fel eira gwyn yn Salmon,
fel yr wyt, fel yr wyt,
Gan hynny, tyrd yn brydlon,
fel yr wyt.

For the sake of this very morning
As a little baby, a little baby
Was born the root of Jesse
As a little baby;
The Strong one who came from Bosra,
The Lawmaker of old on Sinai,
The Redemption to be had on Calvary
As a little baby, a little Baby,
Suckling the breast of Mary,
As a little Baby.

Therefore, sinner, hurry,
As thou art, as thou art,
To ask for his Sanctuary,
As thou art;
For thee the well was opened
Which washes thy black wounds
Like the white snow on Salmon,
As thou art, as thou art,
For that, come promptly,
As thou art.

The eating, drinking and general horse-play (pun intended) are an essential part of the Mari ceremony. It is here that the real work is done—the chasing away of the unwanted spirits. It is a simple matter of raising and focusing energy, both directed and magnified by the bones of the horse. After all, only the dead can chase the dead away.

A Ritual of Liminality

That the Mari Lwyd is a ritual of liminality is clear. Liminal space is the place between two realms of reality and can be physical, psychological or time-bound. The Mari occurs in all three spaces.

- It is physically in a doorway—between inside and out. Between the revellers and the householders.
- It is psychologically between joy and terror—the merriment of the party and the grotesque form of an undead horse. Indeed it is between life and death.
- It is in the liminal time between years. Whilst there is a broad timeframe for Mari to appear all are linked with the New Year in some way, be it the secular, Celtic or even Julian calendar. More broadly it can be seen as a time of seasonal transition.

A clear boundary is created in multiple senses that is plain for all to see. An us and a them. Insiders and outsiders. Those with command over death, and those afraid of its earthly symbolism.

The tension escalates with the challenge and response of the participants. Those familiar with traditional initiatory rites might well consider the Mari Lwyd in light of their own experiences and find some enlightenment as to the ritual purpose of the hooded horse.

In the Mari Lwyd ritual we find complex symbolic interplays which come together in an unusual form of first-footing. Even if the precise meanings of the practices are hidden from sight, just a cursory consideration of horse symbolism can provide insights which transform the Mari Lwyd from a slightly odd Welsh custom to a powerful and transforming ritual.

—BREO

To view the full version of this aricle, as well as others, visit TheWitchesAlmanac. com/almanac-extras/

Marijuana—Da Ma

Cannabis sativa, Cannabis sativa forma indica, Cannabis ruderalis

CANNABIS HAS BEEN used medicinally in Chinese, Egyptian, Indian, African, Japanese, Arabic, Mesopotamian and European medicine for millennia. Cannabis leaf tea has been used for coughs, insomnia, bladder conditions, pain and depression. The leaves have been used to poultice wounds and smoked to ease glaucoma. Not surprisingly, this supremely useful herb has many religious and magical associations.

The ancient Scythians incorporated cannabis into their funerary rites. Writing in about 450 BCE, Herodotus reports that when a king died he was first carried around for forty days in a chariot, accompanied by his relatives. As the chariot made its way among the king's friends, gifts were laid out before the deceased ruler and his family. Then a tipi-like structure was set up so the funeral participants could purify themselves. First the mourners washed their heads and then they entered the tipi structure, placed hemp seeds and flowers on red hot rocks and inhaled the smoke.

During the Hindu Spring festival of Holi, people drink *bhang* which is made with cannabis flowers. According to tradition the *amrita* or elixir of life was created by the *devas* and *asuras* churning the oceans. Shiva created cannabis from his own body to purify the elixir and when a drop of that elixir fell to Earth the cannabis plant was born. Now people drink bhang to unite with Shiva and to have a fortunate reincarnation, but in order for this to happen the drink must be consumed within a respectful religious rite.

The Rastafari consider cannabis a sacrament and equate it with the Tree of Life in the Bible. They say smoking the herb brings them closer to God (Jah) and allows them to see the truth more clearly. It is the vehicle to cosmic consciousness that burns corruption from the human heart.

The Taoist encyclopedic text called *Wushang Biyao* (Supreme Secret Essentials) of 570 CE says cannabis was burned in ritual incense burners and used in hallucinogenic smokes. The Taoist scriptures of the Shangqing School were revealed to Yang Xi by immortals, apparently aided by cannabis. The *Mingyi Bielu* (Supplementary Records of Famous Physicians) states that Taoist magicians consumed the seeds with ginseng to be able to see the future. The sixth century *Wuzangjing* (Five Viscera Classic) says that by eating the flowers one can gain the ability to command demons to appear.

Cannabis was gathered on the seventh day of the seventh month, a day when séance banquets were performed in Taoist societies. The seeds were gathered in the ninth month.

Magu (Hemp Maiden) is a Taoist Goddess of the elixir of life and protector of females. Her name derives from *ma* (cannabis) and *gu* (aunt or maid). The Chinese word *Wu* (shaman) may be a loanword from Iranian *maghu* or *maguš* (magi; magician), meaning an "able specialist in ritual" and may be comparable to Magu.

Magu is called Mago in Korean and Mako in Japanese. She is the creatrix, progenitrix and Great Goddess of creation myths associated with long life, rebirth and good fortune.

Mexican devotees of Santa Muerte (Holy Death) smoke cannabis as a form of purification and use it in incense censers in their church ceremonies. A personification of death, Santa Muerte is also associated with healing, protection, and safe delivery to the afterlife. She is a continuation of the Aztec Goddess of Death Mictecacihuatl or Mictlancihuatl (Nahuatl for "Lady of the Dead"). Mictlantecuhtli and Mictecacihuatl are the Lord and Lady of Mictlan, the realm of those who die of natural causes. In order for the deceased to be accepted into Mictlan, offerings to the Lord and Lady of death are necessary.

Cannabis was carried into Africa by Arab traders. The Bashilenge, an African tribe, have a cannabis-centered religion known as the Riamba Cult. They call themselves *Bena-Riamba*, which means "the sons of hemp." For them cannabis is a deity and the pipe in which it is smoked a peace symbol. They believe cannabis smoke has universal magical powers and can ward off evil spirits.

Sufis, mystical devotees of Islam, enjoy the use of cannabis in the form of hashish. According to Arab legend the Persian founder of one school of Sufism, the Haydar, was a very reserved and silent man. One day he came back from wandering the mountains and was strangely animated and talkative. His disciples asked him why he was so happy and then they went into the mountains to try the herb for themselves. Now the Persian Sufis enjoy the pleasures of hashish.

—ELLEN EVERT HOPMAN

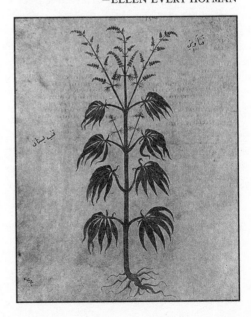

THE DEITIES OF ANIMALS

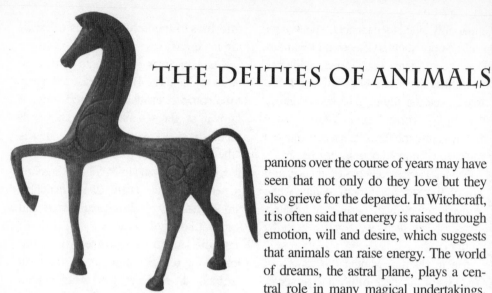

THE MAJORITY OF PEOPLE that identify themselves as Witches or Pagans, as well as many other magickal people, believe that animals have souls, spirits. Indeed, it is common to believe that everything from the soil to the trees to the stars are imbued with spiritual essence. It is also common in these communities to remember that humanity is not the center of the universe, that we are part of a web of inter-related life. To give more than lip service to these ideas, it is necessary to imagine more fully the universe from the perspective of other beings. Among other things, this means imagining that the animals have their own Goddesses and Gods.

Varied Personalities

If you've spent enough time with an animal companion, observed animals on a farm or in the wild, you have probably concluded that they have emotions and personalities. Perhaps you have kept watch on an animal as it was dreaming and wondered what each twitch and sound meant and what it was doing in its dreamscape. Those of you that have had the blessing of animal companions over the course of years may have seen that not only do they love but they also grieve for the departed. In Witchcraft, it is often said that energy is raised through emotion, will and desire, which suggests that animals can raise energy. The world of dreams, the astral plane, plays a central role in many magical undertakings. Animals that dream have access to the astral—the otherworld—and as such can commune with spiritual entities and travel the subtle roads. Love and grief and the longing that arises from both can urge animals, in their own fashion, to seek contact with their beloveds that have crossed over. Some have reported the ghosts of animals, and if humans can sense them surely the animals do so as well. There are a thousand and one human descriptions of the lands beyond the gates of death and their associated pantheons. Surely it is not much of a stretch to think that the various species of animals have done the same.

Many Witches and Pagans will speak of the unity of life and spirit, but also about the many distinctly different Goddesses and Gods. There is no inherent conflict in this continuum of possibilities when it is viewed as a matter of focus and perspective. Are we looking with microscopes, telescopes, our own eyes or x-ray machines? Each will reveal a very different universe, and all will be equally real and true in a relative way. The deities of animals will be shaped by their unique perspectives and lines of sight. Perception and consciousness like giant windows, composed of a myriad of panes of different sizes, shapes, colors, refractions and clarities, looking out onto the landscape of the universe. Each species views the universe and divinity through their individual pane. It may be that like many human deities, many of their deities are like larger, more powerful and perfected versions of themselves. There are also Goddesses and Gods that are perceived by humans as highly abstracted beings. Contemplating what would be entailed in an abstract representation of an animal deity requires spending a good amount of effort gaining insights into animal consciousness.

Environmental Awareness

Animals are often more deeply connected to their environment than humans. Their self-awareness is more blended and balanced with their awareness of the environment wherein they exist. It is possible that some animals have deities that are more like the shape of their environment rather than the shape of the animals. When humans describe Goddesses and Gods, they are described in terms of the colors, sounds, scents, etc., that are in the human range of perception. Animal senses span different ranges and include those outside the confines of human senses. These differences in style of consciousness must influence their perception and awareness of their deities.

More often than not, humans depict their divinities as having genders. Much of what constitutes gender or what is assigned to gender is based on cultural frames of reference. If and how gender plays a role in the deities of animals probably varies from species to species. The pattern of self-identity in the consciousness of a particular animal would most likely be reflected in how they conceptualize their deities. Whether, how and if gender is expressed in that self-identity would be a shaping factor.

Studies have shown that whales, ground hogs and a host of other animals have something equivalent to language and that it varies in accent from one location to another. Something akin to culture also can differ between animal groups of the same species. It would not be surprising if, for example different packs, herds or pods of any given species have variations in how they experience their deities. Humans do this, so it is reasonable to suggest that the same is true for our distant cousins. All humans have distant ancestors,

and perhaps through this connection it is possible to understand something of the spiritual life of animals in the world today.

The following is a matter of belief and doctrine, so you may or may not agree, but it is expressed for the sake of furthering this discussion. The Goddesses and Gods are real and distinct entities with their own reality separate from and independent of incarnate beings. There is reciprocity and an exchange between the beings we call deities and the living beings of the Earth. The divinities have free will and choose when, where and how they will interact with living beings. There are probably some deities whose focus and interest are fully vested with animals. There are those who have a singular focus on humans. Some have an interest in animals and humans in every imaginable combination of arrangements and proportions of relationships. In some cases the human Goddesses and Gods showing animal aspects may be those that we share with the animals. It is also possible that human imagination has given an animal aspect to a deity as a symbolic summary of its nature, and it may not be a deity to the animal guise it wears. It is only through close observation, contemplation, dialogue that we can begin to know their Goddesses and Gods.

There is more to be pondered and explored than can fit in a short article, but there is enough material here for you to begin. So long as you maintain an open and respectful attitude, it may be possible to gain a broader understanding of the spiritual realms of animals. To begin the work, learn as much as you can about specific animals and how they live. Do something tangible to benefit these animals such as donating to a reputable animal welfare or environmental group. If it is reasonable, offer food, water or some form of comfort to animals. Then when you feel it is right, petition the animals to introduce you to their deities using whichever spiritual practices make sense to you. Be patient and continue in all your efforts. When we can recognize the deities of the animals, we may well have the needed clues and insights to know more about our place in the web of life and spirit.

—IVO DOMINGUEZ JR.

Glastonbury's Magic

GLASTONBURY (Somerset, UK) is a place where myth, history and legend collide in a kaleidoscope of spiritual traditions and alternative ways of living—with a sprinkling of fairy dust and rainbow glitter. Walking down the High Street on any given day will take visitors past Druids, Witches, New Age healers, Pagans of every possible variety as well as yoginis, Goddesses, lovers of faeries, Earth mystery enthusiasts and past life explorers. Adventurers sampling the local cider in the 15th century George & Pilgrim are more likely to overhear discussions on ley-lines, stone circles, ghosts or Aleister Crowley than discussions on politics or the weather. The wacky, eccentric and downright odd is mostly considered "normal for Glastonbury" which has been named as one of the strangest places in the UK.

The town has for centuries been a place of spiritual, religious and cultural pilgrimage, drawing to it people of all faiths and none. Glastonbury has generated many legends of magic and the supernatural, and continues to do so today. This is an introduction to a few of the magical places where visitors often leave transformed, or at the very least with a fascinating tale to tell!

The Abbey

In the 12th century monks at the Abbey found what they claimed to be the tomb of King Arthur, thereby securing a lucrative income from pilgrims keen to connect with the "once and future king." Today the location of the tomb is marked with a simple sign, and visitors continue to marvel at the story while posing to have their photo taken in the ruins of the ancient buildings. Said to be built on the site of the first Christian church in Britain and the first to have a chapel to the Virgin Mary, it continues to draw Christian pilgrims today. Pagans visit seeking a connection to the story of the ancient Isle of Avalon, where a pre-Christian Mother Goddess of sovereignty was worshipped, Merlin and Vivienne of the Lake lived and Druids received training.

Arthurian enthusiasts may also wish to visit the nearby Pomparles bridge crossing the river Brue between Glastonbury and Street. Derived from the French *pont perilleux* (perilous bridge) the area was underwater before being drained by monks in the 12th century. Legend tells us that Arthur's sword, Excalibur, was thrown into the water at this spot and taken by the hand of the Lady of the Lake.

The Tor

Visible for miles in the surrounding Somerset countryside, this iconic hill seemingly calls people to it. The word Tor probably originates from the Gaelic *tòrr* meaning "bulging hill," or the Welsh *tor* which means "belly." Contemporary devotees of the Mother Goddess consider it to be the breast or body of the Goddess. Pilgrims interested in Sacred Geometry sometimes walk the so-called "Tor Labyrinth," Neolithic paths forming a maze-like route around the hill. Welsh mythology links the Tor to Gwyn Ap Nudd, God of the Wild Hunt and Ruler of the Faery. The tower at the top is the remains of a 15th century church dedicated to Saint Michael, today interpreted by some Pagans as a phallic symbol representing the Divine Masculine.

Making the ascent is an initiatory experience, a pilgrimage in the footsteps of thousands who have gone before. One of those was Dion Fortune, who lived and worked on the slopes of the Tor. Visitors

inspired by her work often visit her grave in the cemetery on Wells Road.

The White and Red Springs

At the foot of the Tor, separated by a road today, are the renowned White and Red Springs which once flowed out into the landscape. The waters of the Red Spring have a high iron content and mark its path with red deposits. Today the spring forms part of the Chalice Well Gardens, a sanctuary with beautifully kept gardens, meditation areas and a healing pool where visitors can connect with the magical healing properties of the water. The White Spring, with its calcium-rich sweet water, was unfortunately turned into a reservoir in the late 19th century. In recent decades this has been transformed into a watery cave-like temple with Pagan shrines and circular pool in which visitors can bathe. Many healing properties are attributed to both waters, which are highly symbolic, representing the Divine Feminine and Masculine. They can be collected on opposite sides of Well House Lane near the White Spring entrance.

Gog and Magog

These ancient oak trees, thought by some to be as much as 2000 years old, are named after the apocalyptic figures in the Bible. Locals claim they were part of an avenue of such trees which formed a Druidic ceremonial avenue leading to the Tor. Today Gog is still alive, standing next to the remains of Magog which sadly died a few years back. They are gnarled giants, who have witnessed and survived much!

The Holy Thorn

It is said that when Joseph of Arimathea rested his staff on Wearyall Hill, when

he visited following the death of Jesus, it grew into the first Holy Thorn. Today several specimens can be found around the town, notably in the Abbey and the grounds of St John's Church on the High Street, a sprig of whose tree is cut in December each year for the Queen. Visitors also enjoy walking the labyrinth and marvelling at the mysterious unmarked tomb inside the church, said to hold the remains of Joseph of Arimathea.

Adventurers today may also enjoy visiting the Goddess Temple to spend some time in quiet contemplation of the Divine Feminine, browsing the vast esoteric collection of the Library of Avalon and exploring bygone eras at the Rural Life Museum. Glastonbury's magic is conjured in the cracks of its diversity, on the liminal where beliefs are challenged and suspended. Enjoy!

—SORITA D'ESTE

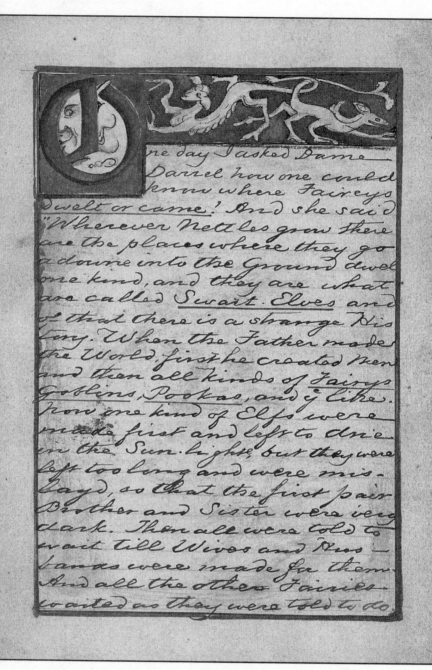

One day I asked Dame Darrel how one could know where Faireys dwelt or came? And she said "Wherever Nettles grow there are the places where they go a downe into the Ground dwel one kind, and they are what are called Swart-Elves and of that there is a strange History. When the Father made the World, first he created Men and then all kinds of Fairys Goblins, Pookas, and ÿ like, now one kind of Elfs were made first and left to drie in the Sun-lights but they were left too long and were mislayd, so that the first pair Brother and Sister were very dark. Then all were told to wait till Wives and Husbands were made for them And all the other Fairies waited as they were told to do

Excerpt from

The Witchcraft of Dame Darrel of York

One day I asked Dame Darrel how one could know where Faireys *dwelt* or *came?* And she said "Wherever Nettles grow there are the places where they go. adowne into the Ground dwel one kind, and they are what are called *Swart Elves* and of that there is astrange History. When the Father made the world, first he created Men and then all kinds of *Fairys, Goblins, Pookas,* and ye like. Now one kind of Elfs were made first and left to drie in the Sun-lighte, but they were left too long and were mislayd, so that the first pair Brother and Sister were very dark. Then all were told to wait till Wives and Husbands were made for them. And all the other Fairies waited as they were told to do."

TAROT'S THE STAR

HERE WE HAVE LEFT the infernal realm as represented in medieval cosmology and ascended to the celestial zones above the Earth in anticipation of the last Tarot trump symbolizing Heaven itself. There are various sets of imagery used to portray the Star trump. Some depict the miraculous star announcing the birth of Jesus which appears in the liturgical play cycle. The imagery used here, however, first appears in the wood block printed partial deck from 15th century Milan, and in modified form in all subsequent Marseille decks. It depicts a nude figure with flowing hair, in modern decks a female, kneeling and emptying jars of liquid into a river or other body of water. Above it shines a large star surrounded by four lesser, while a fifth nestles on the figure's right shoulder. The Milanese original lacks breasts and is arguably male. A dolphin, an allegorical symbol of Hope, has been added to the original design based on marks in the Milanese card suggesting a fish. The origin of the image is likely to be an allegorical representation of Morning Twilight, the large star being the planet Venus, the Morning Star which heralds the coming of the new day. In all instances the Star is seen by cartomancers to represent an optimistic symbol of Hope.

Excerpted from Dame Fortune's Wheel Tarot—A Pictorial Key *by Paul Huson, published by The Witches' Almanac.*

THE KEYS TO THE KINGDOM

MUSIC HAS BEEN utilized in religious rites across the world for thousands of years with each culture drawing upon on theoretical concepts to give it deeper meanings. Religious schisms have occurred over the "proper" use of music, whilst the mathematical relationship between pitches and frequencies first explored by Pythagoras continued to stir the imagination of philosophers into the Baroque era and beyond. Indeed, Charpentier discussed this in 1682 as did Edward Maryon in *Marcotone* (1919) which is believed to be the source of Paul Foster Case's colour and pitch correspondences for the Hebrew letters. However, the change in pitch itself now renders some of their findings useless to the modern-day practitioner who is not aware of it.

Music of the Baroque era (1600-1750) was performed at a lower pitch than we use today where A=440Hz. This is slightly lower than the 430Hz Maryon used and is a semitone lower than the A = 440Hz we use today. This lower pitch for A was by no means a constant and could vary wildly between countries and indeed regions. This therefore calls for consideration on the part of anyone utilizing pitch correspondences in magical work, looking firstly at *when* the correspondences were written or the date of the original source of the correspondences and secondly *where* this evolved from in order to find the most accurate pitch to use.

Another influence on musical composition and theoretical thought from this era, and so in turn its efficiency in magical workings, is that of temperament. Musicians today would, for the most part, consider G sharp and A flat to be two names for the same note, the *enharmonic equivalent*. Indeed, when looking at the pitch correspondences of Case it becomes very apparent that Case regards enharmonic equivalents as being the same pitch. However, in early music the two pitches were different. Before the Renaissance era, music used a system of tuning which was influenced by Pythagoras and focused on pure fifths as the basis of tuning. For this reason, when performing on a tuned keyboard or stringed instrument, movement to keys other than the home key or Tonic resulted in the music becoming audibly "out of tune." In the Renaissance era the interval of a fifth began to be tuned slightly narrower which enabled performers to modulate to different keys without the problems of the Pythagorean system. The *equal temperament* tuning of the 1700s removed the clashes previously caused, but this perhaps also reduced the affect of the different keys and individual pitches.

In 1668, writing in his *Règles de Composition*, Charpentier gave the following associations to key signatures:

C major: gay and warlike

C minor: obscure and sad
D major: joyous and very warlike
D minor: serious and pious
Eb major: cruel and hard
E major: quarrelsome and boisterous
E minor: effeminate, amorous, plaintive
F major: furious and quick-tempered subjects
F minor: obscure and plaintive
G major: serious and magnificent
G minor: serious and magnificent
A major: joyful and pastoral
A minor: tender and plaintive
B major: harsh and plaintive
B minor: solitary and melancholic
Bb major: magnificent and joyful
Bb minor: obscure and terrible

If we compare the associations of C major and the pitch C we find the following:

Author	Association
Charpentier	Gay and Warlike
Case	The Emperor, The Tower, Judgement
Maryon	Red

It can therefore be assumed that a

Salmon of Wisdom

Salm - on of wis - dom. Guar - dian of knowl - edge.

Rise____ Rise____ Rise____ Well spring re - turn - ing.

pitch and a key signature will share associations which can be drawn upon and incorporated into a composition for magical purposes. To illustrate this, a chant which can be used to call upon the elemental and mythological attributes of the Salmon of Wisdom has been included below.

The tonality of the chant, G major and the pitch G, offers the following attributes

Charpentier Serious and Magnificent
Case   Nun, Key 13—Death
Maryon   Green Blue

The magnificence of wisdom is mirrored in the sunrise depicted on Key 13 of the BOTA deck. In the chant the word "leap" rises stepwise in pitch to an E natural, given the association of the colour yellow by Maryon and tied to Key 1—The Magician by Case, a card which is predominantly yellow, to confirm the tonality of G major for the first time in the chant. The earlier pitches could be from G minor or the Mixolydian Mode, an intentional means of representing the hidden nature of wisdom. The fluid, ever-changing and developing current of knowledge is again represented in Maryon's colour and the symbolism of

key 13. The Hebrew letter Nun (meaning Fish) is a perfect representation of the Salmon of Wisdom.

The Salmon of Wisdom lives in a well surrounded by nine hazel trees which are incorporated into the chant through its time signature (9/8) and its length of nine bars. If one wanted, the chant could be repeated nine times giving a total length of 81 bars which can be reduced back to nine to further utilise this symbolism. The time signature, however, is also hidden, disguised by the lack of other vocal or instrumental parts which clearly define the compound nature of the time signature, instead sounding as if written in a simple metre of 3/4.

Two recordings of the chant can be found on *The Witches' Almanac* website, one at the lower pitch suggested by Maryon and another at today's higher pitch. Other audio examples are offered which illustrate the use of different temperaments and percussion to make the 9/8 time signature more obvious.

—JERA

An audio file of the Salmon of Wisdom as well as extended articles can be viewed at TheWitchesAlmanac.com/ almanac-extras/

Why & How Animal Omens Work

IT IS HARD TO find a time in history, a locale or a culture without references to animal omens of some sort. As a result, there is an abundance of lore on the meaning and interpretation of messages, predictions and such delivered by animals. Much of this information is culturally or geographically specific so it may or may not be useful in understanding your encounters with animal omens, though it may provide hints or inspiration. Reading animal omens can be somewhat like analyzing dreams—much of the meaning is unique and set by the mind of the individual and the circumstances of the experience. To understand animal omens more fully and clearly, it is valuable to consider why and how animal omens work.

Bestial Senses

Animals are always listening to nature. Humans, in what we currently think of as civilization, are often distracted or focused on environments and interactions that are created by other humans. Animals take notice of subtle changes in the smell of the air, a shift in the wind or the changing sky. Animals listen to the sounds both low and high that are produced by the

entire landscape and all its inhabitants. Collectively, animal senses cover a much broader range of sound, light, scent, etc., than human senses. They also have senses that humans do not have at all or only in a rudimentary way. When Mother Nature speaks, animals listen, respond and take action. Sometimes these are warnings of events such as earthquakes, storms or other major physical events. At other times, these are forecasts for the long-term weather ahead and so on. Animal behavior can also provide information about the spiritual and energetic conditions of a given place and time. These animal omens are not directed at nor intended for us, but can serve us well if we are mindful.

The world is populated by many varieties of spiritual entities. There are nature spirits, elementals, fey of a thousand forms, ghosts and many other classes of beings that surround us at all times. Humans vary in their awareness of these beings, even when the spirits are trying to get our attention. Many people have reported observing animals interacting with what appear to be unseen presences. It may be that animals are inherently more sensitive to the presence of spirits.

Unified Minds

Another possibility is that animals are better at balancing their inner awareness with their outer perception. People are often so preoccupied with their own thoughts that the outside world, both physical and spiritual, is a low-resolution summary rather than a richly perceived engagement with reality. If a spirit wants to get the attention of a person or to send a message, they may herd or drive an animal across that person's path. A spirit may call out to an animal to encourage it to join in with a howl, caw, squeak, bark or braying so that human ears will hear it as well. Through its actions, a spirit can guide an animal to behave in a way that transmits a message, an omen. This kind of interaction between spirit and animal works regardless of the level of intelligence and self-awareness possessed by the animal. Spiritual entities that have some understanding of human behavior and habits would be more inclined to influence animals that are known to catch our attention.

Some animals have the class of self-awareness and intelligence that humans understand as selfhood. As a result of this perception, humans make the effort to contemplate the meaning of these animals' actions more closely. Animals in this category, such as mammals and some birds, can vocalize or gesture in a way that we interpret as language. Spirits can communicate with these animals and tell them to relay messages to humans. We are more likely to see these animals' actions as communication, as omens, because we view these animals as beings with their own individuality. There is a bit of irony in this focus on individuality. One of the reasons it is harder for spirits to communicate with people is that human identity is so focused on being separate from others. There is also the question of ego and control. Although it is common for spiritual people to ask for guidance, it easily goes ignored or unnoticed when received unless its style and substance are close to what is expected or desired. Animals tend to be more amenable to following the guidance of spirits. If a spirit asks a crow to circle around you twice and then fly away sunward, the crow will simply do it. If a spirit managed to get a message to a human to do something, the human might argue, ask for a full explanation, shrug it off as imagination, and perhaps comply too late for the message to be useful.

Divine Affinity

There are also powerful animal spirits that send omens through their physical counterparts. In many cultures and systems of magick there is the concept of a group mind, a group soul, a monarch, a great spirit, that is the summation of the spiritual nature and power of its species. For example, it is particularly easy for the great spirit of eagles to instruct an eagle to convey an omen. A few years ago, on our drive home from a trip a bald eagle swooped in front of our car several times. We pulled over to the side of the road and

parked. The eagle landed high on a tree and looked down on us as we stepped out of the car. After exchanging glances, it cried and leapt into the sky. One of its feathers spiraled down slowly and landed on the hood of the car. It was an answer to a discussion we'd been having much of the day. I made note of the direction the feather pointed, picked it up, kissed it thanks and placed it beneath the tree. The message was probably from the great spirit of the eagles, based on the question that it answered and the guidance it gave.

When people have a relationship or an affinity with specific animals they are more likely to receive omens from them. In part this is about the psychology of perception and expectation. There is also a greater likelihood that these people also have art, jewelry, statuary or other objects that represent their special animals. These can create an energetic connection to the spirit of that species. Whether intentional or not, the objects can act as altars and conduits to deliver offerings and requests to the spirits. These alliances with animal spirits can also be formalized and long-lasting. When this is the case, the person carries an imprint of that animal within their own psyche. Omens from animals that are your chosen allies can be distinctly powerful because they are facilitated by a connection fueled by human energy.

Disguised Deities

Many Goddesses, Gods and other higher-order beings are associated with specific animals. Some of these beings also have a fully or partially animal form they can assume. Goddesses, Gods and the like can enlist animals in delivering omens—especially those animals that resonate with them. These animals are a part of their entourage, retinue and spiritual court. If the outcome of a situation has many important ramifications or require great precision, an animal omen may be bestowed not by an animal but by one of these higher-order beings appearing as an animal. There are many stories about Goddesses and Gods appearing as humans to test or to bless people. They can also appear as animals to accomplish their work when deemed the best form to enter the mortal world.

The sources, means and reasons for the delivery of animal omens is a longer topic that cannot be addressed in a short article. That said, open your eyes and ears to the guidance animals may offer. In making sense of these omens, in addition to whatever meaning you derive, take some time to contemplate why and how the omen was sent. Think upon who might have sent the omen as well. In doing so, you may discover more layers, clearer resolution and the wisest actions to take.

—IVO DOMINGUEZ JR.

The Holy Guardian Angel
It's a Love Story

MANY OF US are familiar with the term, "Holy Guardian Angel." It entered the popular vocabulary of western occultists in 1888 when Golden Dawn hierophant, S.L. MacGregor Mathers, translated and published fragments of a rather unique 15th century magical grimoire, *The Sacred Magic of Abra-Melin the Mage.*

While most medieval texts were recipe books, filled with spells to conjure and trap dangerous spirits from the infernal regions to serve as the magician's slaves, the *Sacred Magic* was very different. In fact, the text posited that in order to exercise godlike powers the magician must first actually be "God-like," and that true magical power can only be wisely and effectively employed if the magician has first attained a significant level of spiritual illumination.

A spiritually enlightened individual lives and functions in harmony with the supreme consciousness of the cosmos, and the only way to properly harmonize with this infinite consciousness is to mutate one's personal consciousness so that it perfectly reflects and resonates with the universal consciousness.

Hidden Divinity

The Abra-Melin book reveals that each human being is linked from birth to a personal "angel." Although the book talks about this Holy Guardian Angel as an objective being, its nature is perhaps less superstitiously described as being our own projected, perfectly-illuminated self that we are currently too "sleepy" to realize is us. It's a pretty cool concept, and the book goes on to give painfully detailed instructions on how the magician can prepare himself or herself to be wedded to the HGA and achieve this new, expanded consciousness.

At first glance this all seems like a very straightforward and objective endeavor, and in one way it is. After all, magick is facilitated by activating and interacting with colorful and dramatic metaphors of abstract powers and energies. It's easy for me to imagine I have a cool angel hovering around me, and if I could just attract it to my bedroom and somehow get it to permanently mate with me my consciousness would take a quantum expansion. I'd be transmuted into a new, mutated magician on my way to omnipotent, godlike powers and illumination.

But exactly how does this actually work? I'm sure it works differently for everyone. I'm sure if you've read this far you might be curious if it has happened to me?

The answer is, "Yes."

I say this without evasion, equivocation or mental reservation of any kind. And, in case you are curious, I find *Knowledge and Conversation of the Holy Guardian Angel* to be in essence exactly as advertised. Everything I ever read about it, everything I heard about it— it's all true.

But for me, the experience was *nothing like I expected.* In fact, after 40 years of psychedelics, magick rituals, meditations, fasting, initiations, mantras, pranayama, a litany of minor epiphanies and sex magick-ing myself to near blindness, I had grown old and quite frankly, stopped expecting *anything* to happen. But it did happen.

Would you like to hear about it?

Boundless Compassion

It's difficult (impossible, really) to properly describe. Besides, the intensely intimate and personal factors necessary to this equation will vary wildly with each individual on Earth. But I feel I must share what I can, because now it's all I want to talk about. All I want to think about. It's all I want to sing about.

I comb my brain looking for word-vessels capable of capturing even a droplet of the spray from this infinite ocean of love, but I can only come up with four words that begin to say it: "I love all things."

Sorry. That doesn't really say it because it is a sentence that uses parts of speech, and because I love all nouns and all verbs and all adverbs and adjectives and pronouns. I love the silence between the words. I love the space between the letters.

I love you. I love every woman of you. I love every man of you. I love every child, animal, plant and mineral; every cell, molecule, atom, photon and subatomic particle. I exhale and my breath says, "I love you" to the universe… and with every inhalation the universe answers back, "I love you too." I know when I draw my last breath at the end of this Lon-life this mantra will continue, because this love song is all that is holding existence together.

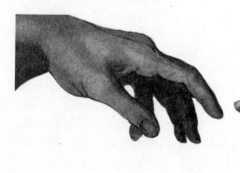

I just want to make love to the firmament!

For years, my wife Constance has said that romance is her religion, and now I say it too, because this is a very romantic tale.

Steps of Fire, Currents of Flame

Not long ago I was in New York City to play a show at Greenwich Village's *Caffe Vivaldi*. I stayed a few days in Queens at the home of a dear friend. For me, New York City is the most romantic city on earth; the city of Gershwin and Cole Porter; the city that has for the last decade been my muse and the venue for my musical rebirth.

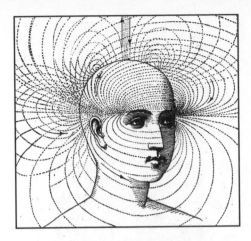

I wasn't doing magick. At least I didn't think I was doing magick. I was simply busy writing new love songs and preparing for my weekend gig. My host had been trying to introduce me to the ecstasies of tango. He is a very serious dancer and travels each year to the sweaty grottos of Buenos Aires. Back in New York he disappears nearly every night into the dark and sultry tango clubs of mid-town Manhattan. That's exactly what he did that night. He left me alone in my Jackson Heights hermitage and suggested I watch a few tango videos featuring Mariano Chicho Frúmboli dancing with Juana Sepúlveda.

This iconic pair are perhaps the most passionate, romantic and exciting tango dancers in the world. As I watched and listened to that tortuously beautiful music, I began to think about love. How all my life I've been really good at loving. Very good. Too good in fact. I fall in love easily, deeply and often. All my life I've had a seemingly boundless supply of love to give to my friends and my lovers and

my art. I've never had a problem loving; no problem *giving* love. But for as long as I can remember, I've had serious difficulty *receiving* love; a problem *accepting* love; a problem *being* loved. My heart could pump out a rich-flowing gusher of love-blood to all the universe, but for some reason would not allow the love to flow back in with equal volume and intensity. That is a magical problem indeed, for love, like the mysterious fifth element, Spirit, is an *alternating* current —an active/passive force.

As Chicho held Juana in his arms and as she put her arm so purposefully across his huge back and shoulders, all the old love songs suddenly made profound sense, as if the voice of God was speaking directly to my soul:

"And in the end the love you take is equal to the love you make."
　　　　　–The Beatles, "The End"

"The greatest thing you'll ever learn is just to love and be loved in return."
　　　　–Eden Ahbez, "Nature Boy"

Then, something very wonderful happened. Between notes of the music, between steps on the dance floor, time

The video orchestra played a dramatic flourish. Chicho violently pulled Juana into his arms and dragged her limp body across the dance floor yet it seemed as if her listless surrender became conquest and was the infinite force pushing them both. Who was active? Who was passive?

There, in the living-room temple, before the altar of a big screen television, while I swooned at the sight of the tips of Juana Sepúlveda's black stilettos being dragged across the dance floor, I gave myself permission to change that moment in *time*. I opened my heart and for the first time in this lifetime I caught the full reciprocal force of love—not my love, not her love—but LOVE.

Perpetual Resonance

Do you know what feedback is? Feedback is when you put an active microphone near the amplified speakers it is connected to. It triggers an almost instantaneous ear-splitting howl. That is what happened at that moment, only it was a feedback of love, and instead of a painful screech getting louder and louder it was a sweet clear note that became sweeter and sweeter and clearer and clearer.

I was thrown back into my chair. It felt as though a fiery pinwheel had been set ablaze in my chest. It spun faster and faster and the sparks it threw off spread throughout my whole body right down to the pores in my skin. My hair stood on end and my hands and fingers and feet and toes were charged with electricity. I was afraid to move my hands for fear

and space liberally collapsed like the bellows of an accordion. My Jackson Heights flat became a time machine and I was taken nearly fifty years into my past. This was not a memory. This was not a boing back. This was now—and I was there. I was there at a moment in time when the full force of my pure love was being joyously and totally accepted, totally received. Instantly the reciprocal ray of love of the exact infinite intensity was being returned back to me.

Nearly fifty years ago I didn't recognize what was going on. It was too pure, too simple, too profound, too subtle for my young heart. I feared annihilation in this awesome, fiery beam. I recoiled and turned aside the catcher's mitt of my heart. I deflected the full force of that pure requited love. And I had been deflecting it ever since.

That was the timeless moment of my fall. That was the moment that I was banished from the paradise love of the Angel. But that eternal moment was back! I was there again! I could change that moment. I could change the past!

I would knock things off the wall across the room.

I had reconnected with the supreme alternating current of life, and I burned with the wall-to-wall, eternally-feed-back-ing LOVE that lights the stars. I knew if I remained seated I would incinerate completely into that light... but I didn't care.

I pulled on my shoes, grabbed my hat and coat and went out into the cool evening and walked and walked. I don't know where. I don't know for how long. I was careful not to bump into people on the sidewalk—I knew if I touched them they would burst into flames!

It was very late when I returned. I was still exploding, but the explosion was now madly centered in a containment chamber roughly in the neighborhood of my heart. It's still there. It hasn't gone away. It was always there. I just had to wake up to realize it.

I suppose the Yogi will recognize the experience as the opening of the Anahata or Heart Chakra; the Magician as the marriage of the microcosmic 5 and the macrocosmic 6; the Qabalist as the raising of consciousness to the sixth Sephirah of the Tree of Life, Tiphareth; the Christian ecstatic as the Mystery of the Holy Grail; the Witch as the cosmic essence of the Great Rite. Call it what you want, it is actually as simple as a song lyric:

And in the end the love you take is equal to the love you make.

The greatest thing you'll ever learn is just to love and be loved in return.

Yes, the Holy Guardian Angel is real, objective and tangible; because when you look at me, you're looking at my Angel.

—LON MILO DUQUETTE

MOON GARDENING

BY PHASE

Sow, transplant, bud and graft   *Plow, cultivate, weed and reap*

NEW	First Quarter	FULL	Last Quarter	NEW
Plant above-ground crops with outside seeds, flowering annuals.	Plant above-ground crops with inside seeds.	Plant root crops, bulbs, biennials, perennials.		Do not plant.

BY PLACE IN THE ZODIAC

In general—plant and transplant crops that bear above ground when the Moon is in a watery sign: Cancer, Scorpio or Pisces. Plant and transplant root crops when the Moon is in Taurus or Capricorn; the other earthy sign, Virgo, encourages rot. The airy signs, Gemini, Libra and Aquarius, are good for some crops and not for others. The fiery signs, Aries, Leo and Sagittarius, are barren signs for most crops and best used for weeding, pest control and cultivating the soil.

♈

Aries—*barren, hot and dry.* Favorable for planting and transplanting beets, onions and garlic, but unfavorable for all other crops. Good for weeding and pest control, for canning and preserving, and for all activities involving fire.

♉

Taurus—*fruitful, cold and dry.* Fertile, best for planting root crops and also very favorable for all transplanting as it encourages root growth. Good for planting crops that bear above ground and for canning and preserving. Prune in this sign to encourage root growth.

♊

Gemini—*barren, hot and moist.* The best sign for planting beans, which will bear more heavily. Unfavorable for other crops. Good for harvesting and for gathering herbs.

♋

Cancer—*fruitful, cold and moist.* Best for planting crops that bear above ground and very favorable for root crops. Dig garden beds when the Moon is in this sign, and everything planted in them will flourish. Prune in this sign to encourage growth.

♌

Leo—*barren, hot and dry.* Nothing should be planted or transplanted while the Moon is in the Lion. Favorable for weeding and pest control, for tilling and cultivating the soil, and for canning and preserving.

♍

Virgo—*barren, cold and dry.* Good for planting grasses and grains, but unfavorable for other crops. Unfavorable for canning and preserving, but favorable for weeding, pest control, tilling and cultivating. Make compost when the Moon is in the Virgin and it will ripen faster.

♎

Libra—*fruitful, hot and moist.* The best sign to plant flowers and vines and somewhat favorable for crops that bear above the ground. Prune in this sign to encourage flowering.

♏

Scorpio—*fruitful, cold and moist.* Very favorable to plant and transplant crops that bear above ground, and favorable for planting and transplanting root crops. Set out fruit trees when the Moon is in this sign and prune to encourage growth.

♐

Sagittarius—*barren, hot and dry.* Favorable for planting onions, garlic and cucumbers, but unfavorable for all other crops, and especially unfavorable for transplanting. Favorable for canning and preserving, for tilling and cultivating the soil, and for pruning to discourage growth.

♑

Capricorn—*fruitful, cold and dry.* Very favorable for planting and transplanting root crops, favorable for flowers, vines, and all crops that bear above ground. Plant trees, bushes and vines in this sign. Prune trees and vines to strengthen the branches.

♒

Aquarius—*barren, hot and moist.* Favorable for weeding and pest control, tilling and cultivating the soil, harvesting crops, and gathering herbs. Somewhat favorable for planting crops that bear above ground, but only in dry weather or the seeds will tend to rot.

♓

Pisces—*fruitful, cold and moist.* Very favorable for planting and transplanting crops that bear above ground and favorable for flowers and all root crops except potatoes. Prune when the Moon is in the Fishes to encourage growth. Plant trees, bushes and vines in this sign.

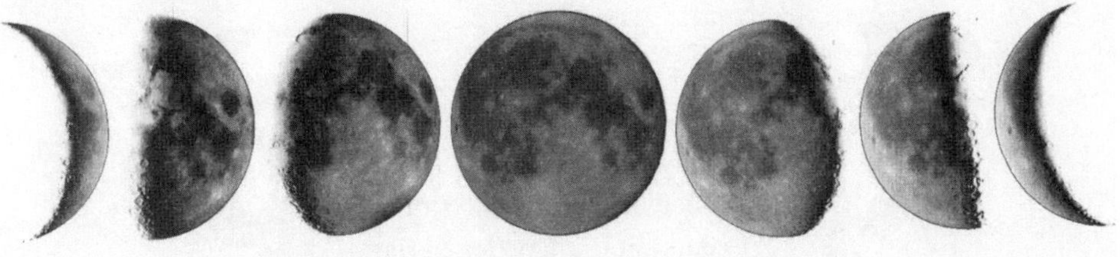

Consult our Moon Calendar pages for phase and place in the zodiac circle. The Moon remains in a sign for about two and a half days. Match your gardening activity to the day that follows the Moon's entry into that zodiacal sign. For best results, choose days when the phase and sign are both favorable. For example, plant seeds when the Moon is waxing in a suitable fruitful sign, and uproot stubborn weeds when the Moon is in the fourth quarter in a barren sign.

The MOON *Calendar*

is divided into zodiac signs rather
than the more familiar Gregorian calendar.

2019

2020

Bear in mind that new projects
should be initiated when the Moon
is waxing (from dark to full). When
the Moon is on the wane (from full
to dark), it is a time for storing
energy and the wise person waits.

Please note that Moons are listed by day of entry into each sign. Quarters
are marked, but as rising and setting times vary from one region to another,
it is advisable to check your local newspaper, library or planetarium.
The Moon's Place is computed for Eastern Time.

capricorn

December 21, 2018 – January 19, 2019

Cardinal Sign of Earth ♍ Ruled by Saturn ♄

S	M	T	W	T	F	S
COMFREY: This is an herb of Saturn, and I suppose under the sign Capricorn, cold, dry, and earthy in quality. What was spoken of Clown's Woundwort may be said of this. The Great Comfrey helps those that spit blood, or make a bloody urine. CONTINUED BELOW					Dec. **21** Winter Solstice ❄	**22** Wolf Moon Cancer
23 WANING	**24** Leo	**25**	**26** Virgo	**27**	**28**	**29** Libra
30.	**31** Be flexible Scorpio	Jan. **1**	**2** Cleanse the house Sagittarius	**3**	**4** Partial Solar Eclipse ⇨	**5** Capricorn
6 WAXING	**7** Have hope Aquarius	**8**	**9** Feast of Janus Know your limits	**10** Pisces	**11** Exaggerate a bit	**12** Aries
13	**14**	**15** Express gratitude Taurus	**16**	**17** Gamble Gemini	**18**	**19** Cancer

The root boiled in water or wine, and the decoction drank, helps all inward hurts, bruises, wounds, and ulcer of the lungs, and causes the phlegm that oppresses them to be easily spit forth: It helps the defluction of rheum from the head upon the lungs, the fluxes of blood or humours by the belly, women's immoderate courses, as well the reds as the whites, and the running of the reins happening by what cause soever.—*The Complete Herbal* by Nicholas Culpeper

Chinese Zodiac Animal Signs

The Chinese Zodiac sign is derived from the birth year.
See the years of each animal below.

Rat	Ox	Tiger	Rabbit	Dragon	Snake
1900	1901	1902	1903	1904	1905
1912	1913	1914	1915	1916	1917
1924	1925	1926	1927	1928	1929
1936	1937	1938	1939	1940	1941
1948	1949	1950	1951	1952	1953
1960	1961	1962	1963	1964	1965
1972	1973	1974	1975	1976	1977
1984	1985	1986	1987	1988	1989
1996	1997	1998	1999	2000	2001
2008	2009	2010	2011	2012	2013
2020	2021	2022	2023	2024	2025
2032	2033	2034	2035	2036	2037
2044	2045	2046	2047	2048	2049
2056	2057	2058	2059	2060	2061
2068	2069	2070	2071	2072	2073
2080	2081	2082	2083	2084	2085
2092	2093	2094	2095	2096	2097

Horse	Goat	Monkey	Rooster	Dog	Pig
1906	1907	1908	1909	1910	1911
1918	1919	1920	1921	1922	1923
1930	1931	1932	1933	1934	1935
1942	1943	1944	1945	1946	1947
1954	1955	1956	1957	1958	1959
1966	1967	1968	1969	1970	1971
1978	1979	1980	1981	1982	1983
1990	1991	1992	1993	1994	1995
2002	2003	2004	2005	2006	2007
2014	2015	2016	2017	2018	2019
2026	2027	2028	2029	2030	2031
2038	2039	2040	2041	2042	2043
2050	2051	2052	2053	2054	2055
2062	2063	2064	2065	2066	2067
2074	2075	2076	2077	2078	2079
2086	2087	2088	2089	2090	2091
2098	2099	2100	2101	2102	2103

aquarius

January 20 – February 18, 2019

Fixed Sign of Air ♎ Ruled by Uranus ♅

S	M	T	W	T	F	S
Jan. **20** Total Lunar Eclipse ⇨	**21** Storm Moon Leo	**22** WANING	**23** Virgo	**24**	**25** Libra	**26**
27 ● Scorpio	**28**	**29** *Contemplate silver wings* Sagittarius	**30**	**31**	Feb. **1** Oimelc Eve Capricorn	**2** Candlemas
3 *Sing to Diana* Aquarius	**4** ● 	**5** Chinese New Year Earth Boar WAXING	**6** *Gaze into dark water* Pisces	**7**	**8** Aries	**9** *Help a friend*
10	**11** Taurus	**12** ●	**13** *Sing an enchantment* Gemini	**14**	**15** *Acknowledge your love* Lupercalia Cancer	**16** *Make wine*
17 Leo	**18** *Cast a Moon circle*					

BEETS: The government of these two sorts of Beets are far different; the red Beet being under Saturn and the white under Jupiter; therefore take the virtues of them apart, each by itself. The white Beet much loosens the belly, and is of a cleansing, digesting quality, and provokes urine. The juice of it opens obstructions both of the liver and spleen, and is good for the head-ache and swimmings therein, and turnings of the brain; and is effectual also against all venomous creatures; and applied to the temples, stays inflammations of the eyes; it helps burnings, being used with oil, and with a little alum put to it, is good for St. Anthony's fire.—*The Complete Herbal* by Nicholas Culpeper

⚜ Looking Back ⚜

Hel, Goddess of Death   Johannes Gehrts, 1883

Daughter of Darkness

THE SCANDINAVIAN goddess Hel made her home beneath the first root of Yggdrasil, the giant ash tree that held the world together. Guarded by her faithful dog, Garmr, Hel ruled the icy-cold underworld of Nifelheim. In early Norse myths all dead souls either spent their afterlife in burial mounds watched over by attendants or joined Hel in her murky domain. Later legends rewarded heroes slain in battle with new life in the glorious halls of Valhalla.

Like the Greek God of the underworld, Hades, whose name and home were the same words, Hel gives us our English word "hell" from an Old Norse root meaning "covered" or "concealed." Hel's world was gloomy, but not a place of torment as penalty for earthly sins. Occasional visits occurred from the fierce wolf, Fenrir, and the serpent, Jörmungandr, for they were Hel's kin. All three were fathered by Loki, the handsome, sly and dangerous God whose actions would, an oracle declared, eventually bring the downfall of the Gods and victory of chaos as the world ends.

– Originally published in the 1998/1999 Witches' Almanac.

46

pisces

February 19 – March 20, 2019

Mutable Sign of Water ▽ Ruled by Neptune ♆

S	M	T	W	T	F	S
		Feb. **19** Chaste Moon Virgo	**20** WANING	**21** Libra	**22**	**23** Scorpio
24 Abandon chaos	**25**	**26** Sagittarius	**27** Walk straight	**28** Capricorn	Mar. **1** Matronalia	**2**
3 Aquarius	**4** Pray for light	**5** Pisces	**6**	**7** WAXING	**8** Aries	**9** Burn frankincense
10 Taurus	**11** Tell a secret	**12** Gemini	**13** Toss a coin	**14**	**15** Cancer	**16**
17 Leo	**18** Light a red candle	**19** Minerva's Day Virgo	**20** Seed Moon			

ALDER-TREE: It is a tree under the dominion of Venus, and of some watery sign or others, I suppose Pisces; and therefore the decoction, or distilled water of the leaves, is excellent against burnings and inflammations, either with wounds or without, to bathe the place grieved with, and especially for that inflammation in the breast, which the vulgar call an ague.
—*The Complete Herbal* by Nicholas Culpeper

The Hawk

Call down the hawk from the air;
Let him be hooded or caged
Till the yellow eye has grown mild,
For larder and spit are bare,
The old cook enraged,
The scullion gone wild.'
'I will not be clapped in a hood,
Nor a cage, nor alight upon wrist,
Now I have learnt to be proud
Hovering over the wood
In the broken mist
Or tumbling cloud.'
'What tumbling cloud did you cleave,
Yellow-eyed hawk of the mind,
Last evening? that I, who had sat
Dumbfounded before a knave,
Should give to my friend
A pretence of wit.'
William Butler Yeats

—WILLIAM BUTLER YEATS

aries
March 20 – April 19, 2019
Cardinal Sign of Fire △ Ruled by Mars ♂

S	M	T	W	T	F	S
			Mar. **20** Seed Moon	**21** WANING Libra	**22**	**23** Spring cleaning Scorpio
24	**25** Write a spell Sagittarius	**26**	**27** Capricorn	**28**	**29** Practice meditation	**30** Aquarius
31	April **1** Nine of Cups Pisces	**2**	**3** Protect yourself	**4** Light a fire Aries	**5**	**6** WAXING Taurus
7	**8**	**9** Use the broom! Gemini	**10**	**11** Protect your home Cancer	**12**	**13** Leo
14	**15** Virgo	**16**	**17** Carry a talisman Libra	**18**	**19** Hare Moon	兔

THE RABBIT: Their grace, style and demeanor makes those born under this sign the most likable of characters. Rabbits are the peace makers among their friends. Their sense of fashion projects style and class. They have the same eye for creative projects. While they are lovable and easy, Rabbits can also be the most pessimistic in groups. They can complicate the simplest of affairs overinflating conditions. They expect to be treated with the same respect they extend to others, clearly bristling when not afforded the same.

The Geomantic Figures: Puer

GEOMANCY IS AN ANCIENT SYSTEM of divination that uses sixteen symbols, the geomantic figures. Easy to learn and use, it was one of the most popular divination methods in the Middle Ages and Renaissance. It remained in use among rural cunning folk for many centuries thereafter, and is now undergoing a renaissance of its own as diviners discover its possibilities.

The geomantic figures are made up of single and double dots. Each figure has a name and a divinatory meaning, and the figures are also assigned to the four elements, the twelve signs of the Zodiac, the seven planets and the nodes of the Moon. The dots that make up the figures signify their inner meanings: the four lines of dots represent Fire, Air, Water and Earth and show that the elements are present in either active (one dot) or latent (two dots) form.

The first of the geomantic figures is Puer (pronounced POO-er), which means "Boy." It belongs to the element of Fire, the Zodiacal sign Aries and the planet Mars. With such correspondences, it's easy to see why this figure stands at the beginning of the geomantic sequence, for it represents the initial burst of energy that sets things into motion. Puer is the flame of masculine sexual energy, by turns creative and destructive. It flares up quickly but has no staying power, unless it finds some other figure to receive its energy.

The arrangement of dots in Puer symbolize the penis and testicles, and also a sword.

Read as symbols of the elements, the dots that form Puer tell a story of their own. The uppermost line, with one dot, shows that Fire is present in active form; the second and fourth lines, with one dot each, show that Air and Earth are in the same active state. But the third line, the line of Water, is latent and passive. Puer lacks the receptive qualities and the inner life that Water symbolizes. Puer seeks its fulfillment outside itself. It suggests the legend of the quest for the Holy Grail: the knights who rode after the Grail had the spear of Fire, the sword of Air and the shield of Earth, but had to go questing for the cup of Water.

In divination Puer is favorable in questions concerning love and also in questions concerning all kinds of competition. It advises you to act decisively and can also warn you of sudden danger.

—JOHN MICHAEL GREER

taurus

April 20 – May 20, 2019

Fixed Sign of Earth ♉ Ruled by Venus ♀

S	M	T	W	T	F	S
THE DRAGON: They are instilled with a sense for power and authority, being a sign of natural leaders. Dragons believe themselves to have intelligence and tenacity, which they indeed do, exercising this in their quests. Dragons set high standards for themselves, aiming **CONTINUED**						April **20** *Plant red flowers* Scorpio
21 Waning ⇦ 	**22** Sagittarius	**23** *Enjoy the clouds*	**24** Capricorn	**25**	**26** ◑ Aquarius	**27** *Use caution*
28 *Take cover* Pisces	**29**	**30** Walpurgis Night	May **1** Beltane Aries	**2** *Dance and sing*	**3** *Wish upon the New Moon* Taurus	**4** ●
5 WAXING	**6** *Full speed ahead* Gemini	**7**	**8** White Lotus Day Cancer	**9** *Fortune smiles*	**10** Leo	**11** ◐
12 Virgo	**13** *Enjoy a sweet* 	**14** Libra	**15**	**16** Scorpio	**17** Vesak Day ⇨	**18** ◯ Dyad Moon
19 WANING Sagittarius	**20**	龍	to exceed their goals. They are the light of the party, bringing dynamism and delight to any event. In seeking perfection, Dragons can be inflexible, stubborn and aggressive. Dragons are not quick to trust, however, once trust is earned it is for life.			

Cookies for the Birds

BIRDSEED COOKIES will help feathered friends get through the winter once their food supplies dwindle. The cookies also make nice, inexpensive, anytime gifts to give those who enjoy bird watching. Decorate a tree out-doors with strings of popcorn and cranberries and add these special cookies for the birds. It's a beautiful, natural and very simple way to attract lovely birds. Also, the aroma is wonderful as the cookies bake.

Recipe
2 cups flour
1/2 tsp baking powder
1/2 cup sugar
2/3 cup vegetable shortening
2 cracked eggs (isn't this ingredient cannibal or vampire/zombie like?)
1 cup birdseed. An option is to assemble extra interesting-looking seeds such as pumpkin or pistachio, as well as peanuts, etc. Select cookie cut-ters and some yarn.

Sift all the dry ingredients together, cut in the shortening. Add eggs and knead until smooth. Chill overnight, roll dough to 1/4 inch, form by hand into rounds or cut into shapes with cookie cutters (stars are nice). Press extra nuts and birdseed into the tops of the cookies, perhaps adding some sunflower, pumpkin or other colorful nuts and seeds for decoration. Bake at 345 degrees for 15 to 20 minutes or so, until the cookies are hard. Fashion a hanger with yarn (the birds might use the yarn later for nest building) and hang the cookies on a tree, fence or windowsill for the birds to enjoy. Get a camera ready. You can snap some lovely photos of the beautiful and grate-ful feathered visitors—and maybe a wayward squirrel or two!

−ESTER NEUMEIER

gemini

May 21 – June 20, 2019

Mutable Sign of Air △ Ruled by Mercury ☿

S	M	T	W	T	F	S
		May **21**	**22** Lessen control	**23**	**24**	**25**
		Capricorn		Aquarius		
26 Pisces	**27** Test the waters	**28** Aries	**29** Oak Apple Day	**30** Read the flames	**31** Taurus	June **1**
2 Admire the stars Gemini	**3**	**4** WAXING Cancer	**5** Night of the Watchers	**6** Leo	**7** Welcome the winds	**8** Virgo
9	**10**	**11** Libra	**12** Look with magic eyes	**13** Scorpio	**14** Enchant a feather	**15** Sagittarius
16 Visions abound	**17** Mead Moon	**18** WANING Capricorn	**19**	**20** Find peace Aquarius		蛇

THE SNAKE: They are gifted a mind that is disposed towards intelligence and wisdom. Snakes provide insight and philosophical views. They are teachers, writers and philosophers of the community. Snakes are known for their beauty and eloquence. In addition to social skills, Snakes have great luck with money. They are also a bit stingy when it comes to lending money. You would be hard pressed to know exactly what a Snake is thinking — they are careful and suspicious, and they often suffer from delicate egos.

FULL MOON NAMES

Students of occult literature soon learn the importance of names. From Ra to Rumpelstiltskin, the message is clear—names hold unusual power.

The tradition of naming full Moons was recorded in an English edition of The *Shepherd's Calendar*, published in the first decade of the 16th century.

Aries—Seed. Sowing season and symbol of the start of the new year.

Taurus—Hare. The sacred animal was associated in Roman legends with springtime and fertility.

Gemini—Dyad. The Latin word for a pair refers to the twin stars of the constellation Castor and Pollux.

Cancer—Mead. During late June and most of July the meadows, or meads, were mowed for hay.

Leo—Wort. When the sun was in Leo the worts (from the Anglo-Saxon wyrt-plant) were gathered to be dried and stored.

Virgo — Barley. Persephone, virgin goddess of rebirth, carries a sheaf of barley as symbol of the harvest.

Libra — Blood. Marking the season when domestic animals were sacrificed for winter provisions.

Scorpio — Snow. Scorpio heralds the dark season when the Sun is at its lowest and the first snow flies.

Sagittarius — Oak. The sacred tree of the Druids and the Roman god Jupiter is most noble as it withstands winter's blasts.

Capricorn — Wolf. The fearsome nocturnal animal represents the "night" of the year. Wolves were rarely seen in England after the 12th century.

Aquarius — Storm. A storm is said to rage most fiercely just before it ends, and the year usually follows suit.

Pisces — Chaste. The antiquated word for pure reflects the custom of greeting the new year with a clear soul.

Libra's Full Moon occasionally became the Wine Moon when a grape harvest was expected to produce a superior vintage.

America's early settlers continued to name the full Moons. The influence of the native tribes and their traditions is readily apparent.

AMERICAN	**Colonial**	**Native**
Aries / April	Pink, Grass, Egg	Green Grass
Taurus / May	Flower, Planting	Shed
Gemini / June	Rose, Strawberry	Rose, Make Fat
Cancer / July	Buck, Thunder	Thunder
Leo / August	Sturgeon, Grain	Cherries Ripen
Virgo / September	Harvest, Fruit	Hunting
Libra / October	Hunter's	Falling Leaf
Scorpio / November	Beaver, Frosty	Mad
Sagittarius / December	Cold, Long Night	Long Night
Capricorn / January	Wolf, After Yule	Snow
Aquarius / February	Snow, Hunger	Hunger
Pisces / March	Worm, Sap, Crow	Crow, Sore Eye

– ELIZABETH PEPPER
Moon Lore

cancer
June 21 – July 22, 2019
Cardinal Sign of Water ▽ Ruled by Moon ☽

S	M	T	W	T	F	S
THE HORSE: They are blessed with boundless energy and passion for life. Horses have a need to travel, being independent. Horses often leave home at an early age for adventure. They **CONTINUED**					June **21** Summer Solstice ☼	**22** Pisces
23	**24**	**25** ◗ Aries	**26** *Roll dice*	**27** Taurus	**28** *Enchant a stone*	**29** Gemini
30	July **1** *Anger is useless today* Cancer	**2** ●	**3** WAXING Total Solar Eclipse ⇦	**4** *Take charge* Leo	**5**	**6** Virgo
7	**8** *Carry coins* Libra	**9** ◑	**10** Scorpio	**11**	**12** *Dance in the rain* Sagittarius	**13**
14 *Summon the Moon* Capricorn	**15** Partial Lunar Eclipse ⇨	**16** Ⓞ Wort Moon	**17** WANING Aquarius	**18** *Fortune wanes*	**19** *Dream* Pisces	**20**
21	**22** Aries	are industrious with a strong sense of ethics. Horses have an ability to handle matters financial; however they hastily leave tasks. They are zealous in pursuing projects, only to move for a newer endeavor. They can be stubborn, ignoring the advice of friends and family.				馬

The Jade Emperor's Race
How the Chinese Zodiac signs came to be

THE JADE EMPEROR, long ago, decided that he would like a way to measure the passing of time. He called upon all the creatures of the kingdom to take part in a race to determine which 12 animals would be granted a zodiac year. The start of the race was along the bank of a fast-flowing river, which the animals would need to negotiate to reach the finish line on the other side.

The rat, seeing that he would have difficulties in crossing the river without being swept away by the currents convinced the kind and good-natured ox to carry him across. Once across, the rat promptly leapt off the back of the ox and claimed first place! Poor, old ox had to settle with second.

Shortly afterwards came the tiger, who was exhausted after swimming against the strong currents of the river. With a hoppity hop, along came the rabbit, who had crossed the river by hopping along some stepping stones before falling into the water and being washed to the shore on a floating log.

In fifth place came the mighty dragon, who flew over the finishing line breathing fire out of his nose. "Why did you not come first?" asked the puzzled Jade Emperor. The dragon explained that along the way, he had to stop and make rain for all the people and creatures in the world, which caused him to be delayed. Then whilst flying over the river, he noticed a little rabbit set adrift on a log, so he blew a puff of wind to carry the log to the shore. Pleased with the dragon's acts of kindness, the Jade emperor granted him the fifth place in the zodiac.

Soon after came the sound of horses hooves. However, the sly snake had hitched a ride by clinging onto one of the horse's legs and when he wriggled out, surprised the horse, giving him time to claim sixth place. Horse had to be content with taking seventh place.

Sheep, monkey and rooster arrived next, having worked together to get across the river on a raft that the rooster had found.

Eleventh place went to the dog, who despite being one of the best swimmers, decided to have a good bath because the clean water of the river was too big a temptation.

Bringing up the rear was the pig, who got hungry during the race and feasted. After the feast, he fell asleep, and it was not until after he woke that he completed the race!

leo

July 23 – August 22, 2019

Fixed Sign of Fire △ Ruled by Sun ☉

S	M	T	W	T	F	S
		July **23** Ancient Egyptian New Year	**24** Taurus	**25**	**26**	**27** *Accept no* *copy* Gemini
28	**29** *Bake bread* Cancer	**30** Lughnassad Eve ⇨	**31** Leo	Aug. **1** Lammas WAXING	**2** *Walk a* *straight line* Virgo	**3**
4 *Be proud* Libra	**5** *Walk* *carefully*	**6** Scorpio	**7**	**8** Sagittarius	**9** *Love* *yourself*	**10**
11 Capricorn	**12** *Wear* *a mask*	**13** Diana's Day Aquarius	**14** *Feeling* *unsettled?*	**15** Barley Moon	**16** WANING Black Cat Appreciation Day	**17** Pisces ⇦
18 Aries	**19**	**20**	**21** *Beware* *of lies* Taurus	**22**	羊	

THE RAM: They are the gentlest mannered and most sincere of the signs. With a sense of compassion, they are easy to be around. The Ram's empathy and sensitivity leads them into acts of social benefit. While they are always eager to help, they are not leaders. Rather than leading, Rams prefer to take direction. They are rarely open about their feelings. Rams are insecure and have a need for love and protection. They are diplomatic, avoiding confrontation at all costs. They will often sink into a sense of pessimism and anxiety.

≳Reed≴

Ngetal

Following the sequence of the tree alphabet, we descend from the highest mountain to sea level, for the reed thrives in streams and marshes. Its other names—marsh-elder and guilder-rose—reveal an affinity for Europe's low-lying coastal regions, especially Holland. "Guelder" refers to Gelderland, a Dutch province bordering the Zuider Zee.

The reed reaches a height of 10 to 15 feet, comes to creamy white bloom in June and is harvested in November to provide thatching for cottage roofs. The herbalist Gerard in 1597 remarked on the beauty of its flowers and lamented its lack of fruit.

The folklore of Northern Europe has little regard for the reed, other than as a water-loving plant through which the winds play and may make sounds that convey esoteric messages. But in more sun-kissed regions, reeds—slender and delicate, steadfast and useful—play significant roles in various myths and symbols.

In ancient Egypt, the tropical canna reed inspired the design of the royal scepter, and arrows cut from its stalk were symbols of the pharaoh's power. In Greece, another variety of reed played a role in Pan's pursuit of the lovely, chaste Syrinx. Pan pursued the nymph from mountain to river, where she eluded him by becoming a reed. The God, bewildered by the myriad reeds and unable to recognize Syrinx amongst them, cut several of the plants at random—and out of these, to turn his lust and sorrow into song, devised the glorious panpipe.

Metamorphosis turns up frequently in ancient Greek stories, especially the theme of maidens transforming into reed to avoid violation. Pan seemed particularly luckless in the sexual chase, and according to myth nymphs would go to any lengths to avoid his embrace. He was similarly thwarted by Pitys, who became a fir tree to escape his attentions. Resigned, this time the God made the best of his loss by cutting a branch and making a crown of the fir, which he wore ever after.

virgo

August 23 – September 22, 2019

Mutable Sign of Earth ♍ Ruled by Mercury ☿

S	M	T	W	T	F	S
THE MONKEY: They are known for being quite intelligent and clever. They are always game for a good amount of fun, exhibiting good cheer and vast energy. Monkeys are problem solvers, always assessing while **CONTINUED**					Aug. **23** Gemini	**24** *Cast a spell*
25 Cancer	**26**	**27** *Look inside yourself* Leo	**28**	**29** *Tempt a love* Virgo	**30**	**31** WAXING Libra
Sept. **1** *Know peace*	**2** Ganesh Festival Scorpio	**3**	**4** *Write poetry* Sagittarius	**5**	**6**	**7** *Bewitch a rival* Capricorn
8	**9** Aquarius	**10** *Be cautious*	**11**	**12** Pisces	**13**	**14** Blood Moon
15 WANING Aries	**16**	**17** *Beware of evil forces* Taurus	**18**	**19** Gemini	**20** *Watch a friend*	**21** Cancer
22 *Protect your own*	simultaneously working out the solution. Owning mental agility, they effortlessly achieve success. They can be given to a sense of privilege and arrogance. The Monkey's drive can border on opportunism. They will seek the pleasures in life regardless of any damage created. Monkeys are often not at all receptive to criticism.					猴

White Raven

Ne'er a hand so sweet I touched,
   Nor looked upon a face so fair;
Beauty is little and yet so much
   When crowned by raven hair.

Thine eyes are pools of clearest jade
   So stunning in their glance;
From moonlight the gods thee made
   More sacred than the dance.

Yea my lady I attest
   I love thee more than night or day,
And wish my heart were on thy breast
   For ever in thine arms to stay.

—ANTHONY P. JONES
A Vision of Sorrows Mystery

libra

September 23 – October 22, 2019
Cardinal Sign of Air ♎ Ruled by Venus ♀

LIBRA

S	M	T	W	T	F	S
雞	**23** Autumnal Equinox ♌	**24** Leo	**25** *Chant*	**26** Virgo	**27** *Draw circles*	**28** ● Libra
29 WAXING	**30** *Take heed* Scorpio	Oct. **1**	**2** *Safety in numbers* Sagittarius	**3**	**4** Capricorn	**5** ◐
. **6** Aquarius	**7** *Psychic powers flow*	**8**	**9** *Carry a feather* Pisces	**10** *Pet your familiar*	**11** Aries	**12** *Shapeshift*
13 (Snow Moon)	**14** WANING Taurus	**15**	**16** *Admire a tree* Gemini	**17**	**18**	**19** *Handle wet stones* Cancer
20 *Don't break glass*	**21** ◐	**22** Leo				

THE ROOSTER: They have the loudest voice in the crowd, for good or for bad. Roosters take the time to observe before accurately capturing what the next step is in any situation. In their group of friends, they are the best dressed. They can at times become self-absorbed with their appearance. In fact, their attention to fashion can be extreme. The Rooster is neither complicated nor profound. They tend to be frank, offering their opinion with economy while eschewing unnecessary flourishes. Those born under the sign of the Rooster value loyalty above all else in their friends. Many will find arguing with them futile as they will always have the last word.

ſexual ßlasphemy

Lovers Desecrate the Temple

APPALLING SISTERS "not to be approached and not to be described" inhabited a murky cavern at the mouth of the Underworld. Euryale, known as "the Far Springer" and Sthenno, "the Mighty," were Gorgons, daughters of ancient sea Gods. The sisters defied description because they were lethally grotesque, for any creature that saw them turned to stone. The Gorgons were rumored to have glares like wild beasts, snakes knotted around their necks and tresses of living, hissing serpents. "Over their heads a great Dread quivers," according to Hesiod.

Medusa, unlike her sisters, was a consummate beauty. Weary of the dreary cave, she begged Athena for a new life in a sunny climate. When Athena denied the plea, Medusa accused the Goddess of jealousy. "Once mortals see me," she boasted, "they will no longer consider you the most beautiful." Athena disdained to take offense at the presumptuous remark, but the insult evoked her fury.

Sea Gods adored loveliness, none more than Poseidon. He found Medusa agleam in the dark cavern, and according to her wish spirited her to the temple of Athena. There Medusa lay with him night and day, the desecration of Athena's shrine adding to the intensity of her pleasure. In revenge for the sacrilege, Athena transformed Medusa into a Gorgon like her serpent-garnished sisters. And like her siblings, all who perceived Medusa turned to stone.

Such evil power would seem to render a Gorgon invulnerable, but never underestimate the ingenuity of a Greek hero, especially a hero aided by a Deity. Athena furnished Perseus with winged sandals for flying, a helmet for invisibility, a curved sword and brightly shining shield. Perseus flew into the dark, foul-smelling cave. Guided by the reflection in the shield, he cut off Medusa's head as she slept. From the blood of the deed sprang Medusa's son by Poseidon, the winged horse Pegasus. He flies the night sky as a constellation—the heavenly progeny of an outlandish union at a sacred site.

—BARBARA STACY

scorpio

October 23 – November 21, 2019

Fixed Sign of Water ▽ Ruled by Pluto♀

S	M	T	W	T	F	S
THE DOG: They are the most faithful of the all of the signs. They are always agreeable when times are good and tend toward a sharp tongue, becoming nasty **CONTINUED**			Oct. **23** *Gaze into a mirror*	**24** Virgo	**25**	**26** *Dismiss a bane* Libra
27 ●	**28** WAXING Scorpio	**29** *Lock your doors*	**30** *Ouija speaks* Sagittarius	**31** Samhain Eve	Nov. **1** Hallowmas Capricorn	**2** *Feast with the dead*
3 *Light a candle* Aquarius	**4** ◑	**5** Pisces	**6** *Read old letters*	**7**	**8** *Honor the deceased* Aries	**9**
10 Taurus	**11**	**12** Oak Moon ○	**13** WANING Gemini	**14** *Watch the Moon*	**15** Cancer	**16** Hecate Night
17 *Taste love* Leo	**18**	**19** ◑	**20** *Dogs sleep* Virgo	**21**		

when situations are stressful. Dogs are driven by a sense of creating situations of equanimity. Those born under this sign often sacrifice to create happiness for others. In the group of friends, the Dog is often given to serving in the most generous of fashions and will go all out in the name of loyalty. They are quite decisive in relationships—you're either his friend or not. Dogs do not deal with their own emotions and, as a result, can become quite moody or short as well as impatient.

ÆSOP'S FABLES

The Vain Jackdaw

JUPITER DETERMINED, it is said, to create a sovereign over the birds, and made a proclamation that, on a certain day, they should all present themselves before him, when he would himself choose the most beautiful among them to be king.

The Jackdaw, knowing his own ugliness, searched through the woods and fields, and collected the feathers which had fallen from the wings of his companions, and stuck them in all parts of his body.

When the appointed day arrived, and the birds had assembled before Jupiter, the Jackdaw also made his appearance in his many-feathered finery.

On Jupiter proposing to make him king, on account of the beauty of his plumage, the birds indignantly protested, and each plucking from him his own feathers, the Jackdaw was again nothing but a Jackdaw.

Moral: Hope not to succeed in borrowed plumes.

sagittarius

November 22 – December 20, 2019

Mutable Sign of Fire △ Ruled by Jupiter ♃

S	M	T	W	T	F	S
THE PIG: They are the altruist always exhibiting the best of qualities; honesty, purity, tolerance and honor. In fact, their path is so good, Pigs are often seen as being too good to be true. They are often the character model in the group. Pigs are generally the most **CONTINUED**					Nov. **22** Libra	**23**
24 Scorpio	**25** *Take your time*	**26** ● Sagittarius	**27** WAXING	**28** *Proceed* Capricorn	**29** .	**30** Aquarius
Dec. **1** *Lay upon the ground*	**2**	**3** Pisces	**4** ◑	**5** *Kiss a star*	**6** *Leave anger behind* Aries	**7**
8 Taurus	**9** *Listen to the wind*	**10** Gemini	**11**	**12** Wolf Moon	**13** WANING Cancer	**14** *Journey safely over water*
15 Leo	**16** *Fairy Queen Eve*	**17** *Saturnalia* Virgo	**18** ◑	**19** Libra	**20** *Read fiction*	豬

loving and caring of friends. It is hard to put them off as friends; their forgiving nature is always in the forefront. The Pig is given to enjoying good drink and good food with their friends. While indulgence in the fineries of life can become costly, this is usually not a problem for them, as the Pig's luck always attracts the wealth necessary to keep life easy. The faults of Pigs are few, though they can become so content with their position that they are not open to change.

capricorn

December 21, 2019 – January 19, 2020
Cardinal Sign of Earth ▽ *Ruled by Saturn* ♄

S	M	T	W	T	F	S
THE RAT: is a hardworking, intelligent type. They are absolutely independent and resolute in the process. They are not satisfied simply to accept anything at a face value; rather their inquisitiveness drives them to have a thorough knowledge of any situation. **CONTINUED**						Dec. **21** Winter Solstice ❄ Scorpio
22	**23** *Create a charm* Sagittarius	**24**	**25** Partial Solar Eclipse ⇨	**26** ● Capricorn	**27** WAXING	**28** *Avoid nightmares* Aquarius
29 *Snap fingers three times*	**30** Pisces	**31**	Jan. **1** *Look both ways*	**2** ◐ Aries	**3** *Eat an apple*	**4** Taurus
5 *Test yourself*	**6**	**7** Gemini	**8** *Talk to the fey*	**9** Feast of Janus Cancer	**10** Storm Moon	**11** WANING Partial Lunar Eclipse ⇦
12 Leo ⇦	**13** *Engage a spirit* Virgo	**14**	**15** *Enjoy music* Libra	**16**	**17** ◑	**18** *Sleep* Scorpio
19	The Rat will watch for situations where they can take advantage. They usually act with speed and are flexible. While the Rat's curiosity can lead it into unsavory circumstance, they are escape artists. The downfall of Rats is they can over examine a situation. Their thrifty ways often devolve into miserly penny pinching. While easily driven to chattiness, the Rat in fact does not trust readily and is in a constant need of assurances that he is liked.					

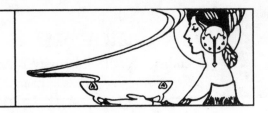

The Star

COOKING IS MAGIC. There is the alchemy of transforming the ingredients, bringing together many elements to create one delicious dish. There is the fugue state achieved when you are eating something amazing. Runners high? That may be a goal for some, but for me tasting a creamy piece of cheesecake topped with the perfectly tart blueberry compote can make my eyes roll to the back of my head. There is also the pleasure you get watching other people eat what you have crafted. That blissful moment when someone who swore they were not going to eat another cookie, looks around to make sure no one else is watching and starts stuffing them in their pocket!

Just like a good spell, there are rules to cooking and baking—you've probably heard them all. Well, sometimes it's best not to measure. You just go with the flow, paying attention to the way things look and feel, and of course the way they taste. That is the case with this eggplant parm recipe. My mother taught me and all these years later, not only am I still making it this way, but I have friends from high school still asking me to make it for them!

The Star tarot card (17) is all about going with the flow. It looks like she is pouring water into the pond, but really the water is flowing through her, creating a circuit. She is relaxed and peaceful. She wouldn't think of measuring ingredients!

If you're feeling really crazy, substitute zucchini for the eggplant! Remember one rule... you can never have enough cheese!

Mom's Eggplant Parm

1 or 2 large eggplants
eggs
flavored bread crumbs
jarred spaghetti sauce (approx 1 jar per large eggplant)
vegetable oil
mozzarella cheese (shredded)
ricotta cheese

Preheat oven to 350°. Slice the eggplant into rounds, 1/4 inch thick. Salt and put in a colander letting excess liquid drain. This takes the bitterness out of the eggplant.

Coat the eggplant with flour, then egg wash (eggs mixed with water) and add breadcrumbs. Heat a large skillet with an inch of oil in it. Fry the eggplant and drain on paper towels. Add oil as necessary.

Coat the bottom of a casserole dish with sauce. Add a layer of eggplant, dollops of ricotta, mozzarella and some more sauce. Repeat the layers, ending with a layer of mozzarella. Bake at 350° until bubbly.

—DEBBIE CHAPNICK

aquarius

January 20 – February 18, 2020

Fixed Sign of Air ♎ Ruled by Uranus ♅

S	M	T	W	T	F	S
牛	Jan. **20** Sagittarius	**21**	**22** *Dance wildly* Capricorn	**23**	**24** ● Aquarius	Jan. **25** Chinese New Year Metal Rat
26 WAXING ⇦	**27** *Your beloved needs you* Pisces	**28**	**29** Aries	**30** *Call a friend*	**31** Oimelc Eve ⇨	Feb. **1** ◐ Taurus
2 Candlemas	**3** *Read the Tarot* Gemini	**4**	**5** *Temperance* Cancer	**6**	**7** Leo	**8** *Read an old almanac*
9 Chaste Moon	**10** WANING Virgo	**11**	**12** *Gather snow* Libra	**13**	**14** Lupercalia ⇨ Scorpio	**15** ◑
16 *Wolves howl* Sagittarius	**17**	**18** Capricorn				

THE OX: They are hardworking, diligent and can stick to an arduous task longer than most. They often put their heart into the job at hand and will dive into a project with vigor that outstrips their colleagues. In the Ox you will find a fiercely loyal partner and friend. In fact, in their book the breaching of loyalty is the most egregious offense. The Ox puts family and friends above all. While they take their time in committing to a situation, they will be unwavering in dedication once the decision has been made. The Ox can indeed be a bit on the stubborn side and fixated on a single issue, sticking to rules even if they become an impediment to progress. They also have a temper that is quick to flare, always needing space and time to calm down.

pisces

February 19 – March 19, 2020

Mutable Sign of Water ▽ Ruled by Neptune ♆

S	M	T	W	T	F	S
THE TIGER: They are born leaders, always exhibiting an air of authority, acting courageously and proudly. They are among the most irresistible, with many being attracted to **CONTINUED**			Feb. **19**	**20** Aquarius	**21**	**22** *Question the dead*
23 ● Pisces	**24** WAXING	**25** Aries	**26** . *Rest the mind*	**27**	**28** *Find what you lost* Taurus	**29** Leap Day
Mar. **1** Matronalia Gemini	**2** ◑	**3** *Relay a message*	**4** Cancer	**5**	**6** *Express passion* Leo	**7**
8 *Drink water* Virgo	**9** ○	**10** WANING Libra	**11**	**12** *Bury a curse* Scorpio	**13**	**14** *Draw with color* Sagittarius
15 *Trust the garden*	**16** ◐	**17** Capricorn	**18** *Don't tempt fate*	**19** *Minerva's Day* Aquarius		

their magnetic personality. The Tiger is calm and warmhearted, but can be tempestuous and terrifying if necessary. The Tiger has an essential need to be dominant in their group. If this need is not met, they can easily become depressed. The Tiger often will act quickly when presented with a task; they will plunge headlong into action without thought. They are often more abrupt and hasty than their peers. Tigers will rebel against authority just to make their point known.

...and that which is especially to be observed in this, the singleness of the wit, innocency of the mind, a firm credulity, and constant silence; wherefore they do often meet children, women, and poor and mean men. They are afraid of and flie from men of a constant, bold, and undaunted mind...
–Cornelius Agrippa

NEW WORLD FAERIES

I begin with this quote about the nature of faeries because I find it true regarding those who tend to have the most faerie encounters. From experience and inference from the testimony of others it seems this is indeed the best mind frame to encounter Them. When you are alone in nature, not thinking about much of anything but the beauty of the day, light of heart, free of expectations and yearnings—is often the moment. Those who have an experience and attempt to recreate it by returning to the same location at the same time of day or year generally don't meet with success, unless it is by the explicit invitation of the Good Folk.

Calling the Fair Folk
Of course, the Witch or any solid practitioner of the magical arts has at their disposal the two things that make such a return possible: the will and the activated imagination. For most occultists, whether learned people or not, the simple will to imagine and return to a state unpolluted by the ideas of human society will be enough, when added to instructions such as those given in Agrippa, to eventually materialize an encounter.

He therefore that will call upon them, may easily doe it in the places where their abode is, by alluring them with sweet fumes, with pleasant sounds, and by such instruments as are made of the guts of certain animals and peculiar wood, adding songs, verses, inchantments sutable [sic] to it...

Burning incense and creating beauty, either through stringed instruments, singing or verses of poetry appear to be the order of the day. One might add the Faerie Throne or "white meal" where a repast laid out on white, with white bread and milk for the consumption of the faeries, placed there, where it is undertaken not to look back once you leave it for their enjoyment. Other taboos such as not speaking, keeping very still and not telling the public in detail about your encounter afterwards in the case where any boons or gifts were given you, are also very helpful.

Whether sprung from the ground natively, being the intelligence of the green world, or having fallen from a more celestial origin, there can be little argument around the strong tie between what we call "nature" and the faerie realm. This is important to understanding the faerie experience of people situated in the New World. For those of us descended wholly or partly from European invasion and settlement of these lands, this shapes our relationship with place and nature in ways which we might not immediately be cognizant of. The bones or ashes of the first peoples are wreathed into the roots of every grove of eucalyptus and sassafras and every pile of rocks a faerie spirit might emerge from.

If you are of indigenous descent and still enmeshed in the cultural inheritance of your people and place, then this topic may not concern you. You might have your own local name for these kinds of spirits. On the other hand, like some indigenous Australians I have met, you might acknowledge that some "Others" came over along with the settlers.

Of course, even if we see faeries as connected primarily to wild nature and the world of the green, there are a large number of humans said to be "taken by the faeries," or families said to be of faerie blood. Human gravesites are haunted by faeries enough so that it's clear—at least in Britain—that just as the bones of the forebears return to the Earth there is a certain admixture between their world and ours.

Devilish Encounters

In all lands it seems there are types of spirits which humans don't readily interact with, and those types are usually only spoken to by sorcerers. This was an idea that existed in Tasmania with the dangerous Wrageowrapper spirit who brought intense destructive winds—only sorcerers would converse with him. Likewise, the women of the Nuenonne people were said to fall pregnant after intercourse with certain "devils" that might have been called faerie instead in the hands of a more sympathetic translator.

This all being said, intermixture between the faerie and the human dead is known in other ways. Some of the little people of the US are remarkably similar to the tales of faeries in Britain and Europe. The Chocktaw and Cherokee stories about their "little people" are in many ways indistinguishable from the stories told across the Atlantic. They involve the ability to tangle a fishing line, just as elves may tangle the horse's mane with elf locks in Britain, with being mainly of smaller stature, with wielding elf-darts which are poisonous, with the ability to change size, dance in circles until disappearing, only living in the pristine wilderness and being seen

sometimes as moving lights. I have heard many people say that whilst they have no doubt these Kwanokasha and Laurels existed prior to contact, the faerie scene as it exists in the Americas today is one of hybridism between introduced and native faeries.

Australia is an entirely alien landscape by comparison, where the bark sheds from the trees instead of the leaves, and all of the animals except for some birds are virtually unrecognizable by comparison to anything from home. Nonetheless there is evidence of how quickly hybridization of a type occurs, in the following tale of an Aboriginal man's sorcerous initiation:

An oony or minychalam, (a bullock-footed devil) came to John at night at the house—not in a dream, it actually came to him. It took him down to the cemetery and right down inside a grave, near that of the missionary Mrs MacKenzie. There was a very long table down there, heaped with money, with oparr (magical substances, "medicines")

for attracting women, for gambling, and for killing and fighting, along with rusty knives, sharp knives—all kind of things. The oony asked him if he wanted to be a rich man, or did he want oparr for women, or to kill people, or did he want to become a 'Murri doctor' healer, a nhoyan. John said that he wanted to become a nhoyan. The oony took out one of John's eyes, and put his own in John's eye sockets. With these eyes, he could then see right through walls and over great distances. Then he showed John tricks; he took his own head off, walked around, then put it back on—all sorts of tricks. The devil then took him out of the grave and they walked back together. When John subsequently healed people, his own spirit shade (maany) travelled in company with his spirit familiar to the sick person as they lay sleeping, but his bodily presence (ngurrp) remained. He is now half minychalam himself, with piercing eyes like those of the bullock-footed devil, and long ears.

The speed with which this spirit seems to have adapted a split-foot when there was no cloven-footed animal anywhere in Australia before white settlement, is interesting, especially given the unique Aboriginal name this split-footed devil is given. It's also potentially significant that the spirit specifically used the grave of a Scottish missionary.

Prior to British occupation, no long tables, rusty knives, money or monetary gambling existed in Australia. Have the same spirits that always lived there become cunning at using the paraphernalia of the neophyte sorcerer's environment? Or have they been altered in some way by the presence of Europeans, bullocks, tables and money?

Shedding Knowledge

Having walked this road, what we know about Them seems even less than when we began and I think that is for the best. Armed with this stripping away of knowledge we can learn the folklore of our local area if any exists, such as taboos of how to treat the Others there, but we must always allow Them to speak for themselves by making ourselves available and silent for long enough periods of time that they may appear to us. When we go down to our bare bones, lay off our words, our categories and walk away into the woods to lay down our idea-load, our firm credulity and innocency of mind. Like the poor and mean man or the child, we may enter their space without making ripples in the waters of awareness.

—LEE MORGAN

To hear Lee Morgan reading this article, as well finding extended articles, visit TheWitchesAlmanac.com/almanac-extras/

Transgender Questions Among Witches and Pagans

Western European Pagan beliefs and practices have survived centuries of deadly persecution and abuse to arrive at last in a time when we can enjoy worshiping the Old Gods in relative freedom. Even in modern times, though, many Pagan people still report experiencing discrimination in societies dominated by mainstream religions, and while oppression serves to strengthen bonds among the victimized, transgender Pagans suffer additional discrimination within the Pagan community itself.

Multiple and complex issues affect transgender Witches and Pagans. The dichotomy of gender-specific events and the dilemma of inclusion or exclusion are keenly felt by those who already feel ostracized in their daily lives. Transgender individuals attending large, public Pagan festivals and gatherings have found themselves barred from some women's or men's rituals and events. Although many Craft groups welcome Pagans and Witches regardless of their gender identity, some accept only cis-gender (genetic) people to participate in their rites. The division that ensues is a thorny problem for the Pagan community at large. Do the rights and desires of either group supersede those of the opposing position?

We cherish our freedom to enjoy the company of kindred souls, to associate and work with others of like mind. This very human need for fellowship with a select group with whom we are comfortable is the foundation of friendships, social circles, clubs and covens. The flip side of the closed-group coin is the exclusion of non-members—the element of exclusion defines a closed group. Private groups have convened throughout human history, and are generally accepted as a normal part of life. At large events, however, which are billed as "public" and "open," attendees may expect featured activities to be open to all, and exclusivity can become a divisive issue. Those attending a restricted event feel they are in their rights to meet with whom they wish while specific exclusion is felt by transgender attendees as transphobic prejudice, sexism and rejection.

In Traditional Witchcraft, the binary division of roles in rituals and initiations can be problematic for transgender Witches. Everything from casting the Circle to the alternating male-female order of Witches in the Dance is defined by gender in Traditional Witchcraft. A Priest initiates a female Witch, a Priestess initiates a male Witch. What happens when a Witch transitions to the gender they identify with after initiation? In Traditions that emphasize the legitimacy of descending lines in rigid terms, some may question the letter-of-the-law validity of roles a transgender Witch filled before their transition. If the transgender Witch was always really the opposite gender, was it actually a priest or was it a priestess who performed that role in a given event? The real question is, of course, does it matter? One perspective adheres to the written rule "once a Witch, always a Witch" regarding initiations; the permanence of the transformation being legendary—it cannot be undone. Another view questions the validity of an initiation if all required elements were not exactly provided: was that Witch really "Witched?"

Some transgender Witches are comfortable with their personal magickal history as it is. If they are in a supportive group or groups that accept their personal experience and assessment, harmony prevails. Other transgender initiates of Traditional Craft choose to go back and repeat the steps of initiation with priesthood they feel appropriate to their corrected gender. After all is said and done, it is up to the Witch.

Rising from the Burning Times, Witches have survived centuries of oppression, violence and death, but in today's world Pagan folk of all walks have the opportunity to forge bonds with each other and build a strong, vibrant alliance. Working together with respect, love and trust, the Pagan community has the strength and solidarity to overcome fear and discrimination and become a place of peace and understanding where we can all come home.

—RHIANNON MCBRIDE

Coiling Serpents

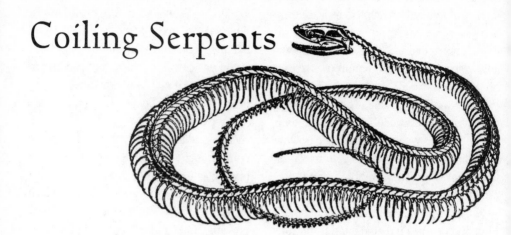

PERHAPS THE MOST famous symbol of Hermes, the Greek messenger God, is the caduceus: a winged staff with an orb on top and two snakes twining around it in a repeating spiral. Certain legends say that Hermes acquired this staff from the blind soothsayer Tiresias, who assaulted a pair of copulating snakes and was turned into a woman for seven years because of it. He was later turned back into a man by finding another pair of snakes and either doing the same or leaving them alone. Another myth credits Hermes with acquiring the snakes personally: finding them in combat, he stuck the staff between them to break up the fight.

Whether the result of a divine peacemaker or a prophetic buzz kill, the caduceus and especially the two snakes on it relate to Hermes in many important symbolic ways.

Transgressing Boundaries

First, as the messenger of the Gods, Hermes is one of the few beings who can move between the mortal world, Olympus and the underworld, Hades, where he must go frequently to con-

duct dead souls. Even other Gods, such as Persephone, can be trapped in Hades, but Hermes can come and go as he pleases. Within the world of the living, Hermes's mobility—aided by his also-famous winged sandals—makes him the patron of travelers, as well as the God of both boundaries and their transgression. The guy, as they say, gets around.

Similarly, snakes, with their thin bodies and flexible skeletons, can get into and out of places most of us large, ungainly bipeds would never expect—emerging from between the rocks in a stone wall, or taking up residence above the drop ceiling in a farmhouse. Folks staying in campsite cabins have had pairs of mating snakes fall on top of them (revenge for that pair interrupted by Tiresias, maybe?) and there are even five species of snakes that can "fly" by gliding from tree to tree.

Being long and narrow also makes snakes symbolic from a phallic perspective, of course, and plenty has been said or written about this in the context of the Garden of Eden. However, this quality also provides another connection to Hermes in his role as God of travelers and boundaries. He is associated with *herms*, phallic structures of stone or wood placed at borders and crossroads to protect travelers. At first, merely the shape of these columns was suggestive; later, when they became statues, the genitals were depicted as well as the head, even though the rest of the body was usually blank.

Perpetual Regeneration

One of the most notable qualities of snakes is the way that they regularly shed their skin. While many animals do this, snakes shed the whole thing at once, leaving behind a ghostly, transparent remnant of themselves. Before shedding, a snake will look dull, stop eating and retreat to a safe place, in part because the cloudy skin over its eyes obstructs its eyesight. Snakes' reclusiveness and lack of appetite at these times is very reminiscent of the dying process. When a snake peels off its old skin and emerges, larger and shinier than before, it brings to mind the process of rebirth, perhaps the closest thing in the natural world to the phoenix emerging from its own ashes.

Due in part to this quality, many cultures associate snakes with death and rebirth—the trip to and from the underworld that forms the transformative hero's journey for so many mortals, but which Hermes makes with ease. This is likely one reason why the Greeks also associated snakes with the healing God, Asclepius—whose rod, bearing a single snake, is the symbol of medicine often confused with the caduceus—and often let non-venomous snakes loose in

rooms where the sick and injured were recovering. Legend has it that Asclepius learned the art of evading death because he saw one snake bringing another back to life with herbs. Just as Hermes can ignore boundaries that most of us consider almost insurmountable, snakes regularly cast off their old selves all in one piece, emerging renewed (and with fewer parasites). They're close to death, life and profound change in general.

This closeness is one of the reasons snakes are associated with wisdom in many cultures—from the forbidden knowledge of traditional Christianity to the benevolent Damballa of some African and Afro-American religions—as is their ability to go long periods without acting, then strike swiftly and decisively when need be. Wisdom is another quality that snakes share with Hermes, who is associated with cunning, and in his role as Hermes Trismegistus, lord of magic and metaphysical knowledge.

—JULIA ATHENA

2019 SUNRISE AND SUNSET TIMES

Providence—San Francisco—Sydney—London

	Sunrise				Sunset			
	Prov	**SF**	**Syd**	**Lon**	**Prov**	**SF**	**Syd**	**Lon**
Jan 5	7:13 AM	7:25 AM	5:50 AM	8:05 AM	4:29 PM	5:04 PM	8:09 PM	4:06 PM
15	7:10 AM	7:23 AM	5:59 AM	7:59 AM	4:39 PM	5:14 PM	8:09 PM	4:20 PM
25	7:04 AM	7:18 AM	6:09 AM	7:49 AM	4:51 PM	5:25 PM	8:05 PM	4:36 PM
Feb 5	6:53 AM	7:10 AM	6:20 AM	7:32 AM	5:05 PM	5:37 PM	7:57 PM	4:56 PM
15	6:41 AM	6:59 AM	6:29 AM	7:15 AM	5:18 PM	5:48 PM	7:48 PM	5:15 PM
25	6:27 AM	6:46 AM	6:38 AM	6:54 AM	5:30 PM	5:59 PM	7:37 PM	5:33 PM
Mar 5	6:14 AM	6:35 AM	6:45 AM	6:37 AM	5:40 PM	6:07 PM	7:27 PM	5:47 PM
15	6:57 AM	7:20 AM	6:53 AM	6:15 AM	6:51 PM	7:16 PM	7:14 PM	6:04 PM
25	6:40 AM	7:05 AM	7:01 AM	5:52 AM	7:03 PM	7:26 PM	7:00 PM	6:21 PM
Apr 5	6:22 AM	6:49 AM	7:09 AM	6:27 AM	7:15 PM	7:36 PM	6:45 PM	7:39 PM
15	6:05 AM	6:34 AM	6:17 AM	6:05 AM	7:26 PM	7:45 PM	5:33 PM	7:56 PM
25	5:50 AM	6:21 AM	6:24 AM	5:44 AM	7:37 PM	7:54 PM	5:21 PM	8:13 PM
May 5	5:37 AM	6:09 AM	6:32 AM	5:25 AM	7:48 PM	8:03 PM	5:11 PM	8:29 PM
15	5:25 AM	5:59 AM	6:39 AM	5:09 AM	7:58 PM	8:12 PM	5:02 PM	8:45 PM
25	5:17 AM	5:52 AM	6:46 AM	4:56 AM	8:08 PM	8:20 PM	4:57 PM	8:59 PM
June 5	5:11 AM	5:48 AM	6:53 AM	4:46 AM	8:16 PM	8:28 PM	4:53 PM	9:11 PM
15	5:10 AM	5:47 AM	6:58 AM	4:42 AM	8:22 PM	8:33 PM	4:52 PM	9:19 PM
25	5:11 AM	5:49 AM	7:00 AM	4:44 AM	8:24 PM	8:35 PM	4:54 PM	9:21 PM
July 5	5:16 AM	5:53 AM	7:00 AM	4:50 AM	8:23 PM	8:34 PM	4:58 PM	9:19 PM
15	5:23 AM	5:59 AM	6:58 AM	5:00 AM	8:19 PM	8:31 PM	5:04 PM	9:11 PM
25	5:32 AM	6:07 AM	6:53 AM	5:13 AM	8:11 PM	8:24 PM	5:10 PM	8:59 PM
Aug 5	5:43 AM	6:16 AM	6:44 AM	5:29 AM	7:59 PM	8:14 PM	5:18 PM	8:42 PM
15	5:53 AM	6:25 AM	6:34 AM	5:45 AM	7:45 PM	8:02 PM	5:25 PM	8:23 PM
25	6:03 AM	6:33 AM	6:23 AM	6:01 AM	7:30 PM	7:49 PM	5:31 PM	8:02 PM
Sept 5	6:15 AM	6:43 AM	6:09 AM	6:18 AM	7:12 PM	7:33 PM	5:39 PM	7:38 PM
15	6:25 AM	6:51 AM	5:55 AM	6:34 AM	6:55 PM	7:17 PM	5:46 PM	7:15 PM
25	6:35 AM	6:59 AM	5:41 AM	6:50 AM	6:38 PM	7:02 PM	5:53 PM	6:52 PM
Oct 5	6:46 AM	7:08 AM	5:27 AM	7:07 AM	6:20 PM	6:46 PM	6:00 PM	6:29 PM
15	6:57 AM	7:17 AM	6:14 AM	7:23 AM	6:04 PM	6:32 PM	7:07 PM	6:07 PM
25	7:09 AM	7:27 AM	6:02 AM	7:41 AM	5:49 PM	6:19 PM	7:16 PM	5:47 PM
Nov 5	6:22 AM	6:39 AM	5:51 AM	7:00 AM	4:35 PM	5:06 PM	7:26 PM	4:27 PM
15	6:34 AM	6:49 AM	5:43 AM	7:17 AM	4:25 PM	4:58 PM	7:35 PM	4:11 PM
25	6:46 AM	7:00 AM	5:38 AM	7:34 AM	4:18 PM	4:52 PM	7:45 PM	3:59 PM
Dec 5	6:57 AM	7:09 AM	5:37 AM	7:48 AM	4:14 PM	4:50 PM	7:54 PM	3:53 PM
15	7:05 AM	7:17 AM	5:38 AM	7:59 AM	4:15 PM	4:51 PM	8:01 PM	3:51 PM
25	7:11 AM	7:23 AM	5:42 AM	8:05 AM	4:19 PM	4:56 PM	8:07 PM	3:55 PM

Prov=Providence; SF=San Francisco; Syd=Sydney; Lon=London
Times are presented in the standard time of the geographical location, using the current time zone of that place.

Window on the Weather

Among scientists, the link between naturally variant systems including solar output, geothermal activity and sea surface temperatures is an emerging topic. All have a profound affect on global temperatures distribution, wind and precipitation, but affect human behavior as well and in a naturally cyclical manner. Fertility rates peak at solar maximums, for example, and diminish during minimums, as a natural response to changes in crop yield and resulting foraging behaviors. The long-term base state shows that populations and individuals tend to be less proximate at high latitudes where birth rates are lower, while the inverse is so at low latitudes, close to the Equator. Solar cycles can also be predictive of economic activity with innovation and general creativity emerging as solar brightness increases from its 11-year minimums.

This is usually a time of relative peace globally and rational thought, while war and dissolution is a risk at solar maximums. At this time, beginning solar cycle 25, weather patterns favor cold winters in North America, Europe and East Asia and warm water in the western Atlantic, bringing an enhanced chance for Fall hurricanes to the U.S. East Coast. Seismic activity along the "Ring Of Fire" near the Pacific Rim also increases, meaning increased occurrences of earthquakes and volcanoes—all part of natural systems variance.

SPRING

MARCH 2019. As solar cycle 25 begins, we note there has been, since 1980, a successive drop from peak to trough for each 11-year cycle. As correlated, there have been more than 25 excessive snowstorms in the eastern United States during the past decade with long-term averages indicating about five for each ten-year period. This year's low solar output and weak El Niño sea surface temperature patterns in the Pacific indicates a high chance for above-normal snowfall this month, from the Mid-Atlantic States south through the Carolinas, Tennessee and Georgia. In fact, odds favor excessive snowfall for much of the nation and arriving relatively late in the season. Such a pattern also supports a southern storm track, supportive of welcome rainfall in Southern California and Texas. A severe weather outbreak or two can also occur in Florida. The Great Lakes states and North Plains are seasonably cold with normal snowfall.

APRIL 2019. As the sun returns, human activity increases at the fastest pace during April. Solar geo-magnetism regulates all mammalian endocrine and limbic systems by engagement with the pineal gland. During Spring, at the low point in an 11-year solar cycle, coastal low clouds and fog are prevalent and activity is slower than inland locations because of diminished sunshine. This will be particularly true this year from Washington D.C. to coastal New England, the Great Lake states, mid Mississippi Valley and from San Francisco to Seattle. Along the Gulf of Mexico through Texas and north to Kansas, an active tornado season is underway as vestiges of an El Niño event bring jet stream wind energy to sharply contrasting pools of lingering winter cold to the north and increasing heat farther south, ingredients for severe weather.

MAY 2019. A nearly ideal growing season begins with a warm and sunny start to the month. That is in sharp contrast to lingering cold April weather in the Northeast, but warmth will quickly spread from Texas to New England. There will be a battleground, however, between contrasting air masses farther west as cold air from the Rockies undercuts building heat across the Plains, bringing hail and high winds. Spring rains will be plentiful farther east from Indiana and Illinois through the Ohio Valley. California reservoirs are bank full, courtesy of abundant late winter snowfall. Florida will enjoy pleasant Spring weather, where heat is less intense than in recent years as La Niña related weather conditions have eased.

SUMMER

JUNE 2019. The highest sun angle of the year is accompanied by warmth and low humidity. Rivers run high in the Rockies and California's Sierra Nevada, where Spring snow melt lingers on longer than usual. An early season tropical storm may grace coastal Texas and Louisiana. Should that occur, rain will spread north as far as Oklahoma and limit early season heat across the Great Plains. Along the East Coast, pleasantly cool nights and warm days are underway, with usual seasonal afternoon cooling sea breezes limited by warm water temperatures. Three outbreaks of thunderstorms accompany cold fronts arriving from Canada, limiting 80 degree temperatures across the Northeast and Great Lakes to just a few days in between modified polar air masses. Afternoon thunderstorms emerge on both of Florida's coasts bringing further drought relief.

JULY 2019. Peak summer heat is reached across the continent, given long-term trends, during the third week of July. Such an occurrence 30 days after the Solstice is attributable to solar variance and difference rates of ultraviolet radia-

tion absorption by the planet that acts as a thermal mass. The net gain in heat lingers after the highest sun angle of the year. In fact, ocean water temperatures peak during the Fall and close to the Equinox. Given that pattern, summer heat is distributed most evenly during July and as a consequence, weather changes are infrequent. Most occur near the U.S. Canadian border, where occasional incursions of modified Summer polar air eases the heat. Fast moving thunderstorms, a few severe, can accompany cold fronts with squally winds. Afternoon rainfall is also common along the inter-mountain west continental divide, mainly during late afternoon in repeated areas and can be planned for by hikers and campers. The tropic stirs off the west coast of Mexico, fueling a few showers in the desert Southwest.

AUGUST 2019. The hurricane season begins slowly in the Atlantic basin and Gulf of Mexico. Tropical storm activity is confined to areas where water temperatures exceed 80 degrees Fahrenheit. During August, such sea surface temperatures are usually confined to near-shore waters off Florida, Gulf Coast States and the South Central Atlantic Ocean. Sometimes, a precursor "monsoon" channel will develop in the eastern United States preceding organized tropical storms and can bring persistent rainfall to that area. Summer heat eases quickly farther east, triggered by a recent 11-year solar cycle minimum. Adequate rainfall promises another bumper corn and wheat crop. Afternoon rainfall is common throughout the Rockies. Cool weather persists in the Pacific Northwest.

AUTUMN

SEPTEMBER 2019. September is the culling season for many biological systems, with naturally variant physical systems initiating those processes. Land-falling hurricanes, which most frequently occur during September, thin woodlands and allow new growth to take seed. Such storms are more common during low solar cycles, now occurring as land areas cool more quickly than oceans, increasing wind speeds as hurricanes advance over land. Similarly, heat from forest fires are a necessary part of a cycle that clears aged tree growth and releases "naked seeds" on pine cones that begin forests anew. In fact, heat that leads to new gene expression extends to humans and all mammals, as the cold and flu season peaks in September and October, a time when the rate of solar decline is greatest along with decreases of vitamin D creation and its influence on the endocrine systems. Inflammation in general and related chronic conditions are most evident during the low point in 11-year solar cycles.

OCTOBER 2019. The frequency of our planet's volcanic activity is part of natural cycle that regulates global temperatures. It is also part of a sequence of events that spreads new and natural soil across growth areas, setting the stage for renewed vegetation growth after the Fall culling season. Not only does volcanic activity correlate with the cyclical low in 11-solar cycles but they tend to occur during the greatest rate of decline in annual solar output, during Fall. Such an occurrence also hastens a drop in global temperatures in October as the amount of atmospheric moisture drops. This is the driest month of the year with rainfall generally confined to the Pacific Northwest, Florida and the Gulf Coast. Fire remains a presence in Southern California, paradoxically because of a robust growing season from Spring rains — another representation of the inverted repetition within nature.

NOVEMBER 2019. Fiery sunsets will signal the afterglow of any global volcanic ash distribution at high altitudes. This should be a welcome sight as it indicates a kind of natural fertilizer for the growing season on the other side of Winter. In fact, this can be an opportunity to spread seed after bird migration and just before the snowfall and work with a gift from nature! Snowfall provides nitrogen in a natural way and with a perfectly even distribution. Both can arrive early this year as a 17-year tendency for increasing snowfalls persists. The first cool fronts of the year advance through Florida with beautiful weather underway there.

WINTER

DECEMBER 2019. Forestalling mood issues and limiting our bodies' inflammation levels becomes even more important in December. According to medical research, vitamin D reserves are essential in such matters and at a minimum each December and during minimums in cyclical solar cycles, now present. A weakening El Niño episode also favors somewhat colder than normal temperatures for much of the country, especially in the east, which is more persistent than during La Niña events which correlate with variant temperatures, with cold centered in the U.S. West. A southern storm track is favored, bringing rainfall to Southern California, Texas and Florida, and snowfall to the Southern Rockies. Arctic air brings lake effect snows to Western New York, Pennsylvania, Northeast Ohio and parts of Michigan. Chicago experiences severe cold for three days mid-month.

JANUARY 2020. Colder than normal temperatures and deep snow can be expected in the Central and Eastern United States this year. A remnant southern storm track will consume Gulf Of Mexico moisture before blanketing areas farther north with snowfall. The pattern favors such storms early and late in the month, with cold and dry weather in between. The greatest cold departure from normal temperatures is still favored in the Eastern United States but the deep freeze extends as far west as Colorado, Utah and Wyoming. Welcome rainfall drenches Central and Southern California, though mudslides are always a concern under such conditions. The Pacific Northwest is quite dry and seasonably cold, while Florida faces a freeze risk by the 20th.

FEBRUARY 2020. Given global sea surface temperature distribution and the current solar cycle, February will likely bring the winter's biggest and most extensive snowfalls. The focus for potential blizzard conditions and record breaking snowfalls will occur along the East Coast, from Washington D.C. to Portland Maine. Such late winter storms also tend to move slowly and produce fierce winds. This is a continuing, naturally cyclical trend established over 15 years ago and similar to one that occurred last in the 1950s and 1960s. The Great Lakes states and Great Plains will be spared deep snow and in fact will be relatively dry with great daily temperature variance. The wet weather pattern persists in Southern and Central California, mitigating drought. Florida is at risk for a brief tornado outbreak.

Magic and the Two Dimensions
of Language

Notes Toward a General Theory of Magic, Part III

IN PART II of these Notes we introduced Sir James George Frazer's two Laws of Magic: the *Law of Similarity* and the *Law of Contiguity*. (The second law he also called the Law of Contact or Contagion).

They are not laws in the sense that lawyers use when they speak of the "laws of the land," or that physicists use when they speak of the "laws of nature." The closest parallels to the Laws of Magic are provided by the laws on which artists rely as they create works of art in various media, for example, the "laws of perspective" in drawing or painting or the "laws of harmony" in music. A painter or musician may, and sometimes does, violate these laws to

good effect. These laws do not *prescribe*, but only *describe*, how artists can give their art the power to rivet attention, to produce rapture, to enhance its emotional power, to force new insights upon resisting minds. Similarly, the two laws of magic guide the magician as he creates compelling, effective rituals, spells, charms, sigils and other works of the magic art.

Like the laws of perspective or harmony, the laws of magic derive from the ways in which we humans receive, perceive and conceive the real world about us. We do this by creating symbols and patterns. **Symbols** and **patterns** are some of our oldest and most useful tools for making sense of the world in which we live and for shaping our lives as we live them. Without these tools, we could not even think or speak to much purpose.

Symbolic Behavior and the Two Dimensions of Language

Scholars speak of the two dimensions of all symbolic behavior, including speech and language. By analogy to mathematical graphs, they also call these two dimensions the two *axes* (the plural of *axis*) of symbolic behavior, and they label them the *axis of similarity* and the *axis of contiguity*.

Since we are talking about magic, let us illustrate this with a very old spell that children still chant—alas, often without effect:

Rain! Rain! Go away!
Come again some other day!

Just nine chanted words, but they are enough for our purpose here.

Note firstly, one can replace some of these words with other similar words. Instead of "Rain! Rain!" an inventive child might chant "Snow! Snow!" when snow is falling. Or instead of "some other day" that child might chant "my next school day" during a school vacation. One word is replaced by another similar word, or phrase by similar phrase. Here the similarity consists in grammar, meaning, and the number and position of stressed and unstressed syllables.

If you replace one word (or any other symbol) by another appropriate word (or symbol) you are working on the *axis of similarity*.

Secondly, the nine words are chanted one after another in time, and in a precise order. It matters hugely which word follows the other. "Rain! Go away! Rain! Again, some day other, come!" sounds more like a child's foolish, clumsy babbling than a powerful magical command that even the rain must obey.

If you move words (or any other string of symbols) around like this, you are working on the *axis of contiguity*.

Below is a diagram that may help to make the two dimensions, or axes, more clear.

The horizontal line, with an arrowhead at its rightmost point, is not only the *axis of contiguity*, but also the "arrow of time," which places all our words and actions in their proper order, from the past through the present into the future.

The vertical line is the *axis of similarity*, and the two short double-headed vertical arrows mark just two of the many possible places where

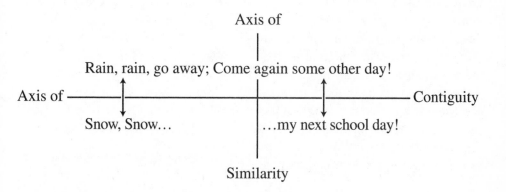

87

one word or phrase can be replaced by another similar word or phrase.

Children's Secret Writing and the Two Dimensions of Language

Children love secrets. Once they have learned to write, they often look for simple ways of secret writing. There are two such ways children commonly use when they want to hide their secrets from others' eyes.

One way consists of scrambling the letters or words of a message in some regular fashion, for example, writing the words and letters in reverse order: "Terces a evah I" instead of "I have a secret." This is called *transposition*, and it works on the *axis of contiguity*.

The other consists of replacing the letters of our usual alphabet with letters from some other, little-known alphabet: "I have a secret" may be written "I have a secret" in the Theban alphabet, or "I have a secret" in the Enochian alphabet. This is called substitution, and it works on the axis of similarity.

Of course, the use of secret writing (in either form) also greatly increases the *coefficient of weirdness* of a child's secret message, tincturing it with hints of mystery and power.

Patterned Behavior and the Two Dimensions of Language

In any chanted spell it is not only the meaning and the grammar of the words that matter, but also the patterns that the words make as they are chanted. The two lines of the children's rain-spell rhyme with one another (...away and ...day). Also, the two lines have the same meter or rhythm, that is, the same alternating pattern of accented (X) and unaccented (—) syllables or pauses:

X	—	X	—	X	—	X
Rain!		Rain!		Go	a-	way!
Come	a-	gain!	some	oth-	er	day!

Rhyme and rhythm are matters of pattern, not symbol. Patterns, like symbols, can be formed along the axis of similarity (for example, rhyme) or along the axis of contiguity (rhythm or meter).

There are many other effectual patterns in magic. They are woven into ritual dances and gestures, the stations taken by men and women inside a magical lodge or Circle, or traced out by their ceremonial movements therein. They can also be seen in the cycles of Heaven and Earth, in the seasons and tides, and in the calendars that we follow.

An Old Charm Against the Night-Mare

In the 1400s and 1500s several English writers wrote down from memory a charm against the Night-Mare, or (as they said in those days) against being Witch-Ridden by night:

> *St. George, St. George, our Lady's knight,*
> *He walked by day, and so by night*
> *Until he found that foulsome wight.*
> *And when it was that he her found,*
> *He her beat, and he her bound,*
> *Until her troth she to him plight,*
> *She would not come thereat that night*
> *Whereat the saint, our Lady's knight*
> *Was named three times—St. George!*

All the surviving copies of this charm differ somewhat from one another, having been written down from imperfect memory long after it was heard. The version given here is a compilation made from all these copies, showing how the charm probably sounded when it was first composed by some unknown Cunning Man or Woman in the 1200s or 1300s.

When the charm was composed, the words "Night-Mare" did not mean any scary dream, but a very specific and frightening condition of temporary paralysis upon awaking from sleep, of difficulty in breathing, of deep weariness despite long sleep, and of a sense that some malevolent being was controlling the sleeper's movements or had been "riding" the sleeper. This old charm was recited in order to free the sleeper from that horrid being. Modern medicine recognizes this same affliction, but calls it "sleep paralysis."

Note how skillfully this old charm was cast into verse, with careful attention to rhyme and rhythm. Note how the fourth and fifth lines fall powerfully on the ear: thrice three strongly accented syllables follow hard on one after another as the charm is recited: "*he her found, he her beat... he her bound.*" The force of these nine hammer-blows is only amplified by the way in which the last two verbs (*beat* and *bound*) begin with the same abrupt sound *b*. And finally, note the suspense that develops at the end of the charm: so far "St. George" has been named just twice, not thrice, as he must be named if the charm is to work. But then, at the very end of the charm, the charmer speaks the last two words with force, striking them home and sealing the magic with a third "St. George!" ("Third time's the charm" is an old adage.)

The charmer who first crafted this charm seems to have been well aware of how skillfully she had joined all these words together for the maximum impact on her patient, and indeed on anyone else in earshot. Whether consciously or unconsciously, she was deploying the resources of both symbol and pattern with all due attention to the laws of similarity and contiguity. Thereby she greatly enhanced the effectiveness of her charm.

What About Our Own Magic?

Just as any spell can gain in power through the skillful arrangement of the various symbols (and words) it uses, so too can it benefit from the skillful use of appropriate patterns.

It is not enough for a Witch to formulate her intention with care and precision. Nor is it enough for her to rivet attention by increasing the *coefficient of weirdness* in her spell. A Witch must also skillfully deploy all the resources of symbol and pattern along each axis—similarity and contiguity—as she creates her spells or designs her magical workings and rituals.

Only then will her spells truly be *performative* acts of magic causing "changes in consciousness in accordance with will."

Looking Forward

Here is a good place to end the third of these *Notes Toward a General Theory of Magic*. The fourth and fifth of these should appear in the next two issues of *The Witches' Almanac*. In them we shall discuss Intention and Attention, the role of the body in magic, and the magic of poppets.

—ROBERT MATHIESEN

Hans Christian Andersen

The Farm-Yard Cock and the Weather-Cock

THERE WERE two cocks—one on the dung-hill, the other on the roof. They were both arrogant, but which of the two rendered most service? Tell us your opinion—we'll keep to ours just the same though.

The poultry yard was divided by some planks from another yard in which there was a dung-hill, and on the dung-hill lay and grew a large cucumber which was conscious of being a hot-bed plant.

"One is born to that," said the cucumber to itself. "Not all can be born cucumbers; there must be other things, too. The hens, the ducks and all the animals in the next yard are creatures too. Now I have a great opinion of the yard cock on the plank; he is certainly of much more importance than the weather-cock who is placed so high and can't even creak, much less crow. The latter has neither hens nor chicks, and only thinks of himself and perspires verdigris. No, the yard cock is really a cock! His step is a dance! His crowing is music, and wherever he goes one knows what a trumpeter is like! If he would only come in here! Even if he ate me up stump, stalk, and all, and I had to dissolve in

his body, it would be a happy death," said the cucumber.

In the night there was a terrible storm. The hens, chicks and even the cock sought shelter; the wind tore down the planks between the two yards with a crash; the tiles came tumbling down, but the weather-cock sat firm. He did not even turn round, for he could not; and yet he was young and freshly cast, but prudent and sedate. He had been born old, and did not at all resemble the birds flying in the air—the sparrows, and the swallows; no, he despised them, these mean little piping birds, these common whistlers. He admitted that the pigeons, large and white and shining like mother-o'-pearl, looked like a kind of weather-cock; but they were fat and stupid, and all their thoughts and endeavours were directed to filling themselves with food, and besides, they were tiresome things to converse with. The birds of passage had also paid the weather-cock a visit and told him of foreign countries, of airy caravans and robber stories that made one's hair stand on end. All this was new and interesting; that is, for the first time, but afterwards, as the weather-cock found out, they repeated themselves and always told the same stories, and that's very tedious, and there was no one with whom one could associate, for one and all were stale and small-minded.

"The world is no good!" he said. "Everything in it is so stupid."

The weather-cock was puffed up, and that quality would have made him interesting in the eyes of the cucumber if it had known it, but it had eyes only for the yard cock, who was now in the yard with it.

The wind had blown the planks, but the storm was over.

"What do you think of that crowing?" said the yard cock to the hens and chickens. "It was a little rough—it wanted elegance."

And the hens and chickens came up on the dung-hill, and the cock strutted about like a lord.

"Garden plant!" he said to the cucumber, and in that one word his deep learning showed itself, and it forgot that he was pecking at her and eating it up. "A happy death!"

The hens and the chickens came, for where one runs the others run too; they clucked, and chirped, and looked at the cock, and were proud that he was of their kind.

"Cock-a-doodle-doo!" he crowed, "the chickens will grow up into great hens at once, if I cry it out in the poultry-yard of the world!"

And hens and chicks clucked and chirped, and the cock announced a great piece of news.

"A cock can lay an egg! And do you know what's in that egg? A basilisk. No one can stand the sight of such a thing; people know that, and now you know it too—you know what is in me, and what a champion of all cocks I am!"

With that the yard cock flapped his wings, made his comb swell up and crowed again; and they all shuddered, the hens and the little chicks—but they were very proud that one of their number was such a champion of all cocks. They clucked and chirped till the weather-cock heard; he heard it; but he did not stir.

"Everything is very stupid," the weather-cock said to himself. "The yard cock lays no eggs, and I am too lazy to do so; if I liked, I could lay a wind-egg. But the world is not worth even a wind-egg. Everything is so stupid! I don't want to sit here any longer."

With that the weather-cock broke off; but he did not kill the yard cock, although the hens said that had been his intention. And what is the moral? "Better to crow than to be puffed up and break off!"

EMBRACING THE WITCH'S BODIES

WITHIN OCCULTISM, there tends to be a heavy focus on exercising the intellectual and spiritual bodies over the physical. Many discussions center around how many or which books someone has consumed to add to their wisdom closet. Or comparing psychic abilities: "What beings were you able to conjure up? Have you achieved spirit flight?"

These things all have their merit and place, but it is foolhardy to dismiss the physical body as unimportant or not worthy of our investigation. After all, isn't part of our spiritual journey to be exploring the physical space, rather than solely trying to transcend it?

The Divine Physical

Numerous traditions and systems acknowledge that we are made up of three components: a physical self, an intellectual self and a spiritual self. The medieval Irish poem *Cauldron of Poesy* asserts that we have three cauldrons within us: the Cauldron of Wisdom in our heads, the Cauldron of Motion in our hearts and the Cauldron of Warming in our bellies. The Feri Tradition of Witchcraft has the concept of the Three Souls: the God-Self, the Talker and the Fetch. In Jewish scripture, we find this threefold concept again describing the life-giving essence connecting God to each human: *neshama* (breath), *ruach* (wind) and *nefesh* (rest). The *neshama* is considered to be affected through thought, the *ruach* by speech and the *nefesh* by action.

Consistently we see a body that is most closely connected to, or is in fact part of the divine essence. The longing to be part of something bigger than ourselves—to be one with the mysteries of the universe or deities—the root of many religious

pursuits. So naturally this body is held with the highest esteem.

The divine self is followed by a conscious body that reasons, imagines and verbalizes our thoughts. Being adjacent to and aware of the divine makes the talker often strive to reach closer towards the divine, even though it is a bridge between our "higher" and "lower" bodies. Many would argue that it is the talking self that makes us human.

Animal Within

The point where our spirit directly connect with our physical body is our animal self. It is the most primal and carnal manifestation of ourselves. It deals with our basic needs that keep us alive and connected to this plane. Pleasures of the flesh (sex and intimacy, eating, drinking, breathing) are its domain. Intuition, "gut-feeling," instinct/impulse and emotions are part of how it communicates.

The animal self has been the most maligned body in recent centuries. The constructs of modern Christianity have launched an all-out attack on the physical body (particularly those belonging to women), decrying it as obscene, impure and ungodly. That its wants and needs are in absolute contrast to the pursuit of the spiritual—and belong to the realm of the Devil. Therefore, the animal self must be denied to save oneself from damnation. Which is essentially a load of manure—especially when you consider where that unhealthy attitude has gotten modern society in terms of physical, emotional and mental well-being. It's insane to loathe such a large part of yourself—this mindset only brings misery.

When you think about it, it's really not surprising that occultists have centered

their focus on the spiritual and intellectual, but they're missing a vital piece of the pie. It's like trying to fly a plane with only ⅔ of the engines turned on. Sure, you might get where you are going eventually, but it can be done more efficiently and quickly if all the engines the plane was designed to run with are turned on.

When we are able to connect all three of our bodies, especially for application in ritual and matters of witchery, the immediacy and the flow of power can be unparalleled. Our bodies are anchors, but not in the mistaken concept that they hold us back or weighs us down. Rather our they root us to the world around us so that we can pull from that energy to sustain ourselves.

Unifying Exercises

Technically it's not even that hard to bring the physical body into the mix: all you have to do is learn to acknowledge it! But we tend to have such a hard disconnect with the very vessels we reside in. We might equate using our bodies with having to workout out at a gym religiously or needing to have the perfect physique. There could be fears about looking silly or feeling stupid in front of others. You don't need a gym membership, a degree in dance or to be a modern Adonis or Aphrodite to be present in your body.

One simple way to engage all three bodies—without even breaking a sweat—is through intentional breathing. To do this, first start by getting in a comfortable, yet stable position, such as sitting (cross-legged or in a chair) or standing at ease. You could lay down as well, but if you're prone to falling asleep or want to get more active past this point, it's not recommended it.

1. Take a deep breath and as you inhale, focus on the sensation of the air as it rushes into your nasal cavity, and visualize it collecting within your skull. As you exhale, imagine your spiritual body taking up residence in and around your head, like a cloud.

2. Before the next breath, place a hand on your chest. Inhale and focus on the air as it goes down your throat and into your heart and lungs region. Feel the beat of your heart for a moment before you exhale, then as you breathe out, visualize the air as your conscious self, flowing around the center of your upper body and mingling with the spiritual self.

3. Move your hands down to your belly. For the third breath, pull in deep, feeling it hit the bottom of your belly where your hands lay and see in your mind's eye an animal nestled there at rest. Perhaps a snake, fox, rabbit or cat—your choice, it's your body. Allow the breath to caress the animal form, then let it flow out to connect with your other two bodies.

4. To firmly unite them all in your mind, let your hands fall to your sides. Take one more deep breath, consciously engaging the regions of your head, chest and belly as you breathe in, and let your hands rise up as you do so. Then let them flow down as you breathe out, feeling the motion of the air flow upward at the same time.

You now should feel fully engaged in a way that you weren't before. If you have problems with visualizations, you can repeat each step 3 times (in a row, before moving on to the next step). Don't get distracted by random thoughts or outside stimuli. Focus on the sensation of the air moving through your body and hold the image in your mind.

Once you have become comfortable with doing this exercise, slowly engaging the rest of your body is recommended— yes, movement! Most people find that it's helpful to put on music that has a slow and steady beat. Start with your feet, becoming conscious of how the toes, balls and heels

connect to the ground, feeling how your weight feels on top of them. Wiggle them, shift from side to side, etc. Next softly bend and straighten your knees, and work up your body to engage your thighs, glutes and pelvic region. Breathe into your belly and be present in your chest. Expand out into your shoulders, elbows, wrists and fingers, stretching and moving them. Connect again down to your feet and bring the movement up through your body, uniting it with your head.

Moving as One

From there you can use your physical body to call upon the Elements, carrying through with your talking self if you feel words are necessary, and using the divine self to see those entities as you move and speak. As you become more comfortable with all three bodies moving as one, you can adopt classic positions and postures of the Gods as you call them into your space. It can be extremely empowering to recreate those iconic poses. Similarly, one can shapeshift or in the very least tap into an animal spirit by simulating their movement

and behaviors. You can also use repetitive movements to build up energy for spellcraft and other forms of magick—yes, you can dance your spells!

You will become more comfortable with movement the more you do it, as is true of any practice. Don't be ashamed or embarrassed by your body—it's you! Tap into the animal part of yourself and regain your power. Acknowledge that taking care of the physical needs of your body is a sacred task. Take pleasure in being aware of your body. Savor the fullness of living as a Witch! Lastly, always listen to your body's needs to avoid injury.

We will leave with a quote from the book *Jitterbug Perfume* by Tom Robbins—highly recommended reading as soon as you get the chance:

I cannot believe that the most delicious things were placed here merely to test us, to tempt us, to make it the more difficult for us to achieve the grand prize: the safety of the void. To fashion of life such a petty game is unworthy of both men and gods.

—LAURA TEMPEST ZAKROFF

Dαrk Lθrδ θf the Fθrest

THE DAY WOULD be peaceful and calm with a soft breeze whispering in the treetops, and the whole wood alive with bird calls. The woodland floor would be carpeted with bluebells in the spring; or summer sunlight filtering through the overhead canopy; crisp, dry leaves crackling underfoot in autumn; or the frozen quiet of a late winter afternoon as a fiery sun began to sink in the west, casting long shadows beneath the trees. Then, almost imperceptibly, there would be the sound of muffled footsteps following quickly in the undergrowth. Your pace quickened and so did that of your stalker. A sudden flurry of old dried leaves would be picked up by a passing zephyr and flung into the air like a mini-whirlwind. All the hair on the back of the neck would be standing on end, heart thundering in the chest, breath almost impossible to take. Then you turned to confront this persistent intruder only to find . . . nothing. The wind died away, carrying with it the faintest sound of laughter and a voice in your head saying: "Gotcha!"

The Wild Wood, however, is the dark, untamed part of natural woodland where unearthly and potentially dangerous beings are still to be found. This is not everyone's favourite place and many urban Witches never get over an "atavistic fear of Nature uncontrolled"… On a magical level, the Wild Wood refers to those strange, eerie places that remain the realm of Nature and untamed by man. Ancient gnarled oaks, festooned with ferns and draped with lichen, carry an air of solitude and remoteness that is deeply unnerving—here birdsong and the trickle of running water are the only sounds to break the stillness. It is the Otherworld of the "unearthly and potentially dangerous." It is the realm of Pan and the Wild Hunt. In modern psychology, it refers to the dark inner recesses of the mind, the wild and tangled undergrowth of the unconscious. Here, among the trees, we are never sure that what we see is reality or illusion.

Excerpt from *Pagan Portals: Pan, Dark Lord of the Forest and Horned God of the Witches*

—MELUSINE DRACO

Purple and Pleasure

The Folklore and Magic of Amethyst

AMETHYST IS one of the best known and most popular members of the quartz family—silicon dioxide coloured by iron giving the distinctive purple colour. Its popularity may be due to its attractive colour, with amethyst charms being found at sites going back to 25,000 BCE, making it one of the earliest crystals used by man in his attempts to engage with and control the unseen worlds.

In ancient times amethyst was frequently used for protective amulets. Heart-shaped amethyst amulets were often placed in the mummy wrappings of the pharaohs, and Egyptian ambassadors would carry an amethyst on them when travelling abroad for protection from treachery and surprise attacks. The Persians

believed that two amethysts engraved with the names of the Sun and Moon together with baboon hairs and swallow feathers worn around the neck would protect against spells; they also believed amethyst would keep away hail and locusts, as well as assist in approaching people of high station (for business or political matters). To the Romans an amulet of amethyst would protect against spells, hail and locusts, and amethysts were commonly cut into intaglio gemstones set in rings for such purposes. It was sacred to Neptune and worn by Roman sailors to ensure safe journeys.

In an allegorical Greek myth written by the sixteenth century poet Remy Belleau in 1576, the story was

told of how Bacchus was annoyed at having been neglected by mortals, and he swore to have his tigers tear apart the next mortal he came across. The nymph Amethyst was on her way to the temple of Artemis to worship, and she was the next mortal he met. Amethyst cried out to Artemis to save her from being torn apart, and Artemis responded by turning her into a pillar of quartz. Bacchus then felt remorse for his actions and libated wine over the stone in atonement, which absorbed the wine giving it the distinctive colour. This is an interesting tale which explains the name of the stone *amethistos* (Gr), *"that which pushes away drunkenness,"* but the name predates this to the ancient world. This tale (*L'Amethyste, ou les Amours de Bacchus et d'Amethyste*) may well be rooted in the belief that amethyst protected the bearer from drunkenness, mentioned by Greek writers including Pliny, and the fact that amethyst was considered sacred to Artemis in ancient Greece. Following on from Belleau's work some sources

suggested binding one into the navel to restrain the "vapour of the wine."

The Pope's Fisherman's ring is made of amethyst, an amusing irony in that the stone is usually attributed to Pisces, whose vice is intoxication (hence "drunk as a fish"), which amethyst is supposed to prevent. A bishop's ring of rank bears an amethyst, unsurprising considering the association since ancient times of the colour purple with power and prestige—the purple of the Caesars became the purple of the Catholic Church. In early Christianity the purple of amethyst was considered a symbol of purity, associated with Christ. This was sometimes associated with his suffering and wounds on the cross, resulting in amethysts being applied to bleeding wounds to attempt to heal them. To the early Christians it symbolized the constant thought of the heavenly kingdom in humble souls. In the Bible amethyst is the twelfth foundation of New Jerusalem and the ninth stone on the High Priest's Breastplate, representing the Tribe of Dan, being placed at the centre of the breastplate. Amethyst was also symbolic of the apostle Matthias, whose attribution replaced Judas. Saint Valentine was said to wear an amethyst ring engraved with a figure of Cupid.

Amongst the many virtues attributed to amethyst in the Middle Ages were the ability to repress negative thoughts and to give good understanding, to help neuralgia and insomnia, to expel poison, to make one vigilant in business, to treat toothache and headache, to treat gout, to protect from poison and plague and perhaps most curiously to prepare an easy capture of wild beasts and birds. An amulet of a bear engraved on an amethyst was thought to put demons to flight and protect the wearer from drunkenness. Soldiers also carried amethyst into battle to keep them safe and give victory over enemies.

In contemporary magic and Paganism amethyst is considered particularly useful for spiritual growth and protection, purification and mental healing. It is commonly seen as one of the prime magickal stones. It is particularly associated with the throat and third eye chakras, hence its use for inspiration, intuition and as a good seeing stone. The throat chakra is the centre of dreaming and amethyst is a good dreaming, stone. Placing one under the pillow may help with insomnia and aid lucid dreaming. When being used in such a manner the amethyst should be carried close to the skin for a period of time of at least a lunar month.

Other popular uses are for developing clairvoyance and astral/psychic vision. Amethyst is thought to work on the immune and endocranial systems, and it may influence the pineal and pituitary glands. Amethyst is used to help ease headaches, including migraines, for which it should be held whilst repeating three times *"Gabriel bind Barisfael"* (the demon of migraines, constrained by the archangel Gabriel). It is a good stone to work with if trying to overcome addiction due to its history of being used against intoxication.

—DAVID RANKINE

101

ANNWFN & THE WESTERN ISLES

In ancient Celtic tradition, everything non-mortal existed in the Otherworld, which was always located to the West. These realms as well as their rulers were an important source of Underworld mythology. After the influence of Christianity, the Otherworld was transformed into an Underworld, namely to punish and lower the power of the old Pagan gods in the eyes of the Northern European peoples."

—DEATH RITES & RIGHTS, FENLEY & ZELL

ANNWFN, OFTEN CALLED the kingdom of shades, is a series of coexisting realms much like a mystical archipelago. It is the Celtic Otherworld, and these realms contain many different beings, Gods and spirits—as well as the dead.

The three major regions are *Caer Wydyr, Caer Feddwid* and *Arran*. These different sectors are separated by seas, mountains, rivers and impassable chasms.

Arran is considered the most divine of the three lands. It is a land of Eternal Summer, with lush grassy fields and sweet flowing rivers. In Arran is found the Cauldron of Plenty, which is linked to the Holy Grail. Only those who are pure of heart, self-sacrificing and spiritual are allowed to enter here. This is the "Summerland" most identified with modern Wiccans, as well as Theosophists. It is a place of peace and beauty, where everything people hold close to their hearts is preserved in its fullest glory for eternity.

Caer Feddwid ("castle of revelry") is ruled by Arianrhod of the Silver Wheel (the Moon), Goddess of time, space and energy. It is also known as *Caer Rigor* or *Caer Siddi*. The air is filled with enchanting music and a fountain flows with magick wine granting eternal youth and health.

Caer Wydyr ("castle of glass"), also called *Nennius*, lies within a glass fort. It is a dark and gloomy place inhabited only by silent lost souls. It is the least desirable place to end up after death.

Different Gods or lords ruled in various national regions of the Celtic Otherworld. The most ancient of these is *Cernunnos* ("horned one") who rules the dead. Images of the horned shaman, etched into cave walls in France, date back to 9,000 BCE. He is also known as Herne the Hunter, leading the Wild Hunt on Samhain Eve. After the conversion of Ireland to Christianity, Cernunnos was identified with Satan and increasingly linked with a dark and foul Underworld, the dwelling place of evil spirits and souls of the damned.

A similar hunter God of the Underworld is *Gwynn*, who claims souls for Annwfn. Gwynn is also associated with fairies, who have been called "the Hosts of Hell" by some Christians.

Donn ("brown one") is the Irish God of the dead who was drowned by the Goddess Eriu after he insulted her. He is the keeper of the first guidepost on the journey to the Otherworld. His realm is a small rocky island called *Tech Duinn* ("house of Donn") off the southwest coast of Ireland, where he welcomes his descendants, the people of Ireland, who briefly visit his house just after the moment of death.

Pwyll was a Welsh prince who chanced to meet *Arawn*, king of Annwfn, and the two of them agreed to exchange kingdoms for a year in each other's bodies. Each ruled the other's land well and were pleased with the arrangement when the time was completed. The full story is told in the first branch of the Welsh *Mabinogion*.

Mider is a benevolent God of the Gaelic Afterworld. His wife is *Etain*. He is a just overlord whose realm is a place of tedium and sorrow rather than pain and torture. Mider had a magic cauldron capable of performing supernatural feats. However, Mider's daughter betrayed him and helped the hero Cuchulain steal the cauldron.

Bilé, on the other hand, is an evil and vicious God who requires human sacrifices to appease his violent nature. His kingdom is a vast wasteland of crushed spirits and broken bodies who must pay him eternal homage.

Bran was a mortal hero in Welsh mythology. His symbol is the raven, a bird of ill-omen associated with death and the grave. Bran angered the Gods, was beheaded and then banished to rule in the Underworld as punishment. Bran's kingdom is filled with failed heroes who must spend eternity in regret.

In the old Irish legends, *Cruachan* was a gateway through which undead legions came to attack the living. Christians later changed the tales, claiming it merely an entrance to Hell. Because of this a cave named Cruachan in Connacht, Ireland, has been considered a gateway to the Underworld for millennia.

—OBERON ZELL

CORVÍÐS

Friend or foe?

DIVINING THE FUTURE by watching birds is one of the most ancient of practices. In traditional British Old Craft, encounters with members of the corvidae family are looked upon as messengers from Otherworld—particularly magpies and crows—since all corvids are highly clever and among the most intelligent of all animals. Persistent, repeated or unusual behaviour is noted, mentally filed away until eventually the penny drops.

If, however, we study the various collections of European folklore, we usually find that those birds whose appearance is deemed evil or unlucky are the ones that were considered "messengers" in the Old Ways. According to *Fauna Britannica*:

> *There are few birds as obvious, noisy and imposing as the six characteristic black species of this [Corvidae] family, nor are the Magpie and Jay likely to be overlooked. They are highly intelligent and are often thought the most advanced and long-lived of all*

birds. All eight are residents and their biology and, to a large degree, their extensive folk-lore are similar, so it is difficult to relate many of the older beliefs to any particular species.

Godly Pedigrees

The poor old raven, for example, gets a lot of bad press but in reality this bird is one of the oldest and most sacred symbols of the ancient Britons, being associated with the Welsh God Bran the Blessed whose name translates to "raven." According to the *Mabinogion*, Bran's head was buried in the White Hill of London as a talisman against invasion and gave rise to the legend that if the ravens were removed from the Tower of London, then England would fall. King Arthur is alleged to have ignored the warnings and removed the head: later Britain suffered the ignominy of the Norman invasion.

Because of its black plumage, croaking call and diet of carrion, the raven has long been considered a bird of ill-omen and of interest to creators of myths and legends. Ravens, which were notorious for gathering at gallows, were once abundant in London and often seen around meat markets (such as nearby Eastcheap) feasting for scraps, and may have roosted at the Tower from earlier times. For an Old Craft Witch the sighting of a raven in the wild would be seen as bringing an important message from Otherworld in answer to our prayer.

If swallows are the voice of summer, then rooks are certainly the voice of winter in the countryside. The call is usually described as *kaah*—similar to that of the carrion crow, but usually much flatter in tone. It is given both in flight and while perched, when the bird characteristically fans its tail and bows on each caw. Calls in flight are usually given singly, in contrast to the carrion crow's which are in groups of three or four. Solitary birds often "sing" apparently to themselves, uttering strange clicks, wheezes and human-like notes.

We can divine the answer to our questions by addressing the rook and waiting for the number of caws in response—one for "yes" and two for "no." One of the most magical of winter sights are a colony of rooks "tumbling" through the air against a blue sky as they ride the thermals and then fall towards the ground, yelling and shouting with *joie de vivre*. The rook is a bird worth getting to know.

Ancient Omens

Carrion and hooded crows are considered to be the same species but they differ in appearance depending on the location. The carrion crow is a handsome, glossy black bird while the hooded crow has a slate-grey back and under-parts and is generally found in Scotland and Ireland or as a coastal winter visitor. For magical and divinatory purposes, they should be

considered the same. The rook is generally gregarious and the crow solitary, but rooks occasionally nest in isolated trees and crows may feed with rooks; moreover, crows are often sociable in winter roosts. The most distinctive feature is the voice. The rook has a high-pitched *kaah*, but the crow's guttural, slightly vibrant, deeper croaked *kraa* is distinct from any note of the rook.

The carrion crow is noisy, perching on the top of a tree and calling three or four times in quick succession, with a slight pause between each series of croaks. The wing-beats are slower, more deliberate than those of the rook. Carrion crows can become tame near humans, and can often be found near areas of human activity or habitation including cities, moors, woodlands, sea cliffs and farmland where they compete with other social birds for food in parks and gardens.

In Celtic folklore, the crow appears on the shoulder of the dying Cú Chulainn and could also be seen as a manifestation of the Morrígan. This idea has persisted and the hooded crow is associated with the Faere Folk in the Scottish Highlands and Ireland. In the 18th century, Scottish shepherds would make offerings to them to keep them from attacking sheep. In Faroese folklore, an unmarried girl would go out on Candlemas morning and throw a stone, then a bone, then a clump of turf at a hooded crow—if it flew over the sea, her husband would be a foreigner, if it landed on a farm or house, she would marry a man from there, but if it stayed put, she would remain unmarried. Since crows are very vocal we can engage them in conversation in a similar manner to that described for the rook.

Sacred Messengers

Magpies are gregarious creatures although they are extremely distrustful of humans. Modern folklore rarely has anything positive to say about them such as one foraging alone in the springtime foretells bad weather and one resting on a house, particularly near a window, foretells a death in the household. "*One for sorrow... etc.,*" But like the rest of the corvid family, these are highly intelligent birds despite the hysterical cackling when someone tells a good joke! Because of their distrust of humans, if they do come close to the house then the message from Otherworld is an important one—especially if they leave a feather for us to find. Also, magpie feathers can be utilized in spells designed to attract the sort of energy magpies are known for: curiosity, trickery, thievery, gregariousness, creativity and communication. Some use magpies to sound the alarm when "danger" threatens—just as the Iceni took notice of their warning that wolves were about. The bird's services were suitably honored by a tribute of heather laid near their nest each year.

The most striking thing about a Jackdaw is its piercing blue eyes. The irises of adults are greyish or silvery white while those of juveniles are light blue, becoming brownish before whitening at around one year of age. Highly gregarious and noisy, jackdaws are generally seen in flocks of varying sizes, though males and females pair-bond for life and pairs stay together within flocks.

Jackdaws are extremely vocal birds and the main call, frequently given in flight, is a metallic and squeaky *chyak-chyak* or *kak-kak*, which is a contact or greeting call. Perched birds often chatter together and before settling for the night large roosting flocks make a cackling noise. They also have a hoarse, drawn-out alarm call, *arrrrr* or *kaaaarr*, used when warning of predators or when mobbing them. If you can get a word in edgeways, ask your question and gauge the response from the bird's reply. The 12th century historian William of Malmesbury records the story of a woman who, upon hearing a jackdaw chattering "more loudly than usual," grew pale and became fearful of suffering a "dreadful calamity," and that "while yet speaking, the messenger of her misfortunes arrived."

Divine Portents

And who can deny the thrill of excitement in witnessing that flash of electric blue when an elusive Jay flies through the oak or beech wood like some Faery fighter pilot on acid, cackling insanely as it vanishes into the undergrowth? The name is believed to come from the Latin word Gaea, for Mother Earth, but it has surprisingly few references in folklore and mythology, in spite of its range across the entire Eurasian continents. These birds, like most corvids, are talented mimics, a talent they share with the mynahs and starlings and many parrot species; there has even been a recording of one imitat-

ing a house cat! The jay is a wary bird and its harsh, explosive call—a shrill raucous cry repeated two or three times—can be used for divinatory purposes.

Last but certainly not least is the chough that is generally restricted to coastal cliffs and mountains in the far west, although it has now vanished from its traditional Cornish haunts.

The bird has its own fair share of folklore, but the most obvious refers to its red legs that associated it with Witchcraft because Witches were said to wear red stockings for identification. Although, as wildlife author Stefan Buczacki wryly observes, why should they wish to advertise their wickedness in such a way is not recorded!

Corvids are common to most parts of the world and developing a close bond with these feathered hooligans could provide you with a hotline to Destiny!

—MELUSINE DRACO

The Spider Thread from Hell

THE BUDDHA was in a lotus-filled garden when he perceived a man named Kandata who was squirming in the depths of Hell. He had been a murderer, an arsonist and thief. A lifetime of these causes had put him in Hell. He was in the company of others like him.

The Buddha looked further into Kandata's life and saw an incident where Kandata came upon a spider. He raised his foot to stomp on it. Suddenly, he reconsidered, thinking, "There is no doubt that this spider is also a living being and it is a shame to take its life for no reason." In the end, he spared the spider.

Knowing this, the Buddha took a spider thread and lowered it into the depths of Hell with the intention of saving Kandata. Kandata reached for the thread and found it strong enough to hold his weight. Using all his strength, he began lifting himself from Hell.

After some progress, he looked down and saw hundreds of others behind him climbing on the same spider thread.

He shouted back at them, "Get off! This is mine!" Just then, the thread broke and Kandata fell back into Hell.

— from a lecture by Masao Yokota

William Gray meets his Inner Light

«*Don't bother with the 'Inner Light' lot either.... Few genuine initiates stay with them for long. True they serve a purpose, but surely you can do better than that dismal and depressing crew of self-righteous and semi-sanctimonious souls... Dion Fortune dead has more vitality and energy than all the I.L. lot have while still in this world.*»   [letter to A.R. August 1969]

DURING THIS TIME, honoured though he was among Druids and Witches, and a sort of Prince of the Apple Lands, as Avalon was called, he was still earnestly (and it almost seems effortlessly) plugging away at the lessons sent by the Society of the Inner Light. He had also made a powerful "inner contact" with his heroine Dion Fortune, founder of the SIL, whom he felt was a much warmer, nicer presence dead than she had been when alive. As we had noted in a previous chapter, he had liked the tone of the initial correspondence from that society, and rather hoped that by joining something from the mainstream of the Magical Tradition, it might ratify and develop the work he had been doing by himself over many long years. It is possible, also, that with the shade of DF behind him, the apparently austere and utterly genuine group would welcome him with open arms as her heir apparent. A conceit, perhaps, but not a particularly unreasonable one given his formidable background

and achievement. He wanted a genuine initiation into the Hermetic Tradition by people who really knew what they were doing. He wanted to be surrounded by real adeptii, in an atmosphere of incense and chanting, overlooked by august and enlightened beings from the Otherworld, where the power was so great within the temple that you could hardly walk. He wanted to be touched by the magic at the very deepest levels of the soul, and transformed by new energies, and find himself—at the last—in a lodge where he truly belonged.

In the event, it was disastrous.

The lessons, which were sent by the Society of the Inner Light on a regular basis, dealt with the Qabalah, the Paths on the Tree of Life, the Archetypes, Group Minds and God Forms, Artificial Elementals, Initiates and Initiations, Character Training... and more, much more. As might be expected the information provided a thorough grounding in the ideas of the Western Mysteries as interpreted by Dion Fortune, and with a lot of emphasis on her obscure and difficult treatise *The Cosmic Doctrine*. After each lesson came a series of meditations or questions. For example:

- Compress into 15 lines the main features of Esoteric Anatomy
- Explain the term 'Astral Consciousness'
- Discuss the conception of Life, Death and Evolution as set forth in this lesson.
- What are the gods of a race?

And so on. Bill's answers were detailed, pertinent, and in-depth. They often showed a quite unique level of insight that must have made his examiner's head spin, although in each case they were returned with the simple comment: "Adequate +. Thank you." And you can't help but get the feeling at times that he was—just a bit—showing off. His own system of attributing the Tarot to the paths on the Tree of Life is unique. It is brilliant. It also highlights the fact that two generations of magicians before him had been using a system of Correspondences which simply didn't correspond. "There may be copyright on this," he added.

Slipped in among the surviving papers were fragments of the work that he was doing at that time, such as the following table which outlines an approach to ritual work within a Circle:

	EAST	SOUTH	WEST	NORTH
Move on and stop	EAST	SOUTH	WEST	NORTH
Breathe in and out	Inhale	Hold	Exhale	Exclude
Call Name	Ooooay	Eeeooo	Hoooah	Hayeeee
See the	Sunrise	Noon	Sunset	Midnight
Think of Moon at	New	Full	Old	Dark
Feel the	Spring	Summer	Autumn	Winter
Greet Archangel	Raphael	Mikael	Gabriel	Auriel
Experience the Element	Air	Fire	Water	Earth
Feel	Pure	Radiant	Flowing	Fertile
Feel as if	Flying	Burning	Swimming	Walking
Take and use the	Sword	Rod	Cup	Shield
Emote	Sorrow	Excitement	Joy	Contentment
Use Magnetism to	Repel	Control	Attract	Hold
Decide to	Will	Work	Want	Wait
Have	Perception	Power	Purpose	Patience
Dedicate	Mind	Spirit	Soul	Body

This list can be added to indefinitely. It is recited and acted upon while circumnambulating...

This was the sort of scheme that he had been working through for years, and honed during his time with the Witches, who generally don't have much time for the Qabalah, and prefer the simple circle-cross with Pagan attributions. Nevertheless, it was probably light years ahead of anything being done by the initiates within the group he was trying to join.

His examiner wrote: "Adequate +. Thank you."

At the end of the course, asked to add his own comments, he wrote:

From a personal viewpoint the objective part of the Course taught me nothing whatsoever, since I was previously acquainted with every single word and idea in it, but the interesting thing is that subjectively from the Inner Planes, a very great deal came through, and quite new vistas opened up.... The course acted as a catalyst which projected existing knowledge and experience into fresh combinations. Again I must re-iterate that this did NOT come through the printed matter of the Course at all, but from contacts at subjective levels which were associated with the consciousness expressed throughout the Course. The subject matter of the Course simply acted as foci through which these Intelligences operated...

What he was trying to say, is that by this time he was well and truly connected with the spirit of Dion Fortune herself, and he damn well hoped that they realised this. Although he got a nice letter from the Director of Studies, dated 15th December 1963, saying he was quite sure that Bill "had what it takes," and looked forward to the interview and likely initiation, it all went downhill from then.

—ALLAN RICHARDSON & MARCUS CLARIDGE

Excerpted from The Old Sod: The Odd Life and Inner Work of William G. Gray *published by Skylight Press.*

THE VULTURE, THE PARROT AND
THE ANTELOPE

Lessons from the Animal Kingdom for Mankind

THE YORÙBÁ of Southwestern Nigeria have long had a unique relationship with the animal kingdom, enshrining behavior, merits and taboos of both man and beast in their rich corpus of myths and poetry. Many modern ethnic Yorùbás, while certainly depending on domestic and bush animals for protein, maintain a deep-seated respect for the life of their earthly cohabitants. Before taking the life of another being, be it for sustenance or sacrifice, the animal is thanked and praised. To do otherwise is a most egregious offense.

As humans feel a gamut of emotions, so too do animals experience the same. For example, it is taboo to kill mating animals while in the bush hunting. In the being of these animals, the Yorùbás will draw an equivalency between humans engaged in love-making. The act of procreation is pleasurable and sacred for all beings. Through the agency of understanding, morality enters the relationship between man and animal. Like humankind, animals are participants in the divine order and are expressions of divinity.

In addition to being part of the divine order, some animals should be neither killed, eaten, nor used for supplication of deities. This taboo is chiefly due to their status as sacred animals. Vultures and parrots are among those that are considered inviolable. Both are believed to interact directly with the high God, Olodumare. In the case of the vulture, their broad wings are said to carry messages to and from earth. In fact, the vulture not only carries messages, it speaks them directly into the ear of Olodumare.

It is taboo not only to kill a parrot—domestication is also forbidden. The parrot is believed to be a being that can only utter truth. It is a common belief that animals and humans in early creation spoke in the same tongue. Of all the animals, the parrot is the only being of the animal world still conversant in the languages of humans. The parrot is also a sign that the beauty of good character comes from within.

The parrot and beauty

Long ago there was a contest among the birds to determine who was the most beautiful. At that time the Parrot was white. He wondered why the others felt the need to add color to their feathers to gain beauty. Parrot felt beauty was unimportant and did not prepare for the contest. All of the birds conspired to eliminate Parrot because of his natural beauty. First they dumped ashes on Parrot; he remained steadfast. The birds then went to a sorcerer who turned Parrot's tail feathers red. On the day of the contest, Olodumare judged that Parrot was the most beautiful, cit-

ing that his beauty was on the inside. Olodumare declared that from that day forward, kings and queens and members of the priesthood would wear a single feather on the day of their crowning. This would remind all that beauty radiates from within.

The Antelope-Woman of Owo

Long ago Renrengenjen the Olowo (King of Owo) went out to the bush to hunt. He ventured deep into the bush looking for game. He hardly noticed how far into the bush he went when he encountered an antelope-skin hanging on the low branches of a tree. He immediately remembered that sometimes the animals of the bush removed their skins and took the forms of humans so that they could enter the town marketplace. Once affairs in the marketplace were accomplished, they would return to the bush, donning their skins and once again transforming into animals. The folk of Owo always stayed vigilant on market day, eyeing strangers well and noticing the reactions of the town's dogs. The Olowo instantly knew that he had come upon such a magical antelope who transformed itself into the form of a human.

With a deep sense of curiosity as well as fear, the Olowo Renrengenjen abandoned his hunting. He wanted to spy the antelope-person who would claim their skin again. He took the skin, rolled it up and placed it at the top of his backpack. He then climbed a tree to keep an eye out for the antelope-person. The Olowo waited a bit of time in the tree, in fact he was just about to take his leave when he heard footsteps signaling the approach of someone. To his amazement a most beautiful woman appeared. He was taken. He watched as she searched the surrounding area to no avail. She searched behind trees and all around the scrub. When at last she realized that it was gone, she began to sob.

The Olowo's heart broke and so he descended from the tree, carrying the skin. The woman looked up as he stood still, captivated by her beauty and grace. The woman looked up at Renrengenjen, noticing that he carried her skin on the top of his backpack. She spoke softly, requesting that he return her skin to him. The Olowo was so awestruck that he could not immediately speak. She again requested the return of her skin, this time with a tear in her eye. The Olowo spoke to her gently, "Why would you again want to resume your form as an antelope? The world of humans is a life of ease. We are not hunted, because we are the hunter. We have plentiful supplies of food and do not need to forage for it. Our weapons are superior and all the animals of the world fear us. You are too beautiful to have to worry where your sustenance comes from. Become my wife and I will provide abundance and safety to you. I am the Olowo of Owo and you will be treated with respect."

The antelope-woman saw the love and trust in his eyes and agreed that she would return with him to Owo to take her place with his other wives. She said, "You must respect my taboos and you must never let the people of Owo nor your wives know that I am an antelope-woman. I will not suffer abuse from your subjects or your wives."

The Olowo answered, "I will keep the secret. I will say that you are from a distant city. Tell me your taboos, and I will instruct the servants of my compound. Tell me your name and I will know how to introduce you."

She revealed the three taboos. She was firstly forbidden to see women pounding spices; second, water was not to be splashed on the ground before her; and lastly a head-load of firewood was not to be thrown down in her presence. Finally she said to him, "My name is Orunsen."

They left the bush together traveling to his compound in Owo. He immediately hid the antelope-skin in the rafters of his house. He took Orunsen as his wife and admonished his other wives that they were to keep well her taboos. While Orunsen was not the senior wife she certainly was the first of wives for his love and affection.

The wives were naturally curious about this new wife among them. They would ask time and again where had this woman come from, for she had customs that were clearly not observed in Owo. The Olowo always kept his word and would simply tell the wives that Orunsen came from a faraway place in the south.

In time there grew a great jealousy in the compound. The senior wives took note of the time that Olowo Renrengenjen spent with Orunsen. They noted he would treat her preferentially and with a softness that seemed to be reserved for her. They would in turn make life for Orunsen more difficult with time. She paid little attention to the actions of the senior wives.

The day came when the Olowo decided to go on an extended hunting excursion. He bid goodbye to all of his wives, but gave Orunsen the most affectionate goodbye. The wives were resolute to make life hard for her in the absence of the Olowo. First they broke each of her taboos. They summoned her to the kitchen where they were pounding herbs. As she left the kitchen, another wife splashed water in front of her as she crossed the compound. Lastly, the least senior of the wives dropped her head load of wood in front of Orunsen. She would not give them the pleasure of knowing that she was bothered.

The wives were even more resolute in the face of Orunsen's calmness. They resolved that they would discover Orunsen's origins. Surely there was something the Olowo was hiding. They searched each building of the compound for clues. They almost gave up, when they happened upon Orunsen's antelope-skin in the rafters of the Olowo's residence. They immediately began to taunt Orunsen with calls of "bush creature." From that moment they refused to call her by her name. They would say "let the creature do that chore." They also made it known in Owo that the junior wife of the Olowo was a bush animal.

Orunsen remained cool and would not answer the insults the wives and now the whole town cast at her. Instead she quietly gathered her belongings and her antelope-skin, went into the bush and disappeared from the sight of residents of Owo.

On his return from his hunting expedition, the Olowo Renrengenjen sought out his junior wife Orunsen, but she was long gone. He summoned his servants questioning where she was; they did not know. He then summoned his wives, questioning if they knew where his junior wife was. They sneered at his query telling him "She went into the bush where she belongs. She donned her antelope-skin that we found and leapt off to be with her own." They continued scoffing at him for bringing a beast into the house as his wife.

The Olowo was overwhelmed with sorrow, feeling an emptiness not only in his compound but also in his heart. Before long he ordered his servants, guards and townsmen to find his missing wife. They searched everywhere even going into the bush. They questioned all in the town and reported back to the Olowo that none had seen her and they could not find her.

With anger in his voice, the Olowo commanded that they return to the bush to continue to search for Orunsen, admonishing that they should not return without his wife. Even as he barked his orders, the town heard a booming voice coming from the sky, "My love Renrengenjen, abandon the search. Where I am now, you cannot find me. I have gone to the sky to live under the protection of Olodumare. Here no one taunts me for being an antelope-woman." She continued retelling the offense that she suffered at the hands of his wives and the townsfolk. She said this was the reason for her departure, but knew that Renrengenjen loved her and was good to her. She said she would now be a patron of the town, further instructing him to yearly offer sacrifice and prayers to her. In exchange she said that Owo would flourish and be renowned, the people of Owo would not suffer poverty and the women would be fertile.

Renrengenjen went into his house and remained there for seventeen days without giving audience to anyone. His loss of Orunsen weighed heavy on his heart. On the eighteenth day he emerged and ordered the town to set the sacrifice for Orunsen and hold a festival to honor her. All of the townspeople joined in song to praise their new benefactor, and bells celebrating Orunsen could be heard even in the bush. Orunsen blessed Owo in return with prosperity and fertility.

This was the beginning of the annual festival called Igogo, meaning bells. Just as the Olowo Renrengenjen grieved for seventeen days, so do the townsfolk of Owo celebrate for the same, in remembrance. During this festival no drums are heard in the town, only the sounds of handbells. The activities of the Igogo celebration are led by priests called Ahgoros, who represent the search party that many years ago conducted an expedition to look for Orunsen, the missing wife of the Olowo who then ruled over Owo.

As you travel in the wild places and encounter the animals that share space with us, remember that they too are part of the divine scheme and deserve respect. Take lesson and pay homage to the diversity Olodumare and the Orisa have created.

—IFADOYIN SANGOMUYIWA

Etu Òbèjé

Elésè osùn

Arítete gbón-on-ni

Eranko tíí lé tìróò

Eranko tíí wa gònbò.

Antelope Òbèjé

The one who has legs painted red with camwood

The one who has thighs with which to touch the dew

The animal that puts on eyelashes

The animal that wears gònbò tribal marks

Excerpt from traditional Oriki - praise poem

Codex Gigas

The Devil's Bible

THE LARGEST MEDIEVAL book ever written weighs an astonishing 165 pounds. It stands 36 inches tall and is 20 inches wide. It is almost nine inches thick. No wonder it is known as *Codex Gigas*, which is Latin for *"The Giant Book."* It was written in a monastery in Bohemia (now the Czech Republic) in the early 1200s CE. Except for a few later notes, every word in this gigantic manuscript was written by the hand of one and the same scribe, who was surely a monk. It has been estimated that this monk spent some twenty or thirty years of his life writing out the *Codex Gigas* by hand, from its first page to its last.

The *Codex Gigas* has another name as well: *The Devil's Bible.* Since it seemed an almost superhuman task for a single monk to have written every word of so gigantic a book by hand, people who wondered at its size it began to ask themselves whether that monk might have had supernatural help from God… or, just maybe, from *someone else.*

And so legends gathered around the Giant Book. In their final form, they told of a monk, a scribe, who had committed some very great sin, and had been sentenced to be walled up alive. He bargained with his judges: "Will you spare me if in a single night I write a manuscript containing all knowledge, to glorify our monastery forever?" Thinking this impossible, his judges agreed. Alone in his prison cell that night, the monk called on the Prince of Hell and made a pact. With Lucifer's aid, the monk wrote out the entire Giant Book by hand in the course of a single night. Thereby he escaped punishment, but lost his soul.

These legends were inspired by the single most striking feature of the *Codex Gigas*. If, by accident or design, the book falls open at a certain place, the two facing pages will show a pair of utterly compelling, full-page illustrations.

On the left-hand page is a great walled city—the New Jerusalem—the Heavenly City that will descend from God at the end of time, according to the Revelation of St. John. On the right-hand page crouches the Prince of Hell himself, poised to leap right out of the page and seize the reader. That dread being is clad only in a loincloth made of royal ermine fur. His long, sharp horns and claws are red with blood. His eyes are beady and their pupils, too, are red. His face is green. He bares his teeth, and from his mouth protrude two long red tongues. Surely the Devil had a hand in the Giant Book's making and placed his frightening portrait there as a signature.

The five pages directly before the illustration of New Jerusalem contain a detailed ritual for a monk to confess all his sins, written in letters much larger than the rest of the manuscript. The six pages directly following the illustration of the Devil, also written in large letters, contain five magic spells. The first three spells are for healing, the other two are for identifying a thief (by scrying in the first spell and revelatory dreaming in the second).

Apart from these pages, the *Codex Gigas* contains the following, all in Latin: (1) the Old Testament, (2) *The Antiquities of the Jews* by Josephus Flavius, (3) *The History of the Jewish War*, also by Josephus Flavius, (4) Isidore of Seville's *Etymologiae*, a far-ranging encyclopedia, (5) nine medical treatises, (6) the New Testament, (7) the *Chronicle of Bohemia* by Cosmas of Prague, and (8) an ecclesiastical calendar. The ritual of confession, the full-page illustrations of New Jerusalem and the Prince of Hell, and the magic spells are placed between the New Testament and Cosmas of Prague's *Chronicle*.

For much more information about the *Codex Gigas* or *Devil's Bible*, visit the website of the National Library of Sweden in Stockholm: http://kb.se/codex-gigas/eng. There you can also leaf through the entire *Devil's Bible* page by page if you are so inclined, and download as many pages as you like, one page at a time. One can also find CDs with images of all the pages for sale in various places online.

—ROBERT MATHIESEN

DOG MAGIC, CANINE SHAMANISM AND DREAMS

WANDER BACK in time to the arctic tundra of nine thousand years ago. The environment was a harsh one and life was usually short and difficult. Bleak surroundings made the personal quest for security and stability an elusive one. This was the time when wolves and human beings first explored the benefits of living close to each other. People had scavenging done for them while the wolves always had scraps to eat. A partnership began which continued and intensified for two thousand years.

The theory that we become a part of all that we touch is an important magical axiom. Both the wolves and the people they traveled with slowly began to change. The first breeds of dogs developed. Bones dating to 5100 BCE were discovered in Illinois at the Koster archeological site. The bones were definitely not those of wolves, they were more dog-like and were found intermingled in funerary sites with the bones of people.

The partnership of living in close proximity had created a permanent physical and spiritual bond between humans and dogs. Further archeological evidence indicates that dogs helped hunters pursue game and provided companionship for adults. Puppies were the playmates of youngsters. Some tribes gave dogs a ceremonial position that included sacrifice before being ritually eaten. Dog skeletons have been found throughout North America buried with special honors.

In the desert Southwest and along the Northwest Coast long-haired dogs evolved, and their hair was used to weave blankets and ornamental belts. In 1778 John Ledyard, the explorer described the local natives as being dressed in garments made of plant fiber interwoven with the hair of their dogs, which were primarily white in color.

Ancient Friends

For many hundreds of years dogs were the only domesticated animal in North America. In the Great Plains they would carry loads of belongings on special pole frames called *travois* for their human friends. It's curious to note that dogs tended to be small in warm climates and would grow larger in the north. The very largest dogs of all lived in the far north among the Eskimo.

Legends of talking dogs who faithfully reported to their owners of betrayal come from the Eastern Woodland Indians. The dog pleads that he is the only companion to be trusted. Then he snitches to his human companion about the thievery or infidelity perpetrated by other people.

This illustrates the longstanding tradition of love and loyalty shared between dogs and human beings.

The Shawnee, a tribe of the Eastern Woodlands, always recognized a Grandmother deity who was accompanied by a small dog familiar near her sacred magical campfire. Dog-headed people are described in a variety of legends. These beings were the sinister offspring of a young girl who had taken an unknown lover. He was actually a dog by night and a human by day. Reflective of the werewolf tradition of Eastern Europe, these dog heads could become beastly. They were capable of cleverly attacking and murdering travelers, then fleeing with their plunder to the End of the World. Combining a mixture of human and dog abilities, the dog heads overpowered people. They each had one eye in the center of their forehead and could either walk upright or on all fours. Their hind feet or legs were dog-like and their arms or front feet were those of a human being. Variations of this traditional tale come from

Alaska, Siberia, and throughout the Northern United States.

In Northern Wisconsin in the late 1950s a local legend existed about a woman who had given birth to triplets who were actually a litter of half-dogs. The description was quite believable. Perhaps it was illustrative of the very intimate bond which can form between a human and a beloved dog. Possibly that love can grow so deep that the treasured dog will truly merge with a human being. This mirrors the way marriage partners merge, grow to resemble each other and eventually become two halves of the same soul.

The ancient Greeks portrayed the dog as an emblem of courage and devotion. The China of Fo-Hi saw dogs as messengers of joy and good fortune. An Egyptian ritual tells of five dog amulets buried on each side of a house to assure its safety and security against intruders. Recognized as the very epitome of loyalty, dogs have always claimed a unique position in the human heart and psyche.

Canine Dreams

Dream books always give great significance to the appearance of dogs as a dream symbol. A dream of a vicious dog warns of enemies and other misfortunes which can't easily be avoided. Affection given by a dog in a dream augurs great success and many friends, while dreaming of a purebred show dog promises wealth. If a dreamer is "dogged" by a blood hound temptation must be avoided. The blood hound represents a spy who is observing the dreamer's movements and plotting a downfall.

—ELAINE NEUMEIER

Merry Meetings

*A candle in the window, a fire on the hearth,
a discourse over tea…*

DOLORES ASHCROFT-NOWICKI can be counted amongst the most influential occult minds of the last two centuries. Few are able to find their true path in life, even fewer are able to embark on that path at a young age under the watchful eye of their parents. Dolores took a moment out to share her life experiences and how they informed her occult practice with us. Talking with Dolores belays the fact that we are interviewing an occultist that has been a teacher of teachers.

We understand that there is a strong connection to natural magic on both maternal and paternal sides of your family. Can you tell us about the magic and your early training?

It would take a day to tell you. My father was a natural medium, at one time a materializing medium. But it began to play havoc with his health, so he put a stop to that, he withdrew from that. But he remained a very strong psychic right up until his death in 1999. My mother was not a psychic, but she did have the ability to pass energy. I don't know quite how they did it, but they were very close my mom and dad, and sometimes if he was really, really tired, she would just put her hands on him, over his heart and she could just pass the energy to him. Within a few minutes he would be fine. My father's mother, my nana, she was the Witch of the family. Absolutely from top to bottom. She never really belonged to a group, except during the war, she was a solitary, but she was very powerful. And she had the ability to shall I say influence

people. And she was not always kind of careful about who she influenced... Nevertheless she taught me a great deal. She was the one that used to sit and tell me stories that were never fairy stories. They were, she would say "now this happened to me one day when I was such and such age" and she would go off into telling me all about the things she used to do when she was little. Because her grandmother was a Romani, a gypsy. And she never used a crystal and she didn't do palmistry. But she would use a bowl with water in it, a black bowl. And she would put a tiny drop of milk in the bowl and as it spiraled down, she would go, I suppose you would call it into a light trance. And then she would look up at you and just go off into whatever it was that she was seeing...

Can you tell us about your families' occultists endeavors outside of family passed practices?

...My nana and my father and my mother and two of my father's

friends, Robin and Gerty, comprised, you might say, the family group. It was mainly that we would come together and somebody would start the conversation going, and everybody would join in. They would read what they were reading at the time. They would bring it with them, and they would read bits and it would be discussed. But they didn't do ceremonial magick as I have done in my time. It was in a sense kind of, shall I say, almost a series of lectures. Everybody would offer an opinion. Even by now I would be five or six, they treated me as an adult. They would say, "Dolores, what do you think?" I'd say, "I think so and so and so and so and so and so, but I didn't understand so and so and so and so." Then it would be explained to me. But I was never treated like a child. They got a bit

worried when my mother found out that whenever the Moon was full, I used to get out of my bed, take all of my clothes off and go and dance on the lawn. She would say to me "Dolores, you're going to catch cold!" "No mum, I'm not going to catch cold because the Moon keeps me warm, and she likes being danced to, she calls me out." That was my little effort. That was really all that was done in these early days, because in Jersey you kept your head down. Mind you, the place is alive with people who keep the old traditions. They just don't talk about it. I still get the occasional phone call from a farmer saying his cow is sick or there is something in the barn that he does not like, I would come out and see to it. They never pay cash. I am given cauliflowers and potatoes and vegetables and [unintelligible], oc-

casionally homemade jams and things like that. It's the old traditional way.

How is it that you entered Dion Fortune's Society of the Inner Light?

Well, I was going to London and my friend asked me to collect a set of Tarot cards. She gave me an address to go to. It was the very, very young Aquarian Press. They had two rooms on the third floor of a big office building in Victoria Street. I trotted all the way up those stairs to this dingy little room. There was a desk, a couple of book shelves of second hand books and kind of middle aged man sitting at the desk. He said, "Can I help you?" I said, "I'd like a pack of Tarot cards please." He said, "I think I still have some left" so he went off into the other room. I looked at the books and found a grimoire, and I thought, oh this looks interesting. I was thumbing through this, when all of the sudden this hand come over my shoulder and plucked it out of my hands and said, "You do not need that, you need this." handing me a little book, a book by a certain Walter Ernest Butler and it was called Magic its Ritual Power and Purpose. *I bought that and I bought the Tarot cards. As I went out he said "Read carefully." Now that was actually the guy who started the Aquarian Press. I read it on the train down to Southhampton where I was catching the plane back home. I read it in a single sitting and there was an address in the back. What I read changed my life completely. I got out*

of that plane, a friend was picking me up and she looked at me and said "What's happened to you? You look as if you lit up inside." I said "I think I found where I must go in my life." I took it back and showed it to my then husband and within six weeks we had joined the Inner Light. It was just sitting there waiting for us.

Now, the strange thing is that about two years before, no about a year before, we had been in London, living in London, I went to the library and picked up a book called The Magicians Training and Work. *I thought "Oh that sounds like the other book and it's by the same person." I took it back and we both read it. Because it was a library book I had to take it back. The girl said "You can always take it out again, you know." So, I went back two weeks later and said "Can I have this book?" and a differ-*

ent girl said "We've never had that book." I said "I've read it, this is why I'm asking for it." She went all the way through and said "No, we've got no record of the author or the book."

When we joined the Inner Light and we finally met up with Mr. Butler. I told him about this and he said "You couldn't possibly have read it, I hadn't written it yet. Not at that time." Strange things happen.

How did your time with Society of the Inner Light change practices that you learned in childhood?

It organized me. Its lessons were very, very familiar in the sense that I knew already that I had a lot of learned knowledge. This was giving me ways in which to use what I had learned in a very practical way. I learned the practice of—well you can't really say that you learn the practice of meditation, you either do it or you don't. I learned how to go deeper into myself than I had ever been before. Then I had to write out what I had brought back from these meditations. I had to learn to put it concisely. I had to learn to put it in a way, how can I say—it would mean something to the supervisor who was going to read it—and when I read it back, I would be able to extend it even more. I would read what I had written and thought "Oh, I should have put in that or I should have put in this or that's strange, I wonder how that would fit in." ...With the Inner Light I was finally getting organized training and I lapped it up. It was there that I learned exactly what pathworking was. I was told very specifically that it was inner-level stuff and it was never ever to be spoken about outside. Well I soon broke that law. That is how it changed me. It made me more disciplined, I think.

You have on occasion mentioned your participation in the Craft. How has this changed or enhanced your magical work?

I love the Craft. I love the lightness. I love the laughter. I love the music and the dancing. The old Pagan ways are still alive and well. They are foundation stones. They are what modern occultism is built on. They are the ancestors. We don't look back on the ancestors enough. We don't thank them enough. We don't work with them enough. When you do go back to them, and I love participating with some of the Pagan rituals and with the Craft groups. I really, really enjoy that because there is a freedom, there is a lightness of heart and spirit there. It contrasts so much with the Quantum Physics. It's like Ma'at and her scales. On the one side you have this lovely lighthearted almost childlike power of the Pagan groups, and their power is enormous because it's a nature power. Then on the other side you've got the more scientific one, the Quantum Physics and

the what have you. They're both beautiful in their ways and they both have so much to give. Yet, it's wrong to try to separate them. It's wrong for someone who works with Quantum Physics to look down on the Pagan. It's wrong for the Pagan to say: "You're too high and mighty." This is why Ma'at balances them. We can learn from both of them. The Craft can learn from the physics and physics can learn from the Craft. What comes in the middle this is laughter. You know, laughter is such a precious gift...*

What first steps advice would you give the budding magician as he or she begins their journey?

Find a damn good school and stick with it—but don't take the first one.

Look at several. Ask people who are running the school. Ask them to put you in touch with somebody that is in the school and ask them how is it. "Is it easy? Do you think I can do it?" Ask questions. Don't just go into it because somebody says, "Oh, we go out into the woods and dance naked and drum all night and drink beer." You know this is fun, this is not the occult kind of thing. You've got to find someone who knows more than you do but is ethical. Because, this is why the occult and magic as a whole got a bad name for so long. Ethics weren't part of it. Magic, Quantum Physics, whatever you want to call it, it has to have ethics. People have to be doing things for the right reason, not just so that they can get to wear the purple robe with a collar deco-rated with something and a magical hat and have a wand with a crystal on it. That's not magic. Every one of the magical tools are merely symbols. What they really are, the power of that symbol is in you. I keep telling people, stark naked and in a desert you can do a ceremony. You've got two forefingers. You've got a sword and you've got a wand. The flat hand open is your pentacle and your cupped hands is a grail. This is all you need...

Dolores took the time to truly share her experiences through life in a very in-depth manner. Rather than edit down such an important review, we thought it best to share the entire audio file: TheWitchesAlmanac.com/almanac-extras/

Notable Quotations
ANIMALS

The early bird gets the worm, but the second mouse gets the cheese.

Willie Nelson

To insult someone we call him "bestial." For deliberate cruelty and nature, "human" might be the greater insult.

–Isaac Asimov

The wagon rests in winter, the sleigh in summer, the horse never.

–Yiddish Proverb

Some people talk to animals. Not many listen though. That's the problem.

–A. A. Milne

Some birds are not meant to be caged, that's all. Their feathers are too bright, their songs too sweet and wild.

–Stephen King

Not my circus, not my monkeys.

–Polish proverb

Love the animals: God has given them the rudiments of thought and joy untroubled.

–Fyodor Dostoyevsky

But ask the animals, and they will teach you, or the birds of the air, and they will tell you; or speak to the earth, and it will teach you, or let the fish of the sea inform you.

–Job 12: 7-8

And the fox said to the little prince: men have forgotten this truth, but you must not forget it. You become responsible, forever, for what you have tamed.

–Antoine de Saint-Exupéry

Edible, adj.: Good to eat, and wholesome to digest, as a worm to a toad, a toad to a snake, a snake to a pig, a pig to a man, and a man to a worm.

–Ambrose Bierce

Quotes compiled by Isabel Kunkle

Sirius

The Dog Star

THE FIXED STAR featured this year is Sirius, the famous Dog Star. Currently located at 14°05' of Cancer, stargazers can observe it sparkling in the mouth of the Greater Dog, Alpha Canis Major. Sirius is a brilliant, white-yellow binary star and emits the brightest starlight in the heavens. Honor, renown, goodwill, the power to pacify leaders, devotion and faithful love are linked to the Dog Star when it is favorably placed. Its heavenly glow offers hope and encouragement during these times of personal and earthly changes.

Sirius is one of the fifteen Behenian stars which were invoked in medieval magic practices. These special stars were thought to be the power sources for planetary energies. Hermes Trismegistus and Cornelius Agrippa were among the legendary practitioners who used special diagrams to call upon the celestial energy of Sirius and the other Behenian stars. In Agrippa's *Three Books Of Occult Philosophy*, the stone beryl and the herb juniper are used in ritual magic to court the favor of Sirius. Agrippa related Sirius to Venus in magical workings.

In ancient Akkadia, Sirius was seen as angelic and associated with the heavenly host. Sirius is illustrated in the ancient zodiac discovered in the Temple of Hathor in Dendera, Egypt. It was revered as a source of Jupiter's benevolent energy and a blessing from the Egyptian gods Osiris and

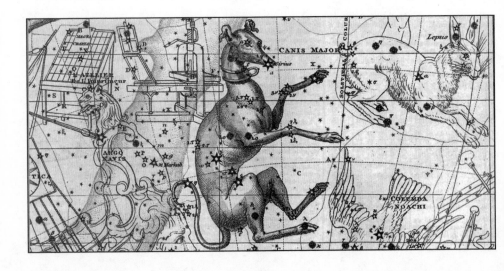

Thoth. Later, Virgil related Sirius to "a pestilence in the sky" when it was afflicted, and Homer wrote that the Dog Star's "burning breath taints the red air with fever and plagues." Chinese astrologers felt Sirius was a celestial canine deity and a star of great significance. They named it *Tseen Lang*, the Heavenly Wolf. When it was especially brilliant, Chinese astrologer-magicians observed it would bring protection from evildoers.

Sirius rises during the legendary "dog days" of summer, in July and August, signifying great heat and the need to adapt to seasonal changes. On July 5 each year, during the early to mid-21st century, Sirius will be exactly conjunct the Sun. Using an orb of two degrees, this extends to also impact July 3–7, promising great success and an overall positive personal turn of events. For the whole story, though, it's necessary to factor in all of the transits aspecting the 12–16° of Cancer, remembering to consider that two-degree orb.

During the coming year the eclipses on July 2, 2019, and January 10, 2020, will be quite close to the orb allowed with conjunctions with Sirius and will be marginally impacted by the Dog Star. Transit Venus conjuncts Sirius July 13–17, 2019. This can be quite a fortunate cycle for many.

Whether Sirius functions as a favorable fixed star influence or not depends upon the astrological energies it is linked with at a given time. Sirius rising with Mars can indicate competition, anger, impatience and injury. Sirius at the midheaven is very fortunate, drawing protective friends and fame. Linked to the 8th house, Sirius indicates longevity and/or honors after death as well as great wealth.

Check with your astrologer to see which planets or zodiacal house in your own personal horoscope span 12–16° of Cancer for more insight into exactly how you can recognize the influence of Sirius, this powerful, faithful and heavenly canine companion, in your own life.

A Guide To Interpreting Sirius

With the Sun: great success, wealth and status

With the Moon: good health, intimate relationships, a beneficial parent and home

With Mercury: business success, but a tendency toward stress and worry can cause illness and accidents are possible

With Venus: a life of ease, luxury, inherited wealth

With Mars or Pluto: recklessness, adventurousness, turmoil, work in manufacturing or the military, injury from blades, power tools or natural disasters

With Jupiter: travel, great success, helpful people, connection with churches or higher education

With Saturn: perseverance and the passage of time brings progress, a favorable heritage and legacies are accented

With Uranus: gain through connections and networking, interesting friends and associates, sudden changes in fortune

With Neptune: spiritual and occult inclinations, intuition, creativity, ease in old age

—DIKKI-JO MULLEN

RAIN SPELL

RAIN: OUR BODIES need it, animals need it, the crops need it. Without precipitation, dry vegetation makes the land vulnerable to wildfires. Search the news reports for the last two years and you'll see what happens when large swaths of countryside become combustible.

Weather magic can bring needed precipitation. Traditional spells often employ imitative magic, magic that works by mimicking the desired results. To bring rain, a village shaman or witch doctor would sprinkle or spit-spray water while chanting the appropriate words and drumming to mimic the sound of thunder.

With one small modification, modern Witches can help bring drought relief to areas thousands of miles away. The following is a simple spell that anyone with good intentions and the power of visualization can perform.

What You Need

Assemble the following items:

Container full of water—Traditionally, this is a bowl or a cauldron. The water can come from your faucet or from a stream, pond or well. Purists prefer natural sources, but work with what you have.

Aspergillum—An aspergillum is something used to sprinkle water. You might have read recent reports of a Mexican priest using a water gun to dispense holy water, but you don't want anything as directed or forceful. Remember that you're doing imitative magic and using too much force is asking for a deluge. Consider using a feather or a sprig of an evergreen tree.

Map—This is the modern addition mentioned earlier: a map showing the location in need of rainfall. Using your own drawing skills, a map site like Google Maps or an illustration from a newspaper, create a paper map.

Rain chant—Using your local library or Internet, look for a rain chant used by the indigenous people of the area. If you feel it would be better to invoke the aid of your own deities, find or write one that suits your pantheon or try this: Rewrite that old nursery rhyme "Rain, rain, go away" to call the rain. "Rain, rain, come today / Sprinkle down a gentle spray / Make the drought go away." If the area is being ravaged by wildfires, change the last line to "Make the fires go away." Resist the temptation to make the rain come down too hard in a burned area— with no vegetation to hold it, the runoff can cause flash floods.

The Spell

1. Cast your circle or do whatever creates sacred space in your practice. Ground and center yourself.

2. Pick up the container of water. Consider what you are doing: bringing gentle rain to a place that needs it. Keep that image in your mind—gentle rain. You don't want floods and you don't want to rob surrounding areas of the rain they need.

3. When you have the intent and image firmly in mind, pick up your aspergillum and dip it in the water. Shake some of the water off so that you're not spraying a downpour. Gently shake it onto the map while chanting the words of your spell. Visualize a gentle rain falling steadily over the area.

Continue to chant and sprinkle until you feel the spell taking effect. Know that the rain will appear, but it may take time.

—NEVROM YDAL

Mysterious Feather Crowns

Omens of Death or Angelic Blessings?

THEY CAN BE FOUND in museums throughout Appalachia. The mysterious circles of feathers evoke amazement. Always the quill points turn inward while the feather tips swirl out, forming a circle which is usually about the size of a bird's nest. Sometimes called angel crowns, feather crowns or more often, death crowns, they can be found carefully preserved under glass display domes, in cabinets or picture frames. These peculiar artifacts have been found tucked away in drawers, kept by families for genera-

tions. Vintage photographs show them positioned near funeral cards with other photos of mourners or even the deceased in a casket, prepared for eternal rest. The museum in Clinton, Tennessee offers an explanation which reads in part:

"When a person died there was sometimes found in the bed pillow a closely woven mass of feathers. Called an angel crown, it indicated that the deceased had gone to heaven."

Sometimes, though, the lumpy mass would be noticed in the pillow of someone who had fallen ill, but was yet alive. Then the feathers were called a death crown and were dreaded omens indicating that death was imminent. The crowns are only found in the pillows of the recently deceased or seriously ill. Skeptics might say the masses form while the dying person tosses and turns, perhaps in the grip of a fever or chills. Those who see the odd formations as conveying something deeper might counter the cynical remarks with other anecdotes.

There is one about a healthy and beloved father who was killed getting off the bus by a speeding car. When clearing away his bedding the grieving family found a large death crown in his pillow. Another account was offered by a man who was undergoing treatment for heart disease. He was terrified when, one night, he felt a lump and opened his pillow to find a sinister feathery wreath. He promptly destroyed it and slowly his condition improved. For many years he told of how he cheated death. Part of the tradition of death crowns does involve breaking them apart when found in the pillows of those still living to offset death. The feather formations have also been found in the pillows of children who have passed away. One poignant report from the 1940s tells of three small feather death crowns cherished for decades by a mother who lost her three small children due to illness in the early 1900s.

In the United States, the tradition of death crowns seems to be limited to accounts stemming from Appalachia—especially Tennessee—as well as Indiana and Missouri. Perhaps that's due to the isolated lifestyle of rural folks in generations past. However further research shows that a belief in death crowns is also prevalent in Germany and neighboring countries. Scholars speculate the tradition was perpetuated by immigrants who settled in the mountains. The feather circles do have a widespread link with accounts of deaths and witchery in Central Europe throughout the ages. A touching account was shared by a 17 year-old mountain boy, a member of the McCoy family. Mourning the death of his grandmother, he found a crown in her pillow while clearing away her bedding. Upon burning the blankets, sheets and pillows, he noticed that one pillow would not burn. Inside and intact was the circle of feathers. He interpreted it as a sign that she was in heaven with the angels.

Another memory comes from a man whose little brother passed away in 1942 at age 8. He found a feather crown in the brother's pillow and has kept it throughout his life, believing it to be good luck.

With feather pillows becoming a rarity in modern times, actual accounts of discovering angel crowns are more and more infrequent. However, they still remain a topic of nostalgic conversation among those who are over the age of sixty or so. There is a 1993 novel titled *Feather Crowns* by Bobbi Ann Mason. It's set in Kentucky during the early 1900s and beautifully weaves this tradition into a parable about an amazing family.

A truly impressive display of actual death crowns and their histories can be enjoyed by visitors of The Museum of Appalachia, 2819 Andersonville Highway, Clinton, Tennessee.

—MARINA BRYONY

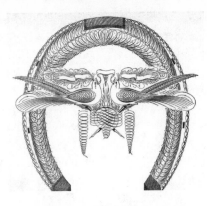

Horseshoes

A farmer travelling with his load
Picked up a horseshoe in the road,
And nailed it fast to his barn door,
That Luck might down upon him pour

The Lucky Horseshoe
James Thomas Fields

A HORSESHOE NAILED over the door protects against harmful magic, bad luck, contagious disease and other evil influences. Images of horseshoes are displayed where games of chance are played, invoking luck for a win. As a general good luck talisman, people hang miniature versions on charm bracelets, necklaces and key rings. We see references to horseshoes in literature and media. In the early days of silent films, a movie called *The Lucky Horseshoe* (1925, starring Tom Mix) got its title from a horseshoe charm the heroine gave to a ranch foreman, saying it would bring him luck. But why are horseshoes considered good luck? Where does the luck come from?

According to a legend involving Saint Dunstan (909–988 AD), before he became the Archbishop of Canterbury, Dunstan worked as a blacksmith. One day the Devil came to his smithy, asking him to shoe

his horse. Dunstan recognized him, but agreed to shoe the horse. When the shoe was ready, he instead nailed the shoe to the Devil's hoof. He screamed in pain, pleading with Dunstan to remove the shoe, which he did only after the Devil promised to never enter a household with a horseshoe nailed to the door.

Ancient Iron

Long before Saint Dunstan, blacksmiths were held in esteem because of their ability to transform metals employing fire. Hephaestus in Greek mythology and Vulcan in Roman mythology were the blacksmiths of the Gods. In Celtic mythology, Boibhniu of the Irish Tuatha de Danann cycle was a blacksmith god. Gofannon of the Mabinogion was his Welsh counterpart.

Ancient blacksmiths worked with iron, believed to ward off danger from malevolent spirits and those Witches who wanted to cause harm. Iron acquired that magical power when it was extracted from ore and worked into objects using the element of fire. If iron could withstand fire, it was reasoned, it could withstand the power of Witches. Seven iron nails added

136

to the horseshoe's power due to the extra iron and the magic of the number seven.

Even the shape of the horseshoe contributes to its luck. The crescent shape is sacred to various Moon Goddesses, conferring protection and fertility.

Lucky Finds

The material the horseshoe is made from and how it is obtained affect the luck-bringing qualities of the shoe. It must be made of iron and found, not removed from a horse. That is, it must be thrown by the horse. In the Thuringian Forest region of Germany only a horseshoe forged by a bachelor of wholesome life and good character on Saint John's Eve will do.

Ozark hill folk believed that if you found a horseshoe with the closed end toward you, it should be left at the spot. If the open end was toward you, you could take it as is or pick it up, spit on it and throw it over your left shoulder. Another option was to place it in a tree or on a fence, saying: "Hang thar, all my bad luck!" Whoever touched the hanging horseshoe inherited the misfortune of the person who placed it there.

In UK and Western Europe, the people commonly referred to as "Gypsies" (Roma) believed that if you found a horseshoe with the nails still in it, it meant a year's worth of good luck, though some believed that each nail counted for a single year of good luck. Like the Ozark hill folk, if they found the horseshoe in an inauspicious position, they would spit on it and throw it over their left shoulder. For them, though, the inauspicious position was the opposite of that in the Ozarks: they considered it bad if the ends were pointing toward them. If the ends were pointing away from them, they'd keep it to hang over the door of the *vardo*, the traditional horse-drawn wagon used by English Roma.

Horseshoes were also hung on ships for good luck. In 1898 a folklorist reported that in Shrewsbury, the ancient county town of Shropshire, horseshoes were hung on the barges which navigated the River Severn. Even today you can see iron horseshoes hand-painted in a traditional style on English canal boats.

Seafaring sailors nailed a horseshoe to the mast not only to ward off evil entities, but to protect them from severe storms. Lord Nelson reportedly had one nailed to the mast of his ship, Victory.

Hanging the Horseshoe

The proper way to hang a horseshoe has long been a matter of debate. Though some believe that if you hang it with the ends pointing down, the good luck will rain out on those below, most believers say that it should be nailed with the opening at the top (that is, like the letter U) because it prevents the luck from falling out.

In the poem *The Lucky Horseshoe* by James Thomas Fields, written in 1903 and quoted at the top of this article, a farmer had bad luck after hanging a horseshoe he found on the road. His hens wouldn't lay, the wheat crop failed and his cattle all died or wandered off. A great drought prevailed the following spring. Despondent, he sat ruminating over his misfortune. An old man walking by asked why he was so sad. The farmer told him of his difficulties, lamenting "what a desperate state of things/a picked-up horseshoe sometimes brings."

The stranger asked to see the horseshoe and when the farmer showed him, the man laughed and said,

"No wonder skies upon you frown — You've nailed the horseshoe upside down!"

He urged the farmer to turn it around, which he did and was rewarded with gentle rain, sunshine, thriving crops and healthy, obedient cattle.

Where you hang the horseshoe is just as important as its orientation. Hung on the outside, it effectively bars evil spirits. Older texts often say that a horseshoe protects against Witches and Witchcraft. A modern Witch might wonder if the horseshoe, would then prevent Witch friends from entering and prevent spells of healing and good energy from afar doing their work.

The answer is no. The older texts meant evil Witches and baneful Witchcraft.

Hung on the inside, a horseshoe is less useful because it cannot expel the evil. However, all is not lost if the inside is the only place the horseshoe can be hung; it is still an emblem of good luck and if hung over the bed or over the bedroom door, it prevents nightmares. An article in *The Times*, March 5, 1917, says that it should be a pair of horseshoes covered in blue and red cloth that you hang over the bed.

Hung over a stable door, a horseshoe prevents hag riding. Hag riding (riding by evil Witches during the night) was suspected if a farmer discovered his horse bathed in sweat in the morning. Three horseshoes hung in a triangle pattern were even more effective.

Disappearing Talismans

If you're hoping to find your own lucky iron horseshoe, act fast. Modern shoes are made from steel, aluminum or composite material. There are even hoof boots and clip-on shock-absorbing plastic shoes, neither of which are nailed into the hoof. There's also a move to abandon shoes altogether: the barefoot movement.

Proponents of the barefoot horse movement believe that with proper trimming, the hoof is better off unshod. There are exceptions, of course, depending on the terrain and the normal activities of the horse, but when unshod, they say, the hoof and foot become stronger and healthier. There is still an ongoing debate over horses going barefoot versus horses being shod, but it may not be long before horseshoes made of any material become a thing of the past.

—MORVEN WESTFIELD

Wedjat—The Eye of Horus

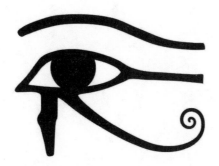

THE WEDJAT EYES ARE two of the most recognizable icons of the ancient Egyptians. The single eye was connected to many different roles throughout Egyptian mythology and as a result had many uses as a talisman. Just as there are two eyes to every human, so too are there two Wedjat eyes—either right or left.

We will concern ourselves with the left eye, known as the *Eye of Completion*, considered to be lunar in nature and associated with the mighty falcon-headed deity Horus. It was Horus who came to the defense of his father Osiris when he was murdered by his brother Set—the jackal-headed God of the night. In the battle to avenge his father, Horus' left eye was lost. The God of wisdom, Thoth, restored his eye, after which Horus was able to provide for the ascendency of his father.

Because of the regeneration of the eye of Horus, it was thought that the likeness his eye had healing powers and could bring safety, healing and protection. It was thought that as Horus was able to guide Osiris into afterlife, allowing him to become the Lord of the Dead, the eye constructed as a talisman would be placed in mummies to help the dead through the tribulations they would face.

For the land of the living, wearing the Eye of Horus was believed to protect the wearer from adversity as well as provide for good health, endurance and wisdom. It is also certain that it would protect the wearer from an untimely death.

In constructing the Eye of Completion, today's talisman maker might want to add an accent color of significance as the ancients did. They were often painted green or a blue-green, the color of fertility and rebirth. Accents of red were sometimes added to contribute significance. The Eye could very well be painted onto vellum/parchment or fashioned out of clay or sculpey.

—DEVON STRONG

NIKOLA TESLA

The Benevolent Wizard and Futurist

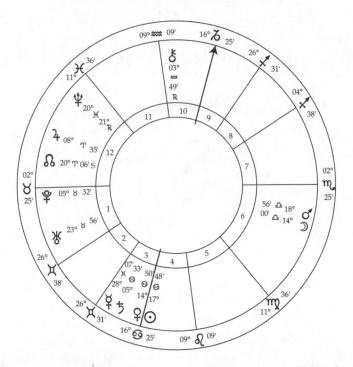

IT HAS BEEN PREDICTED that at least another thousand years will pass before the rest of the world will comprehend the depth and breadth of Nikola Tesla's genius. His legacy is our entire modern world. Tesla didn't just touch on the concept, he actually invented technology. Alternating electrical current, radio, television, X-rays, robotics, wireless communication, refined lasers, remote controls and more can all be linked to his tireless efforts and the genuine magic of his inventiveness. Frequently described as the most influential, inventive, enigmatic and purely brilliant individual who has ever lived, Nikola Tesla was born at the stroke of midnight on July 9-10, 1856 in Smilijan, Serbia (now Gospic, Croatia).

The Fixed Star Sirius, located in the sign of Cancer, is the brightest star in the sky and its impact is pivotal in Tesla's birth chart. This powerful star, which has been linked with evolution and inspiration at least since the times of Ancient Egypt, activates Tesla's Cancerian Sun, his Venus (ruler of his Taurus ascendant) and Saturn in the 3rd and 4th houses of his birth chart. As is true with many Cancerians his mother seems to have had an especially strong influence on him. She was locally famous as an inventor of clever household gadgets. Tesla's father was a Greek Orthodox priest. An ethic of service to humanity and working for the common good, a major motivation stimulating Tesla's efforts, might be traced to early religious training.

Mercury is in its ruling sign of Gemini and dignified by placement in the 3rd house. This points to a quick wit and communication skills. Tesla spoke 8 languages and excelled in his early schooling. As a teenager he enrolled in an engineering program at Graz University, Prague, completing his degree early—in just a year. Illness and a complete nervous breakdown followed, since he accomplished this by studying 19 hours daily, barely taking time to eat or sleep. While recovering Tesla observed strange and unbelievable phenomena. His vision and hearing which had always been sharp, intensified beyond any normal human capacity. He could sense objects in the dark in the same way as a bat. It was a period in which his sensitivities were so heightened that the flashes of light he had seen from childhood now filled the air around him with tongues of living flame. Their intensity, instead of diminishing, increased with time.

His responses were so keenly tuned that a word would become an image that he could feel and taste. It was during this time that he had one of his most famous ideas, that of the rotating magnetic field and alternating current induction motor. Tesla retained an extremely acute sense of hearing, exceptional eyesight and a vivid power of visualization. He described inspirations and inventions that would come to him in a flash, fully complete.

Pluto rising in Taurus, coupled with the 1st house Uranus in Taurus suggests the sensitivity to sound, a transformative experience, intensity and originality. His Venus, ruler of the ascendant, is in Cancer, in a fortunate mutual reception with the 6th house Libra Moon. This enabled his recovery from the health crisis and enabled the eventual positive outcome.

He began a career working for the Central Telegraph Office in Budapest before eventually emigrating to the

United States. There he soon met Thomas Edison who recognized young Tesla's potential and hired him. The two later became bitter rivals, when Tesla correctly insisted that alternating, not direct current, was the secret to the future of expanding the use of electrical power. Many inventions credited to Edison were actually Tesla's. Retrograde Chiron in Aquarius in Tesla's natal 10th house describes shifts in direction as well as complex learning experiences through his career path. Friendships, patronages or business relationships with John Jacob Astor, Mark Twain, George Westinghouse, Rudyard Kipling and J.P. Morgan waxed and waned during the course of Tesla's life. The strongly aspected Libra Moon gave him charm and a flair for showmanship. Tesla hosted dinner parties punctuated by sparks flying and spectacular displays of his inventions. Tesla wanted to make power available for free to benefit all of humanity. His powerful connections tended to reject this concept. Banker JP Morgan summed it up, saying, "But where is the meter?"

The strong Taurus influence reveals Tesla was a person of habit. For many years he usually dined at 8:00 pm at the same table while living at the Waldorf Astoria Hotel in New York City. A fresh white table cloth and napkin were essential. He took pleasure in calculating the volume of his meal, which included honey, bread, milk, fresh vegetables and juices—mostly vegetarian fare—which he promoted as the key to wellness and longevity. His 6th house Moon and Mars describe his fastidiousness. Tesla was known as a germaphobe, always concerned with the cleanliness of his food, clothing and surroundings.

Retrograde Neptune in Pisces and Jupiter in Aries along with the North Node in Aries in the 12th house all reveal how progressive, otherworldly and futuristic Tesla's visionary ideas really were. He left notes describing ecological concerns and the dangers of global warming unless the burning of fossil fuels would be eliminated. He claimed to be able to discern communications coming from aliens who were always watching planet Earth. The strong 12th house shows Tesla's preference for spending time alone. He usually slept just two hours each night while absorbed in his various projects. He stated that no great inventor had ever married and shunned intimate relationships of all kinds. His own claim was that he had been celibate for his entire life. Perhaps the canvas of his work and mind were just too vast for anyone else to truly share. This was a disappointment to many of his acquaintances, who were romantically attracted to the tall, handsome and intriguing scientist. Tesla was 6'2" and maintained a lifelong weight of 142 lbs.

Although he became a millionaire, his business decisions and choices left him in constant financial difficulty. He was forced to move from hotel to hotel in New York City, leaving behind cases of his notes as security for unpaid debts. After his death these papers surfaced and have since posed many questions concerning who Tesla really was. He had many truly prophetic visions about the future and life today.

At the end of his life Nikola Tesla became increasingly confused and alone, living in poverty. He spent his last days at the New York City Public Library. The birds he fed out front, he said, were his only remaining friends. His cause of death was recorded as heart failure on January 7, 1943. Looking again at his birth chart, the Moon, which rules his 4th house, shows his circumstances at the end of life. The Moon conjoins Mars and forms a cardinal T-square with his natal Jupiter in Aries and his Sun-Venus conjunction in Cancer. Jupiter rules the 8th house which describes the manner of death. The ruler of the 8th is in the 12th house, which shows that he passed away alone. He was found in his ramshackle hotel room by the maid.

Nikola Tesla's story doesn't end here though. Over 2,000 mourners attended his funeral in New York City. He continues to become more well known, receiving posthumous recognition to this day. An airport in Belgrade, Serbia is named for Tesla. The founder of Tesla Motors was inspired by his work and this 21st century company also honors him. During 2019–2020 transiting Neptune will be moving toward a conjunction with Tesla's natal Neptune. Uranus will be transiting Taurus, the sign of Tesla's natal Uranus. These powerful outer planets, which relate to mystery, creativity, inventions and electricity might coincide with a new appreciation for Tesla's amazing life.

The Tesla Society in New York City (phone 718-417-5102) and the Tesla Museum in downtown Belgrade, Serbia offer an array of resources for those who would care to learn more.

—DIKKI-JO MULLEN

NIKOLA TESLA
Born on July 9-10, 1856 CE
NS, at the very stroke of midnight
in Gospic (Smilijan, Serbia) Croatia
44N33 15E23

Data Table
Tropical Placidus Houses

Sun 17 Cancer 18'—4th house

Moon 14 Libra 00'—6th house—waxing Moon in the crescent phase

Mercury 28 Gemini 07'—3rd house

Venus 14 Cancer 50'—3rd house

Mars 18 Libra 56'—6th house

Jupiter 08 Aries 35'—12th house

Saturn 05 Cancer 33'—3rd house

Uranus 23 Taurus 56'—1st house

Neptune 20 Pisces 21' (retrograde)—12th house

Pluto 05 Taurus 32'—1st house

Chiron 03 Aquarius 49' (retrograde)—10th house

N. Moon Node (true node) 20 Aries 06—12th house

Ascendant (rising sign) is 02 Taurus 25'

The Black Dog

IT'S LATE AT NIGHT and the mist is rising. You're chilled to the bone, so you walk faster. In the fog, a large shape emerges. As your eyes adjust, you realize that it's a dog the size of a calf or even a horse, with glowing red eyes. Animal lover or not, you shiver with more than the cold.

Phantom black dogs are sometimes viewed as benevolent creatures, but the most common belief is that they're malevolent. Where and when they appear seem to confirm this suspicion. They're known to frequent crossroads and places of execution, and you're most likely to encounter one of these dogs at night, especially if there's an electrical storm.

Association with the Devil
In Germany and most Scandinavian lands, the Black Dog is believed to be the Devil. In most of the British Isles, the Black Dog can also be the Devil's familiar. Witches of the Highlands, however, believed the canine to be Old Nick himself.

In *Tam O'Shanter*, first published in 1791, poet Robert Burns tells a tale of an eerie sighting of Witches dancing wildly in the ruins of an old church. Watching from a distance, farmer Tam can see a large black dog sitting in an alcove.

There sat auld Nick, in shape o' beast;
A towzie tyke, black, grim and large

"Towzie" or "tousie" means disheveled, shaggy or unkempt, a common attribute of the Black Dog. "Tyke" is an old Scots word for a mongrel or cur; "Ane black tyke" is one of the phrases Scots used when referring to the devilish Black Dog.

Other names for the creature illustrate a curious connection to Witches. In Dunstable it was usually referred to as Old Shuck, in Suffolk it was Old Shock, and in East Anglia it was Black Shuck. "Shuck" may derive from the Old English word *scucca* meaning "witch," though in some dialects the word just means "shaggy." Since Witches were thought to be in league with the Devil, it's possible that people believed Witches shapeshifted into the Devil's form, especially while traveling to the Sabbat.

According to a local folktale, on Sunday, August 4, 1577, Black Shuck burst through the doors of Holy Trinity Church in Blythburg during a thunderstorm. He killed a man and a boy and left scorch marks on the north door, which can still be seen. The scorch marks, of course, suggest the Devil.

In 2014, archaeologists discovered the skeleton of a massive dog in the ruins of Leiston Abbey, approximately eight miles away from Blythburgh. It would have weighed 200 pounds and stood seven feet tall on its hind legs. Was this Black Shuck, or just the remains of a non-supernatural dog of unusual size whose feats were reported inaccurately?

Omens of Death

In Welsh mythology, Cŵn Annwn are the spectral hounds of the Otherworld, Annwn. Hearing the hounds on the mountain of Cadair Idris, a mountain near the town of Dolgellau, foretold your death. Welsh folklore maintains that the hounds sound loudest at a distance, becoming quieter as they draw near.

In East Anglia, Black Shuck, who is said to have only a single eye in the middle of his head, haunts dark lanes and deserted field footpaths. His paws make no noise as they hit the

ground, but you know he is there by his howling. To encounter him means you will die in the year. However, if you shut your eyes before you actually see him, you can avoid your demise. Be forewarned: in the legends of the Maldon and Dengie area of Essex, the death occurs immediately and there is no mention of escaping harm by closing your eyes.

Psychopomps

Spectral dogs can often be guides to the realm of the dead. Their role is not to cause death, but instead to escort the souls of the newly dead to the afterlife.

The ancient Egyptian God Anubis is a well-known example. Depicted as either a man with a dog's head or a dog or jackal, he attended the Weighing of the Heart that determined whether a soul would be allowed to enter the realm of the dead. He was depicted as having black fur.

Guardians of the Gates

Dogs also guard the entrances to the world of the dead. An example from Greek mythology is Cerberus, the three-headed watchdog who guards the gates of Hades and prevents the dead from leaving. The Twelfth Labor of Heracles saw him capture Cerberus and remove him from Hades. Eventually, though, Cerberus returned.

Hellhounds, another form of black dog, are guardians of the realm of the dead who also hunt down lost souls and guide them to their destination.

Protector Dogs

Not all phantom black dogs are malevolent. Some even act as supernatural

guardians, though it's possible that these creatures are not the mysterious phantom black dog, but instead are ghosts of formerly natural canines.

In one story, a man was riding a mile-long path through lonely woods. A black dog silently joined him, following by his side. At some point the dog left him. Upon arrival at his destination, he conducted his business and then turned around to go home. At the same point where the dog had left him, the mutt rejoined him, once again making no noise except for the sound of his feet softly padding along.

Later he heard that some robbers had been arrested. They had been hiding in the wood, accosting travelers on that very path. However, when they saw the dog accompanying the man, they determined it was too risky and let him pass.

—MORVEN WESTFIELD

147

The Infinity Symbol

Secrets of the Lazy Eight

One of the most powerful and mystical of all symbols can be observed masquerading, incorporated within everyday objects. Take a rubber band which is merely a simple one-dimensional circle. The circle is a zero. It has no beginning or ending, it goes around and begins again. But now give the rubber band a twist, just once in the middle. Presto! Two circles, zero atop zero, flexible and mobile, appear. You will be holding the figure 8, the infinity symbol, also called the cosmic lemniscate. When looking into a good camera lens the 8 will appear again, indicating the infinity of the focus.

Infinity is the concept of endlessness; it never changes size. There is no other symbol like it. Everything else has a beginning and an ending, but not infinity. It is everywhere and yet nowhere. Those who would bless dwellings consider the figure eight most fortunate when incorporated into an address. Careful observation when visiting the home of a mystic will often reveal the eight symbol subtly penciled in near the threshold to invoke a blessing. The idea is that this sign, which can be drawn with a single sweep of the hand, is an oscillating figure. The back and forth movement suggests many pairs of opposites. Thought and imagination, night and day, chaos and order. In studies of brain wave activity the infinity symbol is linked to epsilon waves (0.5) which indicate meditation, ecstasy and cosmic consciousness.

Divine Interpretations

In many Tarot decks the infinity symbol will appear on several cards, usu-

THE MAGICIAN.

ally on its side as a "lazy eight" figure. It hovers overhead as The Magician (Key 1) and Strength (Key 8) are portrayed focused on seeking truth beyond appearances and transcending illusion. On the Two of Pentacles the lemniscate often turns up again. The fluid eight is outlined by a juggler balancing two coins. This illustrates the idea of the endless motion of balancing pairs of opposites, in values and duality. Perhaps infinity is the single symbol which most aptly describes the complete meaning of life. As an endless outpouring of radiant energy it is a reminder that it all goes on and on. The changes in consciousness proceed, showing the way to understand true being. Health and happiness are found while living within the layers of order and chaos.

Contemplation on the figure eight brings attention to the important goal of self-mastery. It traces critical boundaries to keep in mind. Swinging from side to side, the path of the eight suggests mortality—life then death followed by reincarnation or new life. Though eventually, if the boundaries are stretched too far beyond its limits, the eight will split. The result is an unpredictable future. The wise will keep this in mind while pursuing free will within limits. Explore and experience all that life has to offer, yet "don't tempt fate" might be the ultimate message conveyed by this profoundly significant symbol.

Numeric Endlessness

Those who seek truth in esoteric number codes will find that the Fibonacci number series addresses infinity with the magic of eight. For example divide 89 by 55. This equals 1.61818181818... In mathematics infinity is the term for a number sequence that goes on and on. This is just one of the messages of the infinity symbol eight that can't ever be visualized or resolved. There is the Big Bang theory, maybe an explosion which began the universe, then there is curved space, the ever-collapsing distant black holes beyond our solar system and so much more. What does eight suggest to you as you picture infinity?

—GRANIA LING

Horse Creatures

PLANNING A TRIP to Great Britain or Scandinavia? Have you searched all the travel sites for places to go? Picked up a book on flora and fauna? You're not done yet! Familiarize yourself with the local water horses.

Though distinct in lore, these supernatural creatures share many traits. For example, most appear as horses, though some can shapeshift into human form. Most inhabit freshwater locations like lakes, lochs and rivers, though the *Each-uisge* (Scotland) also frequents the sea and sea lochs and the *Nykur* (Iceland) may emerge from the ocean.

Many are docile at first, their gentle demeanor inviting you to come up to them and mount. If you are foolish enough to mount, the water horse runs into the water, drowning you. Why don't you just jump off? Some water horses' skin becomes sticky when you ride them, preventing you from dismounting. The *Ceffyl Dŵr* in Wales has a different tact altogether. Read details below.

Kelpies and *nykurs* can breed with regular horses. *Kelpie* hybrids appear normal, but are more muscular, have wilder temperaments and are impossible to drown. *Nykurs* who breed with regular horses give birth like a regular mare, but in the water. The offspring look normal, but lie down when splashed with water or when led through belly-deep water.

Here are just some of the fantastic beasts you may encounter on your travels.

Bäckahästen (Sweden). A version of the *nykur*. Usually appears as a majestic white horse. The name translates as *"brook horse."*

Ceffyl Dŵr (Wales). In North Wales, it's a fierce creature with fiery eyes and a

sinister presence, similar to the *kelpie* or *bäckahästen*. It appears solid, but if you mount it, it flies into the air and evaporates, dropping you to your demise. Alternately, it may leap from the water to trample you to death as you walk. In South Wales, it's a more innocuous creature, who is at worst an irritant to travelers.

Colt Pixie (South and Southwest of England—especially the New Forest and Dorset). Appears as a scruffy, pale horse or pony. Like the will-o'-the-wisp, it recedes if approached. The curious follow it off the beaten path, where they may stumble off a cliff or into a bog where, impossibly lost, they perish from exposure or thirst.

Each-uisge (Scotland). Called *Aughisky* in Ireland. Appears as a fine horse or pony. Can shape-shift into a handsome man or an enormous bird. If it's in horse form, you're safe as long as you stay away from water. However, at the merest glimpse or smell of water, the *each-uisge's* skin becomes adhesive, preventing you from dismounting as it gallops into the nearest deep water. The *each-uisge* tears its drowned victims apart and devours the entire body except for the liver, which floats to the surface. In its form as a handsome man, the indication that it's not human is the presence of water weeds or profuse sand and mud in its hair.

Kelpie (Scotland). One of the most well-known water horses. Usually appears as a powerful and beautiful black steed with backward-facing hooves, but can shape-shift into human form. In addition to killing by drowning, *Kelpies* are sometimes known to tear people to pieces and eat them. A New England variant called the *Kalpie* is said to come from the sea. Made of wrack and foam, it is cast up on the beaches at night. In Great Britain some people use the terms *water horse* and *kelpie* to refer to any supernatural *water horse*, but others use *water horse* for loch-dwellers and *kelpie* for those who haunt turbulent water such as rivers, fords and waterfalls.

Nuggle (Orkney Islands). Also called Neugle. Called *Shoepultie* or *Shoopiltee* in the Shetland Islands. Nocturnal, always male. A shape-shifter, it usually takes the form of a magnificent horse with a wheel-like tail. Fairly gentle disposition.

Nykur (Iceland). Also called *Nóni* or *Nennir*, a sinister creature that usually appears as a grey horse form with ears and hooves facing backwards. Can shapeshift into anything except lambs' wool or peeled barley. The sound of cracking ice on frozen lakes in winter is said to be the *nykur* neighing. Like the *each-uisge*, its skin becomes sticky if you mount it. To dismount, draw a cross on its back. Another method is to speak its name '*Nykur*,' at which it rears maniacally, throwing you off its back before galloping to the water. If it does not respond to that name, try the water horse's other names—'*Nennir*' or '*Nóni*.'

—MORVEN WESTFIELD

Understanding Familiar Spirits For What They Aren't

WHAT IS A FAMILIAR SPIRIT? If you ask four Witches this question, you're sure to get at least five different answers. Familiar spirits are interpreted differently among various Witches, just as the word "Witch" is defined differently amongst cultures, time periods, and even groups of Witches themselves. The term "familiar" is a large umbrella term, with the most basic definition being that it is any spirit familiar to the Witch with whom there's a strong relationship and alliance. Therefore, a protective spirit is not a familiar if that spirit is unknown to the Witch herself. With this definition, it only becomes a familiar once the Witch knows the spirit and the bonds of relationship have been established.

However, in certain traditions such as the Sacred Fires Tradition of Witchcraft, the familiar is a very distinct spirit unlike that of others. Despite interactions a Witch may have with the familiar spirit, defining it is not as simple as it may first appear. Sometimes the best way to define something is to look at what something is not rather than what it is. Through the process of elimination and through drawing parallels to the approximation the subject has to a thing it isn't, one can sometimes better understand what it actually is.

Spiritual Allies

A modern concept is the idea that the familiar is a physical animal, if not a pet, which is often an ally to the Witch in their magick. There's a bit of history to back up this idea and Hollywood has definitely perpetuated it. However, if you really examine the historical stories of Witches with their physical animal familiars there are two common themes. One is that the Witch's interaction with the animal is much more like the relationship between a Witch and a spirit instead of a human and an animal. The familiar animal will often have paranormal abilities more commonly attributed to a spirit. The second theme is that the animal in the lore is often a "vessel" which the familiar spirit possesses. If this is indeed the case, then the familiar is not the physical animal itself, but merely a vehicle which it can occupy.

This is a common theme as well these days, and most likely influenced by the rise of neo-shamanic practices. The main difference is that the familiar spirit is an individual spirit with its own identity and personality as opposed to the animal spirit. While it may appear in the form of an owl it is not the Spirit of Owl, which is an animal spirit. Animal spirits are more like the overarching monadic soul of an animal species instead of a singular personality.

Familiar spirits are also often not static in their forms and appearances. They can appear in various guises, shapeshift, and can also appear in chimeric form. It is common for them to take a predominant form—usually that of an animal—but this is more of a way of interacting, a mask or costume they appear in to interact with the Witch. While spirits do not have genuine forms in the way we think of them, being unbound from the realm of the physical world, they usually maintain or hold onto one when they approach us or when we work with them. The difference between the familiar spirit and most other spirits is that there's a more regular "costume change."

There are more similarities between the familiar spirit and spirit guides. However, there are still some stark differences. Spirit guides can come and go depending on the work they are meant to do for us. Familiar spirits seem to be there until the end. It is possible for familiar spirits to work with a Witch through many lifetimes, and this is often reported.

Matthew Hopkins Witch Finder Generall

My Imps names are

1 Ilemauzar
2 Pyewackett

Jarmara

Sacke & Sugar

3 Peche in the Crowne
4 Griezzdl Greediguit

Newes

Vinegar Tom

Fetching Friends

Like the word "familiar," the word "fetch" has various definitions. Sometimes the fetch can refer to the lower soul itself. Sometimes the fetch can refer to a servitor spirit that one has created to do their bidding. Sometimes the fetch can refer to the vessel the lower soul takes on when shapeshifting into an animal while traveling in other realms, particularly in shamanic journeying. It's clear why the familiar and the fetch get confused and conflated, as there are many parallels. The fetch is usually related to our lower self, our animalistic self, our connection to nature, and our physical nature. It acts very much like an animal or pet.

It seems that everyone has a unique looking fetch that appears to them in animal form. Though a Witch may have different symbols or animal totems that represent the fetch soul in different traditions of Witchcraft, it is believed the familiar spirit takes on the primary form familiar to the Witch's own fetch, as a primary form of interaction— though it's not limited to this. For clarity it would be more appropriate to refer to the fetch as the familiar soul or familiar self and not the familiar spirit for this differentiation. The familiar spirit is external but linked and understood primarily to the familiar self.

The largest difference is that spirit guides tend to be lofty and moral with a focus on your spiritual evolution. The familiar spirit is not so much concerned about this and historically we see this as well. The familiar spirit tends to be mainly concerned with two areas: psychic ability and magickal ability, which are often seen as two sides of the same coin. Their focus is on the Witch's pursuits of these areas and ensuring they're both effective, which sometimes means assisting in areas and practices that aren't full of "Love and Light."

The Witch's moral and ethical lessons are his or her own, and the familiar spirit is willing to help regardless of what forms of magick he or she chooses to engage in. Magickal and psychic aptitude and effectiveness seem to be a stronger focus rather than how they are used. Familiars are more like magickal sidekicks and mentors regardless of what one chooses to do with their magick.

Another common apparition of familiar spirits in history and among modern Witches is that of the imp, which is a much lower self-image. There's also an experience where one merges with their familiar spirit while astral projecting or journeying, where there definitely is a merging of the familiar spirit and the familiar self, but they are not the same thing. Sometimes this is experienced as the familiar spirit becoming a steed for the Witch to ride in the astral, or it acts as guide. Most historical stories involving Witches and the familiar also include journeys to the Sabbath or to a faeryland.

Mystical Assistants

A servitor spirit usually refers to an artificially created spirit that does one's bidding. This is also another usage of the word "fetch." There are some similarities here. The first being that the familiar spirit can definitely assist in carrying out tasks just as a servitor does, but this is where the similarities end for me. The familiar spirit is not created by the Witch, but rather exists independently.

The familiar spirit has its own individuality unlike servitors which function more like robots and in worst-case scenarios as slaves. With the familiar the relationship is more along the lines of co-conspirator, sidekick and friend. There's no sense of being superior to the spirit or vice versa, just that they have an intimate understanding of the nature of the spirit worlds and magickal arts they're willing to coach you in. The familiar spirit doesn't require feeding or offerings either—making them more akin to spirit guides—but will enjoy them when given. They seem to be more interested in the relationship itself, so time, attention and thus energy is what feeds them.

There's an interesting symbiotic relationship between the familiar and the Witch, which is unlike any other spirit. As the Witch's power grows and the relationship is strengthened, it seems the familiar is strengthened as well, giving it an almost egregoric nature in this sense. Sometimes this symbiosis is experienced as sexual interactions with the spirit. This may also well be the origin of the stories of familiars suckling on the Witch's teat, referring to both the Witch providing sustenance from themselves as well as sexual union with a more erotic focus than that of procreation.

—MAT AURYN

155

Moon Cycles

A New Moon rises with the Sun,
Her waxing half at midday shows,
The Full Moon climbs at sunset hour,
And waning half the midnight knows.

NEW	2020	FULL	NEW	2021	FULL
		January 10			January 10
January 24		February 9	Jan 13		Jan 28
February 23		March 9	Feb 11		Feb 27
March 24		April 7	Mar 13		Mar 28
April 22		May 7	Apr 11		Apr 26
May 22		June 5	May 11		May 26
June 21		July 5	Jun 10		Jun 24
July 20		August 3	July 9		July 23
August 18		September 2	Aug 8		Aug 22
September 17		October 1	Sept 6		Sept 20
October 16		October 31*	Oct 6		Oct 20
November 15		November 30	Nov 4		Nov 19
December 14		December 29	Dec 4		Dec .18

*Blue Moon on October 31, 2020.

Life takes on added dimension when you match your activities to the waxing and waning of the Moon. Observe the sequence of her phases to learn the wisdom of constant change within complete certainty.

Dates are for Eastern Standard and Daylight Time.

presage

by Dikki-Jo Mullen

ARIES, 2019–PISCES, 2020

All of us are hoping for a glimmer of light to follow, for guidance in understanding ourselves, others and the world around us. For thousands of years astrology has been a key to finding answers. The Sun, Moon, planets and stars are alive with energy fields. They are potent and magical forces to reckon with and befriend for those who would follow the Old Ways while embracing the future.

The year ahead finds Jupiter transiting Sagittarius until December, underscoring the role animal companions and wild creatures play in our lives. The welfare of animals and secrets about their undiscovered aptitudes can come to light. On December 2 Jupiter shifts into Capricorn for a year-long stay. Economic factors, changing values and ecological issues may be a focus. Amazing revelations about crystals may emerge in late 2019–2020.

There are four eclipses during the year to come, two in Cancer and two in Capricorn. Eclipses augur inevitable, significant and unexpected changes. This year's eclipses affect family life, housing, the water and food supply and economics. Values are in flux. Eclipses encourage growth through change.

When reading Presage, begin with the forecast for your Sun sign. It presents an overview, revealing what the year to come promises for you. Next, consider the segment for your Moon sign to learn about your emotional needs and responses. Finally, consult the forecast for your ascendant or rising sign. This describes your physical presence and appearance in interacting with the world around you. Those born on a cusp may consult both forecasts. The combined information will blend into their lives in unique ways. Read about all of this and more in Presage.

ASTROLOGICAL KEYS

Signs of the Zodiac
Channels of Expression

ARIES: fiery, pioneering, competitive
TAURUS: earthy, stable, practical
GEMINI: dual, lively, versatile
CANCER: protective, traditional
LEO: dramatic, flamboyant, warm
VIRGO: conscientious, analytical
LIBRA: refined, fair, sociable
SCORPIO: intense, secretive, ambitious
SAGITTARIUS: friendly, expansive
CAPRICORN: cautious, materialistic
AQUARIUS: inquisitive, unpredictable
PISCES: responsive, dependent, fanciful

Elements

FIRE: Aries, Leo, Sagittarius
EARTH: Taurus, Virgo, Capricorn
AIR: Gemini, Libra, Aquarius
WATER: Cancer, Scorpio, Pisces

Qualities

CARDINAL	FIXED	MUTABLE
Aries	Taurus	Gemini
Cancer	Leo	Virgo
Libra	Scorpio	Sagittarius
Capricorn	Aquarius	Pisces

CARDINAL signs mark the beginning of each new season — active.
FIXED signs represent the season at its height — steadfast.
MUTABLE signs herald a change of season — variable.

Celestial Bodies
Generating Energy of the Cosmos

Sun: birth sign, ego, identity
Moon: emotions, memories, personality
Mercury: communication, intellect, skills
Venus: love, pleasures, the fine arts
Mars: energy, challenges, sports
Jupiter: expansion, religion, happiness
Saturn: responsibility, maturity, realities
Uranus: originality, science, progress
Neptune: dreams, illusions, inspiration
Pluto: rebirth, renewal, resources

Glossary of Aspects

Conjunction: two planets within the same sign or less than 10 degrees apart, favorable or unfavorable according to the nature of the planets.

Sextile: a pleasant, harmonious aspect occurring when two planets are two signs or 60 degrees apart.

Square: a major negative effect resulting when planets are three signs from one another or 90 degrees apart.

Trine: planets four signs or 120 degrees apart, forming a positive and favorable influence.

Quincunx: planets are 150 degrees or about 5 signs apart. The hand of fate is at work and unique challenges can develop. Sometimes a karmic situation emerges.

Opposition: a six-sign or 180° separation of planets generating positive or negative forces depending on the planets involved.

The Houses — *Twelve Areas of Life*

1st house: appearance, image, identity
2nd house: money, possessions, tools
3rd house: communications, siblings
4th house: family, domesticity, security
5th house: romance, creativity, children
6th house: daily routine, service, health
7th house: marriage, partnerships, union
8th house: passion, death, rebirth, soul
9th house: travel, philosophy, education
10th house: fame, achievement, mastery
11th house: goals, friends, high hopes
12th house: sacrifice, solitude, privacy

Eclipses

Elements of surprise, odd weather patterns, change and growth are linked to eclipses. Those with a birthday within three days of an eclipse can expect some shifts in the status quo. There are four eclipses this year; three are partial and one is total.

July 2, 2019 New Moon total solar eclipse in Cancer, North Node

July 16, 2019 Full Moon partial lunar eclipse in Capricorn, South Node

December 26, 2019 New Moon partial solar eclipse in Capricorn, South Node

January 10, 2020 New Moon partial lunar eclipse in Cancer, North Node

A total eclipse is more influential than a partial. The eclipses conjunct the Moon's North Node are thought to be more favorable than those conjunct the South Node.

Retrograde Planetary Motion

Retrogrades promise a change of pace, different paths and perspectives.

Mercury Retrograde

Impacts technology, travel and communication. Those who have been out of touch return. Revise, review and tread familiar paths. Affected: Gemini and Virgo.

March 5, 2019–March 28, 2019
in Pisces

July 8, 2019–August 1, 2019
in Cancer and Leo

October 31, 2019–November 21, 2019
in Scorpio

February 17, 2020–March 10, 2020
in Aquarius and Pisces

Venus Retrograde

Influences art, finances and love. Affected: Taurus and Libra.

There will be no Venus retrograde this year.

Mars Retrograde

The military, sports and heavy industry are impacted. Affected: Aries and Scorpio.

There will be no Mars retrograde this year.

Jupiter Retrograde

Large animals, speculation, education and religion are impacted. Affected: Sagittarius and Pisces.

April 11, 2019–August 11, 2019
in Sagittarius

Saturn Retrograde

Elderly people, the disadvantaged, employment and natural resources are linked to Saturn. Affected: Capricorn and Aquarius.

April 30, 2019–September 18, 2019
in Capricorn

Uranus Retrograde

Inventions, science, electronics, revolutionaries and extreme weather relate to Uranus retrograde. Affected: Aquarius.

August 12, 2019–January 11, 2020
in Taurus

Neptune Retrograde

Water, aquatic creatures, chemicals, spiritual forces and psychic phenomena are impacted by this retrograde. Affected: Pisces.

June 22, 2019–November 27, 2019
in Pisces

Pluto Retrograde

Ecology, espionage, birth and death rates, nuclear power and mysteries relate to Pluto retrograde. Affected: Scorpio.

April 25, 2019–October 3, 2019
in Capricorn

ARIES

March 20–April 19

Spring 2019–Spring 2020 for those born under the sign of the Ram

Enthusiasm, ambition and leadership, the keynotes of Aries, mark springtime and the beginning of the zodiac. Your animal symbol, the Ram, ploughs through and destroys the stubble remaining from the past winter. This allows fresh, budding greens to appear and nurture new life. Ruled by Mars, the planet of competition and courage, Aries is a trailblazer.

March 21–April 16 finds Mercury whispering in your 12th house. Confidential information is surfacing. Plans must be modified before you can move forward toward new goals. The end of April through May 14 loving and helpful Venus races through Aries. Your creative skills and charm will attract approval and support. From mid-May through June, Mars squares your Sun while creating a stir in your home and family sector. Adapt to changes and seek a compromise involving living arrangements in order to accommodate household needs. Maintain a touch of humor and tolerance if a relative seems stressed or preoccupied. At the Summer Solstice light a blue candle for peace. Prepare a favorite comfort food to share around a communal table.

Venus joins the Sun in your 4th house as July begins. You long to improve your living situation. The solar eclipse on July 2 brings the specifics to light. A possible residential move is on the horizon. Analyze a maze of repeating patterns to find the path to happiness. The Full Moon eclipse on July 16 shifts your concern abruptly from family life to career goals. Stay in tune with current trends impacting your profession as Lammas nears. Decorate your workplace with fresh summer flowers and fruits to symbolize abundance. August finds the Sun, Venus and Mercury clustering in Leo, your fellow fire sign. This creates a favorable aspect pattern in your 5th house of love and leisure. Enjoy a vacation break. Focus on enjoyable hobbies or sports. The accomplishments of loved ones warm your heart.

The New Moon on August 30 accents health. Seek information about fitness and wholesome foods. Affirmations and visualizations focusing on wellness can be very helpful through September while several transits, including Mars, roll through your 6th house. Dedicate the Autumnal Equinox to directing healing toward the body, mind and spirit. Sharing resources and supplies can enhance happiness as October begins. The Aries Full Moon on October 13 brings recognition your way. A cherished project you began around your last birthday nears completion. As late October approaches, Mercury, Venus and the Sun enter your 8th house. Your intuition deepens; connections with the spirit world are present. From Halloween through November 21, retrograde Mercury shifts perspectives. It's a time to reconsider previously held beliefs. Keep expectations modest, make few demands, and live and let live.

From the last week of November through December 1 both the Sun and Jupiter highlight your 9th house. You'll be ready to explore new ideas and activities. Winter travel plans are worth pursuing. Fulfillment comes from learning something new. Jupiter and Mercury cross your midheaven as the Winter Solstice nears. Prospects for fame and fortune are present, a trend which continues throughout the winter. Cultivate new friends and get involved in projects to benefit the common good. Your public persona shines, and you can consider a new career move or avocation following the eclipse in your 10th house on December 26.

The first two weeks of January bring an upbeat Venus influence activating your 11th house. Networking with talented people inspires your plans for the year to come. Music and color are powerful catalysts. Experiment with arts and crafts as a vehicle for manifestation. Early January through February 15 a Mars transit gifts you with great energy. You'll have the confidence and courage to explore new horizons of all kinds. At Candlemas place talismans on an altar dedicated to faraway places. Exploring the Native American path, the old ways of western Europe or Far Eastern mysticism might be worthwhile.

Late February through March 10 retrograde Mercury promises a quieter cycle. You may prefer to withdraw from those who seem too dependent. Extra sleep or time in meditation can be healing. As the winter ends Venus joins Uranus in your financial sector, uplifting monetary matters. A bonus or bargain comes your way.

HEALTH
Cultivating patience helps in maintaining health. Give medical remedies time to work initially without resorting to aggressive treatments. Also, use patience when pursuing workout programs and sports to avoid injury. Your body responds well to exercise. Late January and September favor attending to fitness factors.

LOVE
You are proud of your loved ones and are happy to connect with a talented or successful partner. If you feel disillusioned by a relationship you can experience an abrupt change of heart. Avoid rekindling a flame of love once it has grown cold. August and May promise happiness in love this year.

SPIRITUALITY
An intensely spiritual cycle spans the Spring Equinox through the end of November while Jupiter transits your 9th house. Focus on touring a sacred site and the study of spiritual topics then. Spiritual teachings rooted in other cultures can be especially beneficial near the Full Moon on June 17.

FINANCE
Uranus is in your 2nd house of finances for a seven-year stay. Prepare for some fluctuations involving income and security. New income sources are available. Wealth appeals to you for the freedom it promises. The late spring as well as November 12 through December promise enhanced prosperity.

TAURUS

April 20–May 20

Spring 2019–Spring 2020 for those
born under the sign of the Bull

Practical and determined Taurus is symbolized by the strong, deliberate Bull. Once aroused, this placid creature of habit then plunges relentlessly forward, stopping only upon fulfilling its purpose. An earth sign ruled by Venus, Taurus appreciates nature, beauty and comfort. There is an affinity for the arts, especially music.

Spring's first whisper is unsettling, stirring the status quo. Changes are impending. Uranus is entering your 1st house for a seven-year stay. Observe what is happening near the Vernal Equinox. There are hints of thrilling but unplanned events to come. March 20–30 Mars is in Taurus. Quell anger, and use energy constructively. Your 11th house is highlighted by Venus and Neptune through mid-April. Friends seek to include you in social events. Gatherings will tend to emphasize cultural or spiritual objectives.

Finances, always an important focus for you, will be a source of some stress April–May 15 while Mars transits your 2nd house. Cope by making a point of appreciating all you have instead of resenting what might be lacking. The New Moon in Taurus on May 4 is ideal for planning. Reflect upon how best to use your inherent aptitudes. Mercury dashes through Taurus May 7–20. Make choices; judgment is excellent. Work can be completed skillfully and quickly. This is an optimum time to plan travel.

Late May through early June is brightened by a strong Venus influence in your 1st house. Others will cherish you, opportunities arise and there is a sparkle of romance. As the summer nears, your 3rd house is highlighted. Current events can be a topic of discussion. Resist the temptation to gossip though. New information surfaces with the eclipse on July 2, bringing a change of perspective. The July 16 eclipse in Capricorn favors breaking habits. Prepare for new challenges and adventures by Lammastide.

Venus is in your 4th house for the first three weeks of August. Family life improves. A loved one's happiness is celebrated together. August 11 finds Jupiter turning direct in your 8th house. A partner's finances or career choices can cause concern. The end of the month brings recovery and healing. In September Mercury joins the Sun, Venus and Mars in your 5th house of pleasure. A grand trine in earth signs forms through the Autumnal Equinox. You'll combine business with pleasure while easily achieving a desired goal. Time spent gardening, hiking or observing wildlife enriches the last days of summer. Offer a libation of fresh apple juice. Raise a sincere thank-you toast to the Lord and Lady as you welcome autumn.

October begins with Mars joining the Sun in your health sector. More physical activity is the key to wellness. Sharing workouts with a friend can add enjoyment to exercise sessions. Your 6th house is active, showing that the devotion and companionship of a pet can contribute to improved health. On October 31 Mercury begins a retrograde cycle in opposition to your Sun. Expect a change in plans regarding All Hallows celebrations. Someone close to you is a bit contrary. Be flexible and resurrect your sense of humor. The Full Moon in your sign on November 12 amplifies emotions. Memories, reunions and nostalgia characterize the first three weeks of November. Venus joins Pluto November 26–December 19 to trine your Sun. This is of spiritual significance. Seasonal legends, music and other holiday traditions help you attune to a higher consciousness.

As the year ends, a strong Mars opposition surfaces. Avoid confrontational situations. After January 2 the turbulent mood cools. During the first half of January communication improves. There is a deepening of trust and understanding near the eclipse on January 10. The rest of January finds Venus and Neptune highlighting your 11th house, inspiring a hopeful direction for the future. You'll be enthused about new goals and desires. At Candlemas dedicate white and silver altar candles. Throughout February you will be especially sensitive to status and reputation. Have faith that your hard work and good intentions will be rewarded eventually. A favorable influence from Saturn is operative.

March 1–10 a retrograde Mercury impacting your 10th and 11th houses brings a reminder to economize. Verify and confirm appointments and plans. Winter's final days bring positive change as Venus enters Taurus, brightening both love and work situations.

HEALTH

Detachment plays a key role in your well-being. Be aware of which foods, activities and associates make you feel tired or upset, then resolve to release them. Saturn favorably aspects your Sun all year. This is wonderful for overall vitality and health. September is especially good for reaching health milestones.

LOVE

August 12–January 11 a Uranus retrograde promises a sudden meeting or parting which shifts the status quo. However, late winter brings loving Venus to the rescue. Happiness reigns from March 5 on.

SPIRITUALITY

Nature spirits, especially the earth elementals, will awaken your spiritual insights. On December 4 Jupiter begins a year-long transit in your 9th house of spirituality, where it will join Saturn and Pluto. This points to a significant spiritual quest through the late autumn and winter months. The eclipse on December 26 reveals the specifics.

FINANCE

The stars are promising regarding your money this year. Outer planet transits in the earth signs show that overall economic trends or political situations can have a positive impact on your personal finances. Be leery of taking advice during the Mercury retrograde in opposition to your Sun October 31–November 21. The well-meant ideas of another might not be the best option.

GEMINI
May 21–June 20
Spring 2019–Spring 2020 for those
born under the sign of the Twins

Mercurial Gemini thirsts for mental stimulation and variety. Perceptive, restless, versatile and logical, you thrive on meeting new people and exchanging ideas. There is a duality about you, juggling several projects at once. Gemini is like a butterfly, appearing to live more than one life or be more than one person at a time.

Spring arrives with Mercury retrograde in your career sector. There's a hint of frustration; daily routine is slow, even stale. Following the Vernal Equinox sage your workplace; a feng shui consultation might help. On March 31 Mars enters Gemini, announcing a call to action. This motivating and competitive influence energizes you through May 14. Control anger, focus on constructive action and you will accomplish much during the coming weeks. The New Moon on April 5 shines in your sector of friendships and organizations. A cycle begins when you will feel more camaraderie with colleagues and can network, strengthening your support system.

May begins with retrograde Saturn making a quincunx aspect to your Sun. Fate is at work; heed synchronicities and respect what seems meant to be. Devote a May Day ritual to invoking truth and sincerity. Mercury transits your 12th house during mid to late May. This brings a hidden issue to light and forces you to accept some disappointment. Use discretion in how much you confide.

Venus transits Gemini June 9–July 2, generating a happier cycle. Your birthday accents a loving relationship. At the Summer Solstice honor the Goddess with flowers, ribbons and fragrances. July finds retrograde Mercury creating a stir in your financial sector. Be aware of repeating patterns and habits and get finances in order. Resolve old debts. At Lammas offer thanks for all that you have.

August begins with Venus, Mars and the Sun affecting your 3rd house. This is marvelous for vacation travel. Transportation issues are easily resolved. The New Moon on August 30 begins a month-long focus on family life and home improvements. At the Autumnal Equinox perform a house blessing and prepare a talisman for the hearth; consider adding a tiny kitchen witch to charm the pantry or dining room.

The first half of October brings a cluster of transits to brighten your sector of love and pleasure. Plan events to share with the one you care deeply about. A shared hobby or favorite board game can forge a bond. The Full Moon on October 13 accents long-term goals; discuss the future with a loved one. All Hallows brings healing. Rescue mediumship, to help a restless earthbound spirit let go and move on, can be worth including in a Samhain rite. Honor ancestors, but remember that they are other people who lived in another time. November 1–25 Venus joins Jupiter in your 7th house. You will be proud of a partner's success and talent. Let others make suggestions and finalize plans. Cooperate. On November 21 Mercury completes a retrograde in your health sector. Your vitality improves, and health goals are accomplished as November ends.

December begins with Jupiter changing signs, joining Saturn and Pluto in your 8th house. Investments or estate planning are a focus. You can be intrigued by different financial strategies. The Full Moon in Gemini on December 12 offers insight into how others see you. Wear your best seasonal finery; a spa day or new hairstyle could add to your confidence and sense of well-being as you prepare to celebrate the Winter Solstice. The eclipse on December 26 piques your curiosity. Research reveals hidden truths. An old concern is put to rest as the year ends.

January 1–12 Venus trines your Sun. Travel or visiting a bookstore, museum or art gallery can serve as a catalyst for positive change. Mars trolls in opposition to your Sun during January. You'll be presented with complaints or requests. Avoid involvement in issues that aren't beneficial. The New Moon on January 24 points a way out of entanglements. At Candlemas evaluate what friendship means. Light a peach-colored candle to help you cultivate worthwhile associates. Mercury crosses your midheaven as February begins, accenting knowledge about an important avocation or career. Listen carefully to those who have futuristic ideas. From the New Moon on February 23 through March 10 postpone initiating changes. Patience pays off.

A Venus-Uranus pattern in your 12th house March 11–20 is altruistic. You can find delight in supporting a worthy cause, taking on some volunteer work or contributing to a charity.

HEALTH

Your thought processes are always active. Releasing stress and finding a focus are important factors in maintaining wellness. Pluto, ruler of your 6th house of health, is retrograde April 25–October 3. Change habits or address health issues then.

LOVE

October 4–November 18 passionate Mars transits your 5th house of romance in a favorable aspect to your Sun. An intimate relationship intensifies then. Your birthday month finds Venus in your birth sign. Those who care for you express their feelings then.

SPIRITUALITY

The Capricorn eclipses on July 16 and December 26 impact your 8th house. This can shift your spiritual perspectives. Your perceptions are evolving this year. Ceremonies observing the Winter Solstice and Candlemas encourage spiritual advancement.

FINANCE

The total eclipse on July 2 coincides with a Mars transit in your 2nd house of finance. This sparks new motivation to manifest financial gain. By the end of January your efforts should be rewarded. Be receptive to exploring new income sources.

CANCER
June 21–July 22
Spring 2019–Spring 2020 for those born
under the sign of the Crab

Like the ocean tides, ebbing and surg-
ing, guided by the changeable Moon,
Cancerians live in a sea of emotional
energy. Highly sensitive, imaginative and
intuitive, you are extremely responsive to
your surroundings. The Crab is conscientious and caring. You have a unique ability
to inspire others.

At the Vernal Equinox Mercury
is in your 9th house. Honor the spring
with a traditional celebration. Plans
related to travel and study are discussed. March 27–April 19 brings a
favorable Venus transit. Enjoy spiritual
art and music. Contact with a worldly
person brightens your social life. Late
April–May 6 you'll analyze a compelling career concern as Mercury races
through your 10th house.

During the first two weeks of May,
a 12th house Mars transit compels
you to internalize thoughts and feelings. Time spent in solitary pursuits is
especially productive. May 16–June 8
shifts your focus, and you'll become
more gregarious. Venus joins Uranus
in your 11th house. Friendships add
sparkle and direction to your life.
Interesting plans are suggested regarding the future. During the remainder of
June a forceful and competitive influence develops as Mars moves through
your birth sign. Exercise is a great
outlet for processing excess energy
or releasing stress. At the Summer
Solstice dedicate a fire of sandalwood
or birch twigs for peace. Meditate on
the sunset on the longest of days.

On July 2 a total solar eclipse in Cancer
heralds great change and growth. A residential move or job change can be considered. Adapt to shifts in the status quo.
A second eclipse on July 16 affects your
7th house of partnerships. Alliances are
in flux; a legal matter might have to be
addressed. Your birthday this year marks
a significant turning point. Venus transits
Cancer July 3–27. Both love and money
are favored. Express your creativity. You
can make the world more beautiful. On
Lammas Eve Mercury completes its retrograde. Dedicate the Sabbat to widening
your horizons, perhaps creating a charm
for a journey. August 2–10 promises
exploration and adventure. On August 11
Jupiter turns direct in your health sector.
The remainder of the month brings progress in reaching wellness objectives. A
companion animal, perhaps a cat or horse,
offers renewed hope and strength.

September opens with four major transits, including the Sun, affecting your 3rd
house. Communication is a significant
theme; there are errands to run and lots of
multitasking. The pace quickens. Contact
with a neighbor or sibling is accented.
The Full Moon on September 14 conjoins
Neptune in your 9th house, promising
mystical experiences. Time spent near the
waterfront brings a connection with water
elementals. Gather shells and driftwood
to fashion decorations at the Autumnal
Equinox. The last weeks of September

evoke memories and sentiments. Preserve memories in a scrapbook or journal. Mercury and Venus impact your 4th house. Plan to entertain at home. Prepare a favorite traditional dish. Share copies of the recipe with guests.

During October a difference of opinion with another arises, as a strong Mars aspect is in effect. This culminates near the Full Moon on October 13. Seek a compromise. At Halloween break ceremonial bread and salt. Cast a spell for peace and unity. November welcomes a Mercury retrograde transit in your 5th house, recalling a long-abandoned love. The attraction can rekindle, but history repeats itself. Postpone commitments until after November 21. Mid to late November is an ideal time to enjoy historical sites or collect antiques.

Late November through January 2 Mars trines your Sun. Your strength and vitality are on the rise, and you can develop expertise in a sport or complete a demanding project. Others will see you as a role model. Lead a ceremonial observance at the Winter Solstice featuring a Yule log. The lunar eclipse in Cancer on January 10 promises clarity concerning your future direction. The last half of January through February 7 highlights Venus and Neptune influences in your 9th house. Your words impress others. Write a story or poem to share at a Candlemas gathering. The Full Moon on February 9 affects your 2nd house. Security on every level is an emotional issue through the remainder of the month. Seek the best price when shopping for a costly, long-desired item.

Venus crosses your 10th house from mid-February to March 4. Personal issues with coworkers can generate some sensitive job politics. Employ charm and kindness to cope. As winter ends several planets, including Mars and Jupiter, oppose your Sun. Forceful people offer suggestions. Be open and listen while still honoring your personal values and preferences.

HEALTH
Practice discernment regarding health care. Otherwise, emotions can come into play leading to impulsive choices which you might regret later. From the Spring Equinox until December 2 Jupiter transits your health sector. This pattern promises a gradual improvement to your well-being.

LOVE
Two eclipses affect your partnership sector this year in July and December. Alliances and attractions are about to shift. Seek a nurturing, uplifting relationship. Avoid a new involvement with one who seems too needy or who drains your resources.

SPIRITUALITY
A pilgrimage to the seacoast offers spiritual experiences, especially during April or June. Interpret dreams and follow a regular meditation practice to heighten higher consciousness this year. The Full Moon on September 14 brings a spiritual awakening.

FINANCE
Be very careful with risky financial directions this year. Several oppositions to your Sun, ruler of your 2nd house, warn of a potential loss. Excessive generosity, which might deplete your own security, must be avoided. July and October favor financial matters.

LEO
July 23–August 22
Spring 2019–Spring 2020 for those
born under the sign of the Lion

Visualizing sweeping and regal schemes, the affectionate, cheerful Lion often sets the pace and organizes the lives of others. Sharing jokes and stories, you lighten every chore by combining humor and pleasure with the business at hand. A few words of praise and appreciation will win the Lion's loyalty, for there is a desire to make an imprint, to be noticed and remembered. Ruled by the Sun, Leos are radiant with a unique warmth and brightness.

Venus hovers in your 7th house of relationships during spring's earliest days. A supportive and enjoyable relationship intensifies. Include hearts, flowers and a pair of love birds as altar decorations to celebrate love at the Vernal Equinox. April accents goals, as Mars impacts your sector of plans and wishes. Friends offer encouragement. Chant affirmations for manifestation while dancing around the maypole on May Day.

May 7–19 Mercury joins the Sun in your career sector. Business meetings and travel can be a focus. Gather knowledge by asking business associates questions. Late May through June promises a more secretive and introspective cycle. Planetary transits whisper in your 12th house. You'll find inspiration in quiet reverie. A solitary walk at sunrise on the Summer Solstice helps you to attune to your favorite benevolent solar deities.

July crackles with energy. Mars enters Leo where it remains until August 17. Your motivation is high, and a lot can be accomplished as your birthday nears. Be careful not to let a competitive situation become combative though. At Lammas honor the talents and efforts of a loved one. August 12–28 Mercury races through Leo. Time swiftly passes while summer travel and parties make life especially interesting.

September 1–15 accents security. Several planets gather in your 2nd house of finances. Work patiently. By the Full Moon on September 14 there is much progress. The last half of September accents eloquent speaking and writing. Favorable aspects from Mercury and Venus brighten your 3rd house of communication. Your charming expression of ideas opens an important door near the Autumnal Equinox. Recite a ballad to welcome fall.

As October begins Pluto turns direct in your 6th house. Vitality is improving. Include wholesome, seasonal fruits and grains in your diet. You enjoy quietly relaxing at home this month. Decorate for the Halloween season. The Full Moon on October 13 brings a visit from a sorcerer or witch. As October ends Mercury turns retrograde. Relatives or close friends repeat old patterns. Remember the past to foretell the future. November 1–25 Venus and Jupiter trine your Sun. This happy celestial combination blesses your 5th house of love and pleasure. A romantic

168

connection, sports or enjoyable hobbies make life good.

On November 26 the New Moon brings an amazing creative outburst. Express yourself. Your 6th house will be strong December 5–19. Try not to be overly critical of others if their efforts fall short of your expectations. December 20–31 Venus clashes with your Sun. Dedicate the Winter Solstice to simplicity and peace. The entertainment preferences and other selections made by a loved one might not reflect your own choices. Share and compromise.

January opens with five transits in earth signs. The realities of the daily grind are in evidence. Attend to chores, go back to work, fulfill a commitment and keep promises. The last half of January has a mystical quality, and many coincidences occur as Venus joins Neptune in your 8th house of mystery. An unexpected financial windfall is possible. A prophetic dream or message from the spirit world impresses you. Ignite a purple taper at Candlemas to connect with other dimensions and hovering entities.

February begins a 7th house accent. Promptly resolve any legal or ethical issues which arise. The Full Moon in Leo on February 9 allows you to begin anew. Refresh your wardrobe or hairstyle to create a good impression. Late February–March 10 retrograde Mercury stirs up questions of accuracy and credibility. Verify information and keep receipts and copies of correspondence. Resist the temptation to share a juicy bit of gossip. As March concludes Venus and Uranus square your Sun. Associates are unpredictable and sensitive. Offer help and promote understanding to improve rapport during winter's waning days.

HEALTH

The eclipses on July 16 and December 26 join Saturn in your 6th house of health. This year honesty and humility concerning the realities of your health and fitness are essential. On December 2 Jupiter changes signs and begins a year-long passage through your health sector. This promises healing and improved wellness. Consider dietary choices and supplements which strengthen the bones and joints.

LOVE

Venus, the love goddess of the planets, smiles on you during August and November. Deepen a cherished love connection or cultivate a new one during those times. Arrange a romantic stroll at sunset to set the scene for a loving encounter. Follow up with dinner by candlelight.

SPIRITUALITY

The eclipses on July 2 and January 10 affect your 12th house of solitude and reverie. Spiritual awakening arises from within. Meditation can bring spiritual truths to light. Your most profound spiritual experiences this year will be for you alone rather than involving groups.

FINANCE

Elusive Neptune hovers in the midst of a long, slow transit through your 8th house. Good or bad investments and long-range financial strategies might not be quite as they seem. Heed intuitive flashes regarding financial prospects, especially in September and March. The monetary picture improves then.

VIRGO
August 23–September 22
Spring 2019–Spring 2020 for those
born under the sign of the Virgin

Analytical, systematic and precise, Virgo is both a critic and craftsperson. Your grasp of detail melds into genuine brilliance in meeting challenges requiring technical expertise. Ruled by Mercury, Virgo is naturally studious with a gift for problem-solving and teaching. Your sincere desire to make life better earns the loyalty and respect of others.

The Vernal Equinox finds you mulling over a confusing partnership. Mercury is retrograde in your 7th house, showing that others are giving you mixed signals. Postpone decisions about personal or business commitments until the end of March. In April Venus joins Mercury and Neptune in opposition to your Sun. Associates are fey and imaginative. Appreciate the whimsy and creativity in others. The Full Moon on April 19 brightens your 3rd house of communication and solidifies facts. Late April through May 6 highlights financial planning. An investment, insurance or tax issue can be resolved productively. May Day favors connecting to the earth; spend time outdoors. May 7–15 Mars completes a square to your Sun. A competitive mood prevails. Responsibilities and challenges place demands. The remainder of May through June 8 welcomes a benevolent Venus aspect. Others are kind. Tensions ease.

Your 11th house of hopes and wishes is highlighted by Mercury and Mars as the Summer Solstice approaches. Reflect upon what you really want, both personally and professionally. Friends offer encouragement. The eclipse on July 2 introduces humanitarian goals; you could feel drawn to get involved in politics or other kinds of community service. The Mercury retrograde July 8–August 1 marks a time to rest. Take note of any inspirations which come in dreams. At Lammas collect a sachet of fragrant herbs and flowers to make a dream pillow. Secrets and confidences are important August 1–29. Visit a forest or park. Listen to the sounds of nature and a truth is revealed. The New Moon in Virgo on August 30 conjoins Mars, bringing an abrupt energy shift. You will grow more assertive.

Venus transits your 1st house during the first half of September. Others are charmed by your appealing demeanor. Enjoy the fine arts near your birthday. Attend a concert or other cultural event, perhaps an arts and crafts or fashion show. From the Autumnal Equinox through October 3 strong aspects from Mars and Jupiter to your Sun promise a renewed zest for life. Adventure beckons and new interests are embraced. This might include travel.

The remainder of October switches the focus to cash flow. Financial planning and budgeting are of concern. Be versatile and apply a wider scope, making the most of your salable job skills. At All Hallows Mercury goes retrograde in your 3rd house. Vintage costumes and old-time games or stories appeal. A nostalgic mood prevails. Venus joins Jupiter in your sector of home and heritage November 1–25. Redecorating, repairs and other home improvements might help domestic situations. Visitors arrive and a family member's happiness gladdens your heart. The New Moon on November 26 brings new insights concerning home life and haunting childhood recollections.

Late November through the Winter Solstice several transits cluster in your 5th house. Romance, pleasure and a break from the daily grind are due. Pursue a favorite hobby. You are proud of a very young person's progress. The eclipse on December 26 foretells how the specifics might unfold during the months ahead. During the first half of January Venus impacts your health sector. The healing power of love and beauty is in evidence. An animal companion comforts and cheers you. The last half of January finds Venus joining Neptune in your relationship sector. Be very straightforward with loved ones regarding your wishes and emotions. Otherwise, well meaning people may make assumptions that complicate matters. At Candlemas dedicate a votive candle to clear and sincere communication.

February 1–16 a Mars transit creates a stir in your 4th house. Be patient if a relative is stressed. Check supplies, especially the medicines or food you like to keep handy. Don't postpone the replacement of items needed to maintain a comfortable home. Mercury turns retrograde February 17–March 10. Gather information about health care, and maintain the status quo in a close relationship. The Full Moon in Virgo on March 9 brings new factors to light and empow-

ers your ability to make choices. As winter wanes Venus joins Uranus in your 9th house. New studies interest you. Try journaling or writing for publication. Catch up on correspondence.

HEALTH
Stress can manifest in health symptoms from August through the winter. Try simplifying your schedule to include relaxing breaks. A number of oppositions involving 7th house transits underscore the need for tolerance and how worries concerning others impact your health.

LOVE
On December 3 Jupiter begins a year-long transit through your 5th house of love. Romantic involvements are promising; love deepens. You are happiest when helping and advising those you care about. Shared interests in worthwhile projects can help nurture true love.

SPIRITUALITY
Uranus transits your 9th house all year. This brings a genuine sparkle to your spiritual path. Call upon Mother Earth and earth elementals by including sacred crystals and plants in your spiritual observances. Carry a medicine bag filled with favorite stones and herbs.

FINANCE
Overcoming vacillation regarding financial priorities is helpful. Planning and persistence help vanquish hurdles blocking monetary security. When Saturn turns direct on September 18 a grand trine in earth signs is activated. A cycle of financial improvement begins which gradually strengthens through the winter months.

LIBRA

September 23–October 23

Spring 2019–Spring 2020 for those
born under the sign of the Scales

Relationships always are of prime significance. You enjoy people and companionship. With natural diplomacy, Libra strives to maintain balance and harmony. There is a gift for perceiving all sides of an issue and sharing a fair assessment when asked for advice or guidance. Ruled by Venus, Libra has a naturally romantic and idealistic side. You cherish all that is beautiful and artistic.

Select herbs to prepare a detoxifying spring tonic at the Vernal Equinox. Mars transits your 8th house during late March, bringing a need for release. Purge your surroundings of debris. The first half of April finds Mercury forming a quincunx aspect. Animal companions can be a source of both comfort and concern. Organization and problem-solving play a role in meeting an obligation. Your vitality is heightened from mid-April through May 14 when Mars in Gemini trines your Sun. You easily assume a leadership role near May Day. Your workload seems lighter, yet much is accomplished. The last half of May through early June accents desires and a compulsion, as Venus accents your 8th house. You'll seek depth and fulfillment. The New Moon on June 3 is elevating. Life is less intense.

The future is a focus as the Summer Solstice approaches. A Mercury influence affects your career sector during June. Interesting possibilities, including business meetings or travel plans, arise. Consult the tarot or tea leaves on the longest of days. July begins with a strong 11th house emphasis. Longtime friends suggest a reunion. Projects involving group participation present both joys and challenges. The eclipse on July 16 has you analyzing a confusing home and family matter. A change in residence or living arrangements is one possibility.

Mercury turns direct at Lammastide, allowing greater clarity during early August. The Full Moon on August 15 is favorable for focusing on vacation time or favorite hobbies. As August ends you feel an empathy with those less fortunate. Rescuing an animal in need or donating to a charity brings fulfillment. In September you'll seek simplicity. You might plan a retreat with a close partner. The escapist urges ebb after September 14 as both Venus and Mercury enter Libra, activating your 1st house. You'll be at the center of activity both professionally and in your social circle. Public speaking and published writing are successful. At an Autumnal Equinox celebration your influence expands and recognition is attained.

On September 28 the New Moon in Libra inaugurates a significant two-week cycle of opportunity. Make choices near your birthday. Early October begins with a Mars conjunction to your Sun. An energetic and competitive vibration sets the pace through mid-November. At All Hallows seek support for a cherished dream. Genuine progress can be realized. Throughout November Mercury affects your financial sector. You'll analyze cash flow and seek insight regarding earning power. Reading current publications or attending a conference brings helpful guidance. From November 26 to December 19 Venus joyfully transits your 4th house. Holiday plans revolve around home and family traditions. Share photos and memories while decorating for the Winter Solstice. On the longest of nights resurrect vintage cookie cutters and bake a large batch of traditional sugar cookies. Send extras home with friends as gifts following a midwinter gathering. Near the eclipse on December 26 a family member surprises you. A change in home décor or the schedule at home can be involved. As the month ends, enhance comfortable living by keeping up with basic household maintenance.

January begins with an upbeat Venus aspect. You can enjoy a favorite sport, game or avocation. A loved one's talents are a source of pride and happiness. The eclipse on January 10 generates some change in your professional sector. Heed developing situations involving your status throughout the remainder of the month. During the first week of February spiritual considerations affect health as Mercury joins Neptune in your 6th house. Illuminate a collection of small tealight candles in various colors near Candlemas to bring a subtle healing balance to your chakras.

February 8–March 4 Venus opposes your Sun. Tolerate unexpected differences in taste expressed by others. Cooperate with a partner's plans. Late winter, especially following the Full Moon on March 9, accents earth sign transits. This favors your 8th

house. An investment, estate income or other financial settlement is promising. As winter ends money matters will find you smiling.

HEALTH

Decisiveness is important when making choices and following through with health protocols. Neptune is poised in your health sector this year indicating some uncertainty about health care. Seek factual information. Exercise during April and October.

LOVE

The eclipse pattern this year finds you trying to balance family time with career aspirations. July brings the specifics into focus. Allow loved ones as much freedom as they request. Near your birthday a favorable Venus influence deepens love connections. June and January promise happiness in love as well.

SPIRITUALITY

Uranus transits your 8th house all year. Pursue mystery school teachings as a path to spiritual awakening. Honor the Full Moon on November 12 to facilitate spiritual advancement. Sharing through group rituals and forging social connections while pursuing spiritual topics will strengthen spirituality.

FINANCE

October 31–November 21 the retrograde Mercury cycle in your 2nd house is very significant. Insights are gained then as to what works and what doesn't regarding financial choices. Seek ways to lower overhead on household expenses. Finances brighten as winter ends.

SCORPIO
October 24–November 21
Spring 2019–Spring 2020 for those
born under the sign of the Scorpion

Cunning and efficient Scorpio is a water sign co-ruled by Mars and Pluto. You naturally assume a cloak of secrecy. Others tend to find you fascinating yet unfathomable. You are a determined detective who welcomes challenging puzzles. Your inherent intuition combined with profound analytical ability enables you to perceive what is really of significance. The Scorpion cares deeply and is strongly opinionated. Indifference is alien to you.

Spring dawns to find Mercury retrograde in your 5th house. Thoughts and conversations revolve around love. Dedicate seasonal magic to blessing a tryst with one whom you would woo. A shared journey can be appealing. March 27–April 19 brings a supportive Venus transit. Romantic pleasures and favorite hobbies or a creative project brighten the days. Late April through mid-May ushers in a Mars influence which impacts your 8th house. Accepting endings as new beginnings is the theme. On May Day reflect upon release. There can be some agitation regarding financial management or insurance coverages. May 18's Full Moon in Scorpio brings a conclusion.

The end of May through June 8 marks a Venus opposition in your 7th house. A partner reveals needs and thoughts which are somewhat at odds with your own choices. Put the wishes and welfare of others first. Flexibility turns situations in your favor. Mars highlights your sector of travel and higher consciousness throughout the remainder of June. A journey by sea would be refreshing and exhilarating. At the Summer Solstice prepare a talisman for embracing adventure.

July's eclipses impact your 3rd and 9th houses. Neighbors or in-laws surprise you. Clear communication helps in responding to developing situations. Transportation needs are a focus. At Lammas bless your vehicle or prepare a charm to facilitate new transportation. August 1–16 is hot and fiery on many levels. An angular Mars transit squares your Sun. A career situation becomes turbulent. Keep competitive interactions upbeat and good-humored. It's a time to balance extremes of all kinds. Guard against exposure to inclement weather.

The end of August brings favorable earth sign aspects to your 11th house. Involvement in a community project or service organization is worthwhile. If you're nominated to serve on an advisory board or other position of leadership near the New Moon on August 30, accept. The Sun and five other transits are in mutable signs as September begins. This is interesting, yet scattered and hectic. Prioritize and ask for assistance if you feel overwhelmed. After September 14 situations become less stressful.

As the Autumnal Equinox nears, Venus impacts your 12th house. Take note of dreams. Heed your first thoughts upon waking from sleep. Significant truths and valuable guidance are revealed.

On October 3 Pluto turns direct, auguring overall progress. Mercury begins an important transit through Scorpio which lasts until December 8. Embrace travel opportunities. You'll learn much through conversations, meetings and keeping up with current events. The last three weeks of October are blessed by a pervasive happiness because Venus conjoins your Sun. Focus on companionship, creative projects and enjoyable cultural events.

On October 31 Mercury turns retrograde in Scorpio. Connections with friends or relatives who have been out of touch are rekindled while you celebrate your birthday and honor All Hallows. The first half of November finds Venus and Jupiter moving together through your 2nd house. Extra money flows in. Shop for desired items. Mars enters Scorpio on November 19 where it remains until the beginning of January. This brings a heightened vitality and enthusiasm to the holiday season. Enjoy winter sports or walk outdoors to photograph beautiful snow scenes. Honor the spirit of peace at the Winter Solstice.

January 1–12 brings a lovely Venus transit in your 4th house. Remind family members of your love. Beautify your dwelling. It's also a good time for real estate transactions. The eclipse at the Full Moon on January 10 accents curiosity about new places and concepts. This lunation begins a cycle of emphasis on your 9th house. Writing for publication, educational pursuits or travel can be rewarding.

Candlemas accents love and romance. Dedicate a rose-colored candle to honor tender sentiments. February highlights your 5th house. A young person's talents and accomplishments are a source of happiness. On February 23, the New Moon reveals the specifics. March 1–10 Mercury completes its retrograde. This is the time to tackle home improvements with a good measure of ease. The remainder of winter brings innovative ideas from associates.

HEALTH

High temperatures and the effects of anger or stress can pose some health challenges during August. As a water sign, healing herbal baths, a vacation at the seacoast and drinking plenty of pure water will support wellness. January brings health insights.

LOVE

Venus is favorably positioned in your love sector March 26–April 19. Early spring favors romantic connections. Jet to Paris in April with one who has touched your heart. Love sparks can fly during October and again from mid-January to mid-February.

SPIRITUALITY

Finding forgiveness in your heart is vital to spiritual growth. The total eclipse on July 2 impacts your sector of spirituality. Visiting an historic site of patriotic significance over the Independence Day holiday week could heighten your spiritual outlook.

FINANCE

Jupiter is retrograde in your financial sector April 11–August 11. This is wonderful for correcting old financial habits and fulfilling obligations. September through November promises opportunities to generate extra income.

SAGITTARIUS
November 22–December 21
Spring 2019–Spring 2020 for those
born under the sign of the Archer

Optimistic, enthusiastic Sagittarius is a zealous explorer of new dimensions and experiences. With the directness of an arrow released from a bow, Sagittarius isn't subtle. You may come across as blunt, even tactless. You're extremely independent, yet friendly and helpful. Ruled by Jupiter, the cosmic indicator of luck and growth, Sagittarius tends to recover well from setbacks and plays all games to win.

Health and fitness goals are important as you welcome the spring. Mars transits your 6th house from the Vernal Equinox through March 30. Agitation involving a coworker or a stressful employment situation could undermine wellness. As April begins Venus joins Mercury and Neptune in your sector of home and family life. Relatives offer support and make helpful suggestions. Domestic activities are enjoyable. Jupiter turns retrograde in Sagittarius on April 11, a trend which continues until August 11. You'll benefit from drawing upon past experiences and established connections with those whom you respect during this entire time.

From April through mid-May, a Mars opposition to your Sun complicates relationships. Smooth away tensions with good-natured humor and camaraderie. A bossy person who makes decisions involving you is well intentioned. Say affirmations to facilitate understanding on May Day. A special animal companion brightens your life May 15–June 8 when Venus transits your sector of pets. Assemble an album of keepsake pictures featuring beloved creatures as a conversation piece. Mars and Mercury highlight your 8th house from mid to late June. Nuances are present. Trust your ability to sense what is developing beneath the surface. The Full Moon in Sagittarius on June 17 heightens your sensitivity to the spirit world. At the Summer Solstice an old mystery is solved.

July accents travel and higher learning, as Mercury and Mars transit your 9th house. Make note of random ideas and inspirations. They could evolve into a successful book or presentation, eventually bringing you recognition. As Lammas nears, Venus trines your Sun. This upbeat influence extends through August 20. A friendship with an interesting person from a different country or ethnic group deepens. Travel and exposure to another language or cultural tradition would be enriching.

As September opens, your career demands attention. Keep appointments and fulfill promises September 1–14. The last half of September brings positive aspects involving your 11th house. This is progressive and idealistic. Friendships and support groups help you to manifest goals. At the Autumnal Equinox write a wish list or try treasure mapping. Mercury enters your 12th house as October begins, ushering in a desire for peace and privacy. You'll feel rejuvenated by quiet hours spent enjoying nature or being immersed in solitary pursuits. The New Moon on

October 27 accents a sense of uniqueness. Suddenly you'll realize you've outgrown long-standing relationships or interests. At All Hallows seek guidance from within.

November 1–25 Venus transits Sagittarius, brightening your 1st house. Attend to your appearance to make a good impression. Social prospects are excellent. Beautify your surroundings. The Sagittarius New Moon on November 26 reinforces your confidence and brings insight regarding your life mission. In early December Jupiter changes signs and begins a year-long passage through your 2nd house of finances. A variety of options related to improved income appear as you celebrate your birthday month. You are entering a cycle of steadily brightening finances.

December 9–28 Mercury races through your sign. Information is shared. Meetings and current publications communicate valuable ideas and reveal trends. There is much to learn. Travel opportunities materialize near the Winter Solstice and introduce you to new people and places. Time passes quickly during the winter holiday season.

January 1–16 reinforces financial stability. The eclipse on January 10 brings an awareness of how others affect your security. Life is dynamic from January through mid-February when Mars transits Sagittarius. Much can be accomplished. Your energy level is high. Explore ways to make constructive changes if you experience anger or impatience.

Observe Candlemas by assembling a brightly colored candle garden. Retrograde Mercury complicates family dynamics late February–March 10.

Verify appointments and streamline your schedule. Winter ends with Mars, Saturn, Jupiter and Pluto clustered in your financial sector. Savor what you have. Don't regret what might be lacking.

HEALTH

You have a tendency to challenge your strength and endurance. Use reasonable restraint when pursuing demanding exercise programs or performing laborious tasks during April. September through December a favorable Jupiter conjunction to your Sun promises improved health.

LOVE

The New Moon on April 5 and the Full Moon on October 13 activate your 5th house of love. Romantic bliss can blossom near those dates. Venus transits Sagittarius in November, promising happiness in love. Thanksgiving dinner is memorable.

SPIRITUALITY

July through mid-August finds a parade of transits, including Mars, the Sun and Mercury, playing tag in your 9th house of spirituality. This facilitates awakening. Attend a Full Moon ceremony on February 9 to experience deeper insights. Symbols, poems and drawings honoring the Sun support your spiritual quest.

FINANCE

The eclipses on July 16 and December 26 highlight your 2nd house of income. Promising new monetary trends appear then. Prosperity further improves in December when lucky Jupiter begins a year-long transit in your financial sector.

CAPRICORN
December 22–January 19
Spring 2019–Spring 2020 for those
born under the sign of the Goat

Responsible, persistent and stoic, the Goat
has a flair for organization and a desire
for success. Ruled by Saturn, you dis-
like wasting time or resources. Rational,
patient and constructive, you have a subtle
and wry sense of humor which delights
others. Paradoxically, Capricorns feel that
life is too serious to be taken seriously.

Spring begins with Mars stirring your
5th house of pleasure, bringing passion
and creativity. At the Vernal Equinox
present a loved one with a token of
your esteem. By All Fools Day Mercury
and Venus transit your sector of communication. A cycle of brainstorming
begins. Plans for travel and study generate excitement from early to mid-April.
A neighbor or sibling offers assistance
and encouragement. April 17–30 favors
working or entertaining at your residence. Plan a healing circle or house
blessing on May Day.

Relax during the first half of May;
a Mars emphasis in your 6th house is
worrisome. Before adopting a new pet,
carefully consider whether the creature will be a good fit. From May 16
through the first week of June a favorable Venus aspect deepens love connections. Finalize vacation plans. Mid-June
through the Summer Solstice brings

oppositions to your Sun from Mercury
and Mars. Others are quite contrary.
Issues are resolved through compromise
as the month concludes.

July opens with an eclipse in your 7th
house. A relationship takes a new twist. A
partner offers novel and refreshing suggestions. The lunar eclipse on July 16
in Capricorn augurs a new cycle. Don't
resist change. Welcome growth instead.
July may foreshadow a move or job
change. Lammas finds Mercury turning
direct; conflicting viewpoints can be
discussed. Prepare an affirmation pro-
moting enhanced understanding and
acceptance. Throughout August fate is
at work, as several transits quincunx
your Sun. Embrace synchronicities.
Spiritual energies are active. A dream
or omen offers insight.

August 23–September 30 is refreshing because Saturn turns direct while
Mars, Venus and Mercury play tag in
your 9th house. Travel, new acquaintances, studies and other activities
broaden your outlook. At the Autumnal
Equinox reread notes and journal entries
you've made this year. Your perspectives
might be worth developing into a manuscript to submit for publication.

An accent on your 10th house emphasizes status October 1–12. Various networking opportunities introduce you
to new career options. You'll be at the
center of attention and activity in your
professional life. The Full Moon on
October 13 puts a sudden spin on events.
Family dynamics occupy your thoughts.
Throughout the remainder of the month
you'll sense a deepening loyalty and
emotional commitment to relatives and
an appreciation for home life. A family

reunion or meeting could be arranged by All Hallows. Explain the true meaning of the holiday to the young people in your life.

November 1–21 accents traditions and brings greetings from longtime friends. A visit to an old haunt provides insight into where your life's journey will take you next. The remainder of the month favors finalizing strategies and plans for the future. December promises much happiness in love as well as a financial break. Venus glides through Capricorn during the weeks before the Winter Solstice. You'll enjoy preparing for the holiday season. Play and sing holiday songs while observing the longest of nights. The Capricorn eclipse on December 26 establishes priorities and focuses on the overall direction of your life as you celebrate your birthday.

January begins with Mercury in Capricorn affecting your 1st house. You'll be eloquent and talkative. Significant information is communicated. Travel is likely, placing you with different people in new places. On January 10 an eclipse in Cancer underscores how a partnership affects you and whether a commitment is stable. Mid to late January is all about your 2nd house of finances. Wise management of money January 11–31 will protect assets and stabilize your future security. At Candlemas light earth-colored tapers for practical guidance concerning prosperity. Early February finds you cherishing privacy, peace and quiet. You'll prefer to avoid those who appear intrusive.

On February 16 Mars enters Capricorn, where it remains for the rest of winter. A fiery wave of energy and motivation engulfs you. You can be short-tempered. Simultaneously, the pace of life quickens.

Work independently rather than expecting too much of others. The Full Moon on March 9 brings an elevated consciousness. Altruistic values guide daily life. As the season ends you'll realize how much you've grown during the past year.

HEALTH

Saturn completes a passage through Capricorn this year. Be aware of how both heredity and an ongoing health issue affect your wellness. Select wholesome dietary habits and lifestyle choices. Eclipses in Capricorn on July 16 and December 26 focus attention on health.

LOVE

Your 5th house of love sparkles with excitement at the Vernal Equinox. Uranus begins a long transit which foretells a memorable year regarding love. A relationship grows more lively. Greater intimacy is promised during May and January.

SPIRITUALITY

Sociability and service figure prominently in your spiritual advancement. Animal companions tend to play key roles too. During the retrograde Mercury cycles in July and November, try past-life regression to deepen spiritual insights.

FINANCE

The Full Moon on August 15 brightens your financial sector. Explore income-producing opportunities then. Jupiter enters your sign in December, bringing lifestyle improvements and better cash flow during the late autumn and winter months.

AQUARIUS
January 20–February 18
Spring 2019–Spring 2020 for those
born under the sign of the Water Bearer

Original, broadminded and helpful,
Aquarians focus on changing the status quo for the benefit of all. The waves
streaming from the Water Bearer's
urn represent a stream of supercon-
scious energy to be shared universally.
A visionary and inventive idealist, you
aren't easy to classify. Unpredictable
with an underlying stubborn streak, you
resist conforming to expectations.

As spring dawns Venus is in your 1st
house. You'll radiate beauty and charm.
Reach out to others; they will be receptive
and friendly. On March 31 Mars enters
your sister air sign of Gemini where it
boosts your energy level until mid-May.
Enthusiasm brightens a romantic attraction or creative project. Efforts made to
counsel or tutor children meet with success by May Day.

May 21–June 4 Mercury enters
your 5th house and favorably aspects
your Sun. Your wit and repartee help
express appealing ideas. Relationships
are enhanced by your stellar communication. During the remainder of June a Mars
transit in your health sector accents fitness
goals. Exercising with an animal companion can be productive. A coworker
becomes rather cantankerous near the
Summer Solstice. Consult the tarot or

try crystal gazing to determine the best
course of action. The eclipse on July 2
emphasizes a shift in your daily work pattern. Smile. A troublesome person might
be transferred. Mercury turns retrograde
on July 8. Your 6th and 7th houses are
affected until August 1. It's easy to be distracted by background noise. Others are
chatty. Dedicate a Lammas observance to
setting boundaries.

The first half of August brings a competitive situation to the fore as Mars
opposes your Sun. Keep challenges in
perspective. Don't let a tempest in a tea-
pot brew near the Full Moon in Aquarius
on August 15. Uranus turns retrograde
midmonth, marking a subtle softening of
energies and a return to previously post-
poned projects. September 1–12 a grand
trine in earth signs brings grounding and
aids financial choices. Shop for a bargain.
A lighter mood prevails as the Autumnal
Equinox nears and planetary transits activate your 9th house. You may explore new
ideas through travel or studies in meta-
physics and philosophy. Prepare for fall
by organizing your library.

A cheerful Venus aspect encourages
curiosity September 14–October 8. Colors
and music stimulate creative thinking
and awaken spirituality. Attend a meditation circle or yoga class. The remainder
of October focuses on communication
with professional associates. A Mercury
transit in your career sector brings much
discussion about options and job performance. Mercury is retrograde from
Halloween until November 21. Decorate
your work space with smiling pumpkins
and scarecrows to facilitate humor and
goodwill. Patiently check work and
complete projects you've already begun,

but postpone making a career move for the time being.

Mars crosses your midheaven as November ends. This intensifies career demands and accelerates a competitive atmosphere throughout December. Strive to be productive and don't respond to those who are angry or aggressive. Deliver greeting cards inscribed with original messages of goodwill on the eve of the longest of nights. At the Winter Solstice Venus enters Aquarius. This is a pleasant pattern which lasts until January 13. Gradually a more upbeat mood emerges. Associates will be friendlier and more appreciative as the holiday season concludes.

January finds Jupiter, Saturn and Pluto in your 12th house. Innermost thoughts and concerns can be troubling. Do some good works. Benefit those in need. Charitable efforts on your part will provide a wholesome outlet which in turn will help you. January 16–February 1 Mercury transits Aquarius. Plans for the future are of interest. Conversation becomes a catalyst for making decisions. A journey or get-together with friends would be rewarding. On Candlemas dedicate a cream-colored taper to the power of positive thinking.

Financial security is the theme during February. Several transits highlight your 2nd house. Neptune is influential. This brings a reminder to have faith that your monetary needs will be met. Live within your means and all will be well. The New Moon on February 23 brings clarity to your concerns regarding cash flow. February 24–March 3 Venus impacts your 3rd house. Variety adds spice to life as you happily juggle several projects simultaneously. Several short outings make life interesting. Jot notes in a journal for future reference. From March 4 through the last days of winter a Uranus influence brings some changes in the status quo at home. Visitors might arrive unexpectedly. A family member is pleased about a new opportunity.

HEALTH

Eclipses on July 2 and January 10 fall in your 6th house of health. New wellness programs can improve health near those dates. Be receptive to seeking other medical opinions and changing health care regimens. Innovative approaches to health care are promising this year.

LOVE

Early spring, late winter and mid-September through early October bring favorable Venus influences, promising happy love connections. Attending friendly seasonal celebrations at the Vernal Equinox, Autumnal Equinox and Candlemas can encourage romance.

SPIRITUALITY

Cultivate warmth and emotional connections rather than using an analytical approach to spiritual studies to expand spiritual awareness. Attending friendly spiritual gatherings would gradually awaken deeper spirituality during the coming year.

FINANCE

Security issues have been a source of anxiety during the past 18 months or so due to a Saturn transit in your 12th house. This terminates at the very end of winter. Meanwhile, appreciate simple pleasures. Quell excessive generosity.

PISCES
February 19–March 20
Spring 2019–Spring 2020 for those
born under the sign of the Fish

Adaptable and sensitive, often indecisive, the Fish swims an ever-changing course through the sea of life. You are trying to balance the variable energies which tug from many directions. Ruled by Neptune, the planet named for the God of the Sea, you have hidden depths. Your thoughts and plans are forever churning beneath a surface which mirrors your surroundings. Pisces is a dreamy visionary. An impressionable and complex chameleon, you are seldom confrontational.

Spring begins on a note of uncertainty. Mercury is retrograde in Pisces, hovering near Neptune in your 1st house. Interpret dreams and consider options from the Vernal Equinox through March 27. Mercury fast-forwards through your sign March 28–April 16, favoring travel. Commit to a job or move. Late April through mid-May Mars opposes Jupiter, bringing demands involving both home life and professional aspirations. Keep the most important priorities uppermost in your mind while balancing the two. Mars transits your 5th house May 16 throughout June. There is time for hobbies and a romantic dalliance. Your energy level improves, and it's easier to keep up the daily pace. Plan an outing at the Summer Solstice, perhaps attending a performance of Shakespeare's *A Midsummer's Night Dream*.

July opens with Venus entering your pleasure sector. A creative idea or avocation has the potential to expand. Both love and finances are promising during early July. The July 16 eclipse shifts the focus to your 11th house. Friends take an interest in the future, encouraging you to consider new goals. Politics and community concerns captivate your attention by Lammas. Honor the holiday with a healing ritual dedicated to the environment. August 1–11 a supportive Mercury transit encourages communication with children. Vacation travel would be restful and enjoyable in early August.

During late August and early September Venus, Mars and the Sun impact your 7th house. A decision made by a partner influences you. A legal or ethical issue can be addressed. On September 14 the Full Moon in Pisces accents the roles others play in your life. A choice of loyalties is made. By the Autumnal Equinox your awareness of paranormal activity increases. You can sense the presence of angels and other supernatural helpers at work. Ask them for guidance and healing during evening prayers and meditations.

October begins with Mercury starting a two-month transit through your 9th house. A challenging study program is appealing. You are ready to widen existing parameters. Travel can play a key role in this. Relationships with in-laws and grandparent–grandchild dynamics are favorable October 9–31. Honor All Hallows by including customs from several spiritual traditions at a gathering.

Venus transits your career sector November 1–24. Socialize with coworkers and express concern for their personal worries. Dress well at work. Your appearance deeply affects the way important people perceive you now. As November ends Neptune finishes a retrograde cycle. You'll feel a burden from the past lift. An old door closes and a new one opens near the New Moon on November 26. December begins with Jupiter changing signs and entering your 11th house. Accept invitations to attend winter holiday celebrations hosted by clubs and organizations. You may be asked to join a board or run for an office. Accept. This promises to be a worthwhile opportunity. The eclipse on December 26 is sextile your Sun, bringing changing goals as the month ends. New Year's Eve finds you gently releasing a friendship or interest which you've outgrown. Wishes for the future revolve around cultivating the new and unfamiliar.

Venus transits your 12th house as January begins. Be realistic about your feelings regarding lost love. If love is unrequited or there is a love triangle involved, January is a good time to look elsewhere. January 14–February 7 Venus is in Pisces, promising happiness. Love takes a more nurturing turn. Candlemas brings an ultra-romantic energy this year. Select an array of rose, red and pink candles to attract the favor of Cupid in time for Valentine's Day.

Mercury is retrograde in your 1st house February 17–March 10. Be careful not to overbook appointments. Preparing notes and supplies in advance will help you remain focused. Someone from the past is in touch. Recalling a prior situation

helps you understand how this will affect you. Winter ends with Venus in your 3rd house, bringing a cheerful mindset and pleasant communication. Catch up on writing and correspondence.

HEALTH

Encouragement from others always boosts your determination in meeting fitness goals. The Full Moon on February 9 is in your health sector. This brings insight regarding wellness.

LOVE

On July 2 and January 10, eclipses highlight your love sector. Expect intriguing twists regarding romance. Don't rush into commitments; matters are evolving. Go dancing in April and visit the seacoast from mid-June to mid-July to discover true love. Venus smiles at those times.

SPIRITUALITY

Perseverance is important to your spiritual advancement. Follow through with an established spiritual practice. Pluto rules your sector of spirituality, favoring a quiet and solitary atmosphere for dedicated spiritual studies. When Pluto is direct, from October 4 through March 20, spirituality awakens and deepens.

FINANCE

A difficult Jupiter square is in force from early spring until December 1. This can tempt you to risk security. Avoid a gamble and don't acquire debt during this time. From December through your birthday the financial picture gradually improves. Seek income-producing opportunities during February.

पतङ्गमक्तमसुरस्य मायया हृदा पश्यन्ति मनसा विपश्चितः
समुद्रे अन्तः कवयो वि चक्षते मरीचीनां पदमिच्छन्ति वेधसः
पतङ्गो वाचं मनसा बिभर्ति तां गन्धर्वोऽवदद्गर्भे अन्तः
तां द्योतमानां स्वर्यं मनीषामृतस्य पदे कवयो नि पान्ति
अपश्यं गोपामनिपद्यमानमा च परा च पथिभिश्चरन्तम्
स सध्रीचीः स विषूचीर्वसान आ वरीवर्ति भुवनेष्वन्तः

The wise see in their heart, in their spirits, the bird anointed with the magic of the Asura. The poets see him inside the ocean; the sages seek the footprints of his rays.

The bird carries in his heart, Speech that the divine youth spoke of inside the womb. The poets guard this revelation that shines like the sun in the footprint of Order.

I have seen the cowherd who never tires, moving to and fro along the paths. Clothing himself in those that move towards the same center but spread apart, he rolls on and on inside the worlds.

—RIG VEDA
177.10

Sites of Awe

America's Stonehenge

IT IS A BEAUTIFUL day. It has been over 90 degrees for the last ten days, then we had a thunderstorm last night. Today the temperature has gone down into the 70s. I've decided to visit America's Stonehenge located in Salem, New Hampshire (www.stonehengeusa.com), just a 2-hour ride from here and it promises to be a rewarding trip.

As I pull into the parking lot, I see an outdoor picnic area on the right— tables under some very large white pine trees. I walk down to the Visitors' Center and gift shop first to buy a ticket before having lunch. I think the near two-mile walk through the trails would be better taken after lunch.

The $12.50 cost of the entrance ticket includes a short video about the park's history and development. The clerk at the counter gave me a tour guide map as well. The four-page map contains descriptions of 32 marked sites along the trail. Some of the marked sites include: the Pulpit, the Upper Well, Stone Steps,

the Chamber in Ruins, the 8-ton Roof Slab, the "V" Hut, the Mensal Stone, the Oracle Chamber, the Speaking Tube, the Sacrificial Table and much more. It will take a few hours to walk the entire set of trails and the Astronomical Trail which follows the main trails. The Astronomical Trail surrounds the main stone site, and takes you to 15 more marked sites, including the Equinox Sunset Alignment, Moon Standstill Alignment Wall, Winter Solstice Sunset Monolith, November 1st Sunset Stone, True North Stone, May Day Monolith and numerous others. A map of the astronomical area is included as well.

The short video was informative, but I am eager to get onto the trails. As I walk out the back door of the Visitors' Center, I spot a mailbox labeled "bug spray." Conveniently placed inside the mailbox is a dispenser of spray for those of us who forgot to bring our own... as I did.

Following the arrows that seem to be located everywhere, I start down

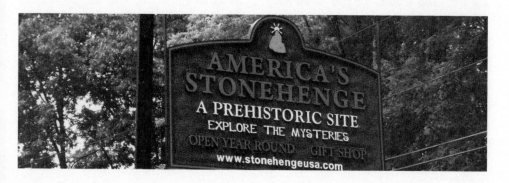

the path toward the stones. Along the way, there are many beautiful trees and undergrowth. I naturally find myself identifying what I can and taking pictures of what I don't recognize so that I can look them up later. In terms of trees, there are a lot of oaks (red and white), white pine, maple and birch.

The markers are clear and easy to locate. I'm following the map I was given and each time I see a site marker I can read the description of the stones at that location. Although dating back over 4,000 years, much of this land feels like it is very much alive and perfectly in harmony with the trees and nature. Several of the very small cave-like structures are covered over with soil and foliage making the entrance only visible from one side.

The area bounded by marked sites #20 (Restoration of East-West wall), #21 (Mensal Stone), and #24 (Large wall on the southern side), is what I have been looking for. Some decades ago—during the early 1970s—a Craft Initiation was

said to have happened here. A High Priestess and three other robed members of a Coven initiated a new member into the Alexandrian Tradition of Wicca. A postcard was made to memorialize the moment and used as part of the advertising materials for Mystery Hill, as it was then known.. A close examination of the postcard will reveal Lady D. (holding two magical tools), R.D. holding the Book of Shadows, two other members of the Coven and the newly made Alexandrian Witch, Ayeisha. I met Ayeisha in the late 1980s and she was a good friend of mine until she passed away in 1998. She was also a founder of K.A.M. and a member of the N.E.C.T.W. Tradition. Examining the postcard further, the altar holds various other tools and candles.

Mystery Hill has long been known as a powerful spot. Other members of the Craft have come here to perform rituals and spells. Recently a Coven visited to perform a Tree Blessing

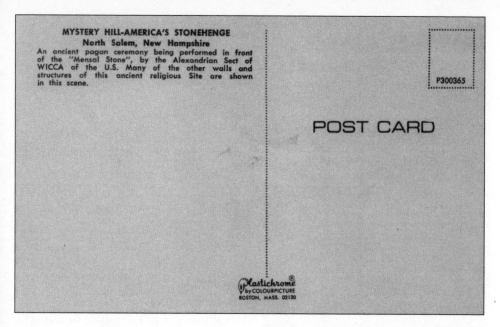

MYSTERY HILL-AMERICA'S STONEHENGE
North Salem, New Hampshire
An ancient pagan ceremony being performed in front of the "Mensal Stone", by the Alexandrian Sect of WICCA of the U.S. Many of the other walls and structures of this ancient religious Site are shown in this scene.

POST CARD

P300365

Plastichrome®
by COLOURPICTURE
BOSTON, MASS. 02130

ritual in the deeper woods behind the Astronomical Trail walk.

I visited here in the 1970s and the power was very strong. Today it feels different. Not less powerful, but definitely different. I might question the original use of the "sacrificial stone," or the actual purpose of the Oracle Chamber. There is no denying the alignment of the astronomical stones or the authenticity of this site as a centuries-old standing stone site of power.

I recall visiting Stonehenge and also the Rollright Stones. At both of these locations, power seemed to radiate differently as well. The tie to astronomy, through the connection to Equinoxes, Solstices, sunrise, sunset, midpoints, etc. is a very powerful thing. I can feel the power here very clearly. This intense energy contains terrestrial and sky aspects—a combination found in many ancient temples and stone circles.

When visiting #30 (Astronomical Viewing Platform, constructed in 1975), you are right in the center—the crossing point—of the 15 astronomical lines which are intrinsic in defining this powerful site. Here at the center, where all lines cross, you can look out in each direction and see a clear path to the marking stone. Trees have been cleared and are continually cleared each year, to provide a clear view of each stone and the rising or setting of the Sun and Moon. I suspect, many years ago when this hill was clear of trees and just a rock outcropping, that standing here would be a very moving experience when witnessing the rising of the Sun at Midwinter!

Stone circles are not unique to England, or to Scotland or Wales for that matter, but can be found around the world. Here in New England, this is the most famous of stone arrangements. If you like to walk trails and you like adventure, I highly recommend you visit Mystery Hill— America's Stonehenge.

—ARMAND TABER

Reviews

Son of Chicken Qabalah:
Rabbi Lamed Ben Clifford's (Mostly
Painless) Practical Qabalah Course
Lon Milo DuQuette
Weiser Books
$18.95
Due to release November 1, 2018

WELL, IT'S DÉJÀ VU all over again. Lon Milo DuQuette has used his wicked sense of humor, deep knowledge and a good bit of wordsmithing in penning his soon to be released volume; *Son of Chicken Qabalah: Rabbi Lamed Ben Clifford's (Mostly Painless) Practical Qabalah Course*. DuQuette's ability to convey profound knowledge seemed to crescendo in 2001 with the publishing of what many concluded was his magnum opus, *The Chicken Qabalah of Rabbi Lamed Ben Clifford*. Needless to say, *Son of Chicken Qabalah* will not supplant the earlier tome, rather it furthers the journey to greater heights.

If you have already read *The Chicken Qabalah*, you will find yourself in familiar territory, even though there is a hard turn off in a new direction. DuQuette takes the reader into a magical lodge where they encounter a Master and a Guide ready to conduct them through a series of initiations, each more profound than what precedes it. Before the conclusion of each initiation, a series of exercises are detailed and a knowledge lecture is given.

Son of Chicken Qabalah explores the deep meanings enshrined in the Hebrew alphabet and their relationship to creation. DuQuette effortlessly scoops up the reader and transports them to an encounter with the profundity of being. The reader can't help but to come face to face with their own divinity as DuQuette adroitly captures the atmosphere of a magical lodge.

While it is not requisite to read *The Chicken Qabalah of Rabbi Lamed Ben Clifford* prior to encountering this new release, it would certainly benefit the reader to do as much. *Son of Chicken Qabalah* is sure to be one those books that peels like an onion, new levels being exposed with each re-read.

Welsh Witches: Narratives of
Witchcraft and Magic From 16th and
17th Century Wales
Richard Suggett
ISBN-13: 978-1999946715
Atramentous Press
£55.00

A CUNNING WOMAN living on the outskirts of town who sells healing charms and potions to the village folk gets bullied by a local ruffian. After striking her across the face, his arm mysteriously goes numb and limp. Soon, members of his household fall ill one by one with no abatement in sight, until the local magistrate is called and the charmer is brought before a grim-faced court on charges of Witchcraft. Though it may sound like the preamble to a Hammer Horror film, this is merely one of the gripping stories of Late Renaissance life found within the pages of this captivating book.

Suggett, a well-respected researcher and historian has been elbows deep in the records of the Court of Great Sessions of Wales, where he's turned up a score of actual trial records, examinations and witness depositions of healers, conjurers, confidence tricksters, midwives and magicians, all while shining a sobering light upon the surprising nuance of those dark times. These alone are worth the price of admission, but Suggett's notes and commentaries bring them all together beautifully.

Spanning two turbulent centuries, *Welsh Witches* is a stark snapshot of religious madness in a land that was comparatively tolerant of (if not indulgent toward) healers and cunning folk at the time. However, the tumultuous conflicts and pontiff-centered politics of the Reformation pushed even the more level-headed toward reprehensible acts of hatred against their fellow citizens.

A fascinating study of Witchcraft, folklore and judicial overreach from the land of the dragon flag.

Sigil Witchery: A Witch's Guide to Crafting Magick Symbols
Laura Tempest Zakroff
ISBN-13: 9780738755854
Llewellyn Publications
$19.99

SIGIL MAGIC OF ONE form or another is a rather common and popular form of mystical expression within occult circles the world over, yet there appears to be few books devoted entirely to the subject. Mostly, one finds a brief chapter or two within a larger tome devoted to spellcraft, listing a couple of quick-and-easy methods for sigil creation that may as well be magical afterthoughts before carrying on about candles, colors or some other such aspect of the Witch's arts.

Inevitably, this book shall be compared to those previously mentioned volumes focusing solely on the subject of magical sigilization. All of these tend to be many things: informative, clever, well researched, practical and instructive. By these rubrics, *Sigil Witchery* shall certainly hold its own, but it deserves an additional adjective: inspirational.

I challenge you to read this book and not draw sigils on whatever piece of chalkboard, tablet or scrap paper happens to cross your path.

Perhaps it's the easygoing nature of Zakroff's instruction, or her barely-stifled joy when describing the various mediums and tools one can use to craft sigils, but her excitement is frankly both palpable and infectious. Haven't picked up a pen or pencil in a while? Start reading this and there's a good chance you'll be blissfully doodling halfway through.

Zakroff greatly enjoys breaking down symbols into their component parts, examining each glyph for what it says intuitively as well as semiotically, and then showing how to use these aspects to build and grow some stunning pieces of art. After the small bits have been dissected, examples of sigils for meditation, spellcraft and protection are provided and interpreted, giving plenty of great ideas and solid advice for even the most boorishly well-informed member of your Coven.

Madame Pamita's Magical Tarot
Madame Pamita
ISBN-13: 978-1578636297
Weiser Books
$18.95

THE HISTORY OF the tarot is veiled in myth and Renaissance mysteries, but as many occultists attest, this enigmatic card-game-turned-oracle is not merely for fortune telling and divination. Dripping with mystical symbolism, this humble pile of cardboard slips can also be used as a potent tool of meditation and spell casting. This is the primary focus of *Madame Pamita's Magical Tarot*, but certainly not the entirety of its scope.

A professional tarot reader with decades of experience and a flourishing "Parlour of Wonders" in Los Angeles, Pamita begins with a brief introduction to the questions each reader should ask themselves, as well as some effective journaling methods. She then successively takes the reader through the cards of the ubiquitous Rider Waite Tarot deck. Tossing aside many of the more Qabalistically saturated approaches to tarot, but still dealing with each card as a miniature pathworking "adventure," she gives keywords, interpretations, journaling questions and affirmations to be used by the budding diviner for each of the 78

cards, so that they may help to manifest their reality rather than merely wait for the Fates to bring things their way.

A lighthearted and entertaining read for any fan of occultism, tarot, cartomancy or the divinatory mysteries.

Traditional Magic Spells for Protection and Healing
Claude Lecouteaux
ISBN-13: 978-1620556214
Inner Traditions
$29.95

HISTORIAN AND researcher Claude Lecouteaux, professor emeritus at the Paris-Sorbonne University and author of over a dozen books on magic and folklore, has done it again. Painstakingly compiling a wonderful catalog of European spells, charms, chants and sometimes strange prescriptions—over 600 of them, to be precise—all while introducing and organizing them into a somewhat slim and unimposing volume.

As the title suggests, every spell therein contained involves either healing or protection, and the reader will likely be amazed at some of the concoctions our early magical ancestors came up with. The sources span nearly the entirety of Europe, with scores of medieval and Renaissance remedies, with some spells being around 2000 years old.

Of special interest to some is the inclusion of spells learned from Transylvanian Romani by Romanian ethnologists in the 19th century, but there's plenty more for everyone, whatever the uncomfortable ailment or unfortunate hex may be. Looking for a Hungarian headache remedy? How about a Slovenian charm against poison? A French rat conjuration? Perhaps Marcellus' scrofula cure is more your speed. Any way you slice it, this book of old antidotes and orisons can be easily cross-referenced thanks to its alphabetized sections, helpful index and rather thorough bibliography—for all the students and scholars out there. Ultimately a discrete treasure for any occult library.

The Museum of Witchcraft and Magic
MuseumOfWitchcraftAndMagic.co.uk

BEING ABLE TO walk into a museum dedicated top-to-bottom to all things magical would probably tickle the fancy of even the most dour-faced occultist, but alas, there are paltry few of them about. The oldest and most well-respected, originally founded on the Isle of Man but moved to the sleepy sea village of Bostcastle on Cornwall's northern coast, is thousands of years of magical history rolled into two floors worth of captivating displays and a research library of over 7000 books.

However, for most of us (especially those in places "across the pond" and further), a quick jaunt to the southwest of Albion is rather cost-prohibitive. Thankfully the museum has provided a most user-friendly website with which to browse its fascinating nooks and crannies. There, one can peruse most of the museum's 3000 objects with high definition photographs, videos and tutorials, delving into their inspired collections with ease. Included is even a search feature allowing one to scrutinize the many documents and books in their considerable library of folklore and occultism.

Thus, Enochian Watchtowers, horse-skull protection charms, poppets, mandrakes and founder Cecil Williamson's scrying mirror can now be easily viewed from the comfort of one's favorite device.

Reflexions
Omnia
Paganscum Records

PAGANFOLK powerhouses Omnia have returned to the scene with their most recent foray. Part greatest-hits album, part inspired remix, *Reflexions* weaves their acoustic-driven classics with layers of electronic soundscaping, re-imagining their songs in new and enchanting ways. The whole thing comes off as a shamanic spirit-journey of melody, bringing one through the hills and dales of a trippy musical sojourn interwoven with rhythm and reverberations of meditative reverie.

The texturing is almost palpable, the mix surrounding the listener in a layer-cake blanket of sound. Weaving medieval European and Middle Eastern folk together with echoing effects, trance-like beats and the occasional spoken word poetry, Omnia's newest is a brilliant reinvention of their older work that transports the listener through an aural odyssey of strength and transformation. Every time you peel back a section of its compositions, a dozen more sonic strata reveal themselves. The well is endless. Drink deeply.

From a Witch's Mailbox

When to begin

Do Pagans and Witches have a New Year and when is it?—Submitted by Andrea Sharp

Yes, Pagans and Witches do have a New Year that is celebrated in one way or another. That is the easier portion of the question—the when is tricky. There are many answers to this simple question. The New Year for each tradition is usually based on the underlying mythology prevalent in their teachings. For example, those traditions that are centered on the British Isles might have one of three potential dates. Some celebrate New Year at the Winter Solstice, citing the many Solstice customs hinting at a time of renewal. Samhain might also be the New Year—Celts started their day/season with darkness before the light. Lastly, Spring Equinox, with is the beginning of the growth season, might be the New Year. If you are solitary, you will need to decide for yourself. If you are with a group, they will indicate their New Year to students.

Witchy Witch

Do you have to be initiated into a Coven to be a Witch?—Submitted by Dan Lin

No you don't have to be initiated or in a Coven to be a Witch. Some would say that a Witch is born, not made. While others will contend that Witches are made. Only you will know if you are a Witch or not. Look deep in your heart and meditate to find the true answer to this question. I would say first, you need to define for yourself what a Witch is. Many define Witch as an individual who has taken the time to dedicate themselves to the study and celebration of the seasonal and lunar cycles, studied Earth and Moon magics, and has fostered their own special innate magical abilities to help themselves and others. No initiation or Coven membership can confer abilities that are not already in your being. Now that being said, you cannot call yourself a Gardnerian Witch, for example, unless you have been initiated by a Gardnerian authorized to initiate. In the end, you must know yourself to be a Witch to call yourself a Witch.

Three times good

What is Karma's role in Witchcraft and Spellcasting?—Submitted by Kelly Rand

It is generally agreed across the board among Witches that there is a cause and effect bounceback to all of our actions, be they magical or not. The basic understanding (as captured by Gwen Thompson The Wiccan Rede found in full at nectw.org/ladygwynne.html) "Mind the Three-fold Law ye should—Three times bad an' three times good." The number three occurs frequently in Wicca. In this case, you are admonished that no matter good or bad, you will be repaid three times what you put out there, be it magical or not. There is one further bit of advice in the The Wiccan Rede, *"Eight words ye Wiccan Rede fulfill—An' it harm none, Do what ye will."* While these are not in the eastern sense of the borrowed word *"Karma,"* they certainly point us towards upright and honest behavior.

To every season

Are Wiccan Sabbats based on astrological events?—Submitted by Gale Ash

Well, the Solstices and the Equinoxes are quite obviously based on terrestrial events that occur annually. The Solstices mark a reversal of the tide of light/dark and Equinoxes mark the peak of the light/dark. They usually occur sometime around the 21st day of their month. The crossquarters are determined by one of two methods. Either by dates that have been absorbed culturally with traditionally set dates—May Day, Lammas, Hallowe'en and Candlemas all having fixed dates on the Gregorian calendar. These same dates can be calculated by the position of the Solstices and Equinoxes of the year. With each being exactly at the midpoint between the Equinox and Solstice of each respective season. We are unsure as to which of the Equinoxes/Solstices/Crossquarter days were celebrated by our Pagan ancestors and I suppose it does not matter. Pick the method that feels most comfortable. If you feel the season as it approaches, you will know best when it should be celebrated.

Cutting through the mess

What are the tools that I will need as a new Witch?—Submitted by Jana Dawes

The single tool that seems to show up in the many traditions of Paganism and Wicca is the black hilted knife, sometimes called the athamé. Most of our work is creating change that conforms to our will. The double-sided blade appropriately captures in symbol the will, cutting through hesitation in both directions.

Let us hear from you, too

We love to hear from our readers. Letters should be sent with the writer's name (or just first name or initials), address, daytime phone number and e-mail address, if available. Published material may be edited for clarity or length. All letters and e-mails will become the property of The Witches' Almanac Ltd. *and will not be returned. We regret that due to the volume of correspondence we cannot reply to all communications.*

The Witches' Almanac, Ltd.
P.O. Box 1292
Newport, RI 02840-9998
info@TheWitchesAlmanac.com
www.TheWitchesAlmanac.com

DAME FORTUNE'S WHEEL TAROT
A PICTORIAL KEY
PAUL HUSON

The Witches' Almanac presents:

- *Illustrates for the first time, traditional Tarot card interpretations unadorned by the occult speculations of Mathers, Waite or Crowley.*

- *Expounds on the meanings collected by Jean-Baptiste Alliette, a Parisian fortune-teller otherwise known as Etteilla*

Based upon Paul Huson's research in *Mystical Origins of the Tarot, Dame Fortune's Wheel Tarot* illustrates for the first time the earliest, traditional Tarot card interpretations as collected in the 1700s by Jean-Baptiste Alliette. In addition to detailed descriptions, full color reproductions of Huson's original designs for all 79 cards are provided, including an extra Significator card as specified by Etteilla that may be used optionally. 200 pages $19.95

For information visit TheWitchesAlmanac.com/dame-fortunes-wheel-tarot-a-pictorial-key/

MAGIC

An Occult Primer

David Conway

The Witches' Almanac presents:

• A clear, articulate presentation of magic in a workable format
• Updated text, graphics and appendices
• Foreword by Colin Wilson.

David Conway's *Magic: An Occult Primer* is a seminal work that brought magical training to the every-magician in the early 70s. David is an articulate writer presenting the mysteries in a very workable manner for the serious student. Along with the updated texts on philosophy and practical magic is a plethora of graphics that have all been redrawn, promising to be another collector's edition published by The Witches' Almanac.

384 pages — $24.95

For further information visit TheWitchesAlmanac.com/magic-an-occult-primer/

Aradia
Gospel of the Witches
Charles Godfrey Leland

ARADIA IS THE FIRST work in English in which witchcraft is portrayed as an underground old religion, surviving in secret from ancient Pagan times.

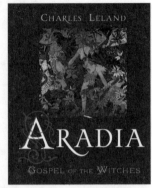

- Used as a core text by many modern Neo-Pagans.
- Foundation material containing traditional witch-craft practices
- This special edition features appreciations by such authors and luminaries as Paul Huson, Raven Grimassi, Judika Illes, Michael Howard, Christopher Penczak, Myth Woodling, Christina Oakley Harrington, Patricia Della-Piana, Jimahl di Fiosa and Donald Weiser. A beautiful and compelling work, this edition has brought the format up to date, while keeping the text unchanged. 172 pages $16.95

⊰ Expanded classics! ⊱

The ABC of Magic Charms
Elizabeth Pepper

SINCE THE DAWN of mankind, an obscure instinct in the human spirit has sought protection from mysterious forces beyond mortal control. Human beings sought benefaction in the three realms that share Earth with us — animal, mineral, vegetable. All three, humanity discovered, contain mysterious properties discovered over millennia through occult divination. An enlarged edition of *Magic Charms from A to Z*, compiled by the staff of *The Witches' Almanac*. $12.95

The Little Book of Magical Creatures
Elizabeth Pepper and Barbara Stacy

A loving tribute to the animal kingdom

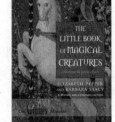

AN UPDATE of the classic *Magical Creatures*, featuring Animals Tame, Animals Wild, Animals Fabulous—plus an added section of enchanting animal myths from other times, other places. *A must for all animal lovers.* $12.95

✣ a lady shape-shifts into a white doe ✣ two bears soar skyward
✣ Brian Boru rides a wild horse ✣ a wolf growls dire prophecy

The Witchcraft of Dame Darrel of York

Charles Godfrey Leland

Introduction by Robert Mathiesen

The Witches' Almanac presents:

- *A previously unpublished work by folklorist Charles Godfrey Leland.*
- *Published in full color facsimile with a text transcript.*
- *Forward by Prof. Robert Mathiesen.*

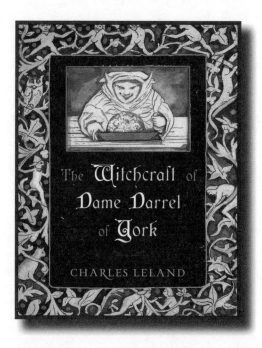

This beautifully reproduced facsimile of the illuminated manuscript will shed light on an ancient tradition as well as provide the basis for a modern practice. It will be treasured by those practicing Pagans, scholars and all those fascinated by the legend and lore of England.

Standard hardcover edition ($65.00).
Deluxe numbered edition with slipcase ($85.00).
Exclusive full leather bound, numbered and slipcased edition ($145.00).

For information visit TheWitchesAlmanac.com/the-witchcraft-of-dame-darrel-of-york/

Atramentous Press
Revealing the inner secrets of traditional practices and occult philosophies

---

The Witches' Almanac is now the exclusive distributor of
Atramentous Press publications in America:

The Witching-Other: Explorations and Meditations on the Existential Witch
by Peter Hamilton-Giles

Welsh Witches: Narratives of Witchcraft and Magic From 16th- And 17th-Century Wales
by Richard Suggett with foreword by Ronald Hutton

Standing at the Crossroads: Dialectics of the Witching-Other
by Peter Hamilton-Giles with Illustrations by Carolyn Hamilton-Giles

Atramentous Press has been initiated as a platform for exploring the mystical and philosophical approaches found in and amongst traditional practices. Encompassing the world of western occultism from Traditional Witchcraft to Ceremonial Magic, from indigenous folkloric practices. It is our aim to open up the debate about how meaning, history, knowledge, magic, superstition, and folklore are understood and applied in various cultural religious practice-based settings. It is by opening up the debate we discover how the meaning, history, knowledge, magic, superstition, and folklore are understood and applied in various cultural religious practice based settings

For information visit TheWitchesAlmanac.com/Atramentous/

≈ MARKETPLACE ≈

The Veiled Crow

MINDFULNESS AND INTENT
FOR A MAGICAL LIFE

WWW.VEILEDCROW.COM
401-919-5499
1830 BROAD STREET
CRANSTON, RI 02905

Dikki-Jo Mullen

The Witches' Almanac Astrologer

PO Box 533024, Orlando, FL 32853
skymaiden@juno.com
http://dikkijomullen.wordpress.com

Seminars, Presentations, Convention Programs

Complete Astrology & Parapsychology Services

Paranormal Investigations

(see the website for astrology articles and information about upcoming events)

Come Join Us at PantheaCon

PantheaCon is a Pagan convention that includes many non-traditional spiritual traditions: Wiccan, Norse, Celtic, Egyptian, Umbanda, Yoruba, & Western Ceremonial Magick.

**February 15–18, 2019
DoubleTree Hotel,
San Jose, CA**

Rituals, Music, Workshops, Celebrity Guest Speakers, & more…

Register online at *www.pantheacon.com!*

Visit the Store

Ancient Ways is your complete metaphysical store and pagan center with books, incense, oils, candles, magical tools, Hoodoo supplies, statuary, jewelry, classes, tarot readings…and much more!

We also do mail order!

ANCIENT WAYS

4075 Telegraph Ave.
Oakland, CA 94609
(510) 653-3244
www.ancientways.com

The Troll Shop

Trolls • Imports • Jewelry
Antiques • Collectibles

88 Main St.
East Greenwich,
Rhode Island 02818
401-884-9800

Alchemy Works

The Materials of Magic
since 2000

❧ Original Magic Oils
❧ Historically Accurate Incense
❧ Vnusal Herbs and Essential Oils
❧ Seeds for the Witch's Garden

www.alchemy-works.com

The products and services offered above are paid advertisements.

Since 1994 Herbs & Arts has served Denver and the region, striving to be a place of healing & sanctuary for the Pagan & Wiccan communities, and all seekers of spiritual living.

We live with a simple intention, to put forth compassion, love & gratitude into the universe with the belief that if we can inspire & empower healing and spiritual connection in ourselves and others, the world will change for the better.

We make 100s of ritual oils, incenses, & bath salts for all your magickal needs. All of our ritual products are made in sacred space and at specific lunar & astrological times. Our webstore also has over 400 herbs, essential oils and other items to support your connection to spirit. Blessed be.

Herbs & Arts

Denver, CO
303.388.2544
www.herbsandarts.com

OpenDoors
Gift & Book Store
Learning & Healing Center

Psychic / Tarot Readings

Best Rates On Telephone Readings

Money Back Guarantee

New Age Products

Largest Selection of Gemstones & Tarot Cards in New England

Wiccan Jewelry, Statues, and Divination Tools

395 Washington St., Braintree, MA, USA
OpenDoors7.com   781-843-8224

SOLAR-LIGHT ONE
A video subscription series by
Dolores Ashcroft-Nowicki

❖❖ ❖❖ ❖❖ ❖❖ ❖❖ ❖❖ ❖❖ ❖❖ ❖❖

How often do you get to listen to an Adept? The answer now is, "Whenever you want!"

For almost 50 years Dolores Ashcroft-Nowicki has taught, trained and instructed students worldwide and is well known for her practical approach to the Art of Magic and her earthy sense of humor.

Now, at 89 she is venturing into the world of technology and is putting her files of over 200 lectures on video. Solar-Light is offering two videos a month, in six monthly periods.

The lectures cover a wide selection of topics and as constitute a valuable and unparalleled archive of knowledge from one of the worlds most highly respected esoteric teachers.

Some of the topics are:
Woman, the original Grail.
Ancient and modern Spellcraft
Psychic Protection

❖❖ ❖❖ ❖❖ ❖❖ ❖❖ ❖❖ ❖❖ ❖❖ ❖❖

For subscription info please go to:
http://www.solar-light.one

The products and services offered above are paid advertisements.

≈MARKETPLACE≈

CHOCOLATE ∗ MAGICK ∗ LOVE

NEW MOON MAGICK

An Intriguing Practitioner's Boutique

A Collection of Hard-to-Find
Quality Items
INCLUDING
Antiques, Jewelry, Herbs, Tools, Candles,
New Moon & Full Moon Sea Salt
ALL NATURAL SEA SALT FROM THE WATERS OF MARTHA'S VINEYARD
THE HOME OF
Enchanted Chocolates™

Martha's Vineyard 508-693-8331
www.newmoonmagick.net

The Museum of Witchcraft

Peter and Judith Hewitt

The Harbour
Boscastle
Cornwall
PL35 0HD
01840 250111

museumwitchcraft@aol.com
www.museumofwitchcraft.com

Now under the care of the
Museum of British Folklore

GAELSONG
CELEBRATING THE CELTIC IMAGINATION

Fine Goods
inspired by
Celtic, Pagan
& Nature
Spirituality

Customer Favorite!
Elemental
Fire Pendant

Apparel
Jewelry
Decor
Journals

Bestseller!
Chakra Journal

Request a Free Catalog!
800-205-5790   www.gaelsong.com

The New Alexandrian Libary

The NAL is a library near Georgetown, DE
dedicated to the preservation of books,
periodicals, music, media, art , artifacts, and
photographs, focused on the metaphysical
and occult aspects of all religions and
traditions.

www.newalexandrianlibrary.com

EYE OF HORUS

Magick & Mindfulness
Supplies, Classes
and Readings

since 2002

Oils, Incense, Candles,
Jewelry, Tools, Gifts

Handcrafted Enchantments

www.EyeofHorus.biz

Visit us online or in Minneapolis
910 W Lake St, Mpls, MN 55408
CALL (612) 872-1292 for orders or to book a reading

The products and services offered above are paid advertisements.

❧ MARKETPLACE ❧

Pyramid Books
— Tools for personal growth —

Books ✫ Tarot ✫ Crystals ✫ Incense
Dream catchers and other new age gifts

Licensed professional readers daily
Psychic phone readings available

214 Derby Street • Salem, MA 01970
978-745-7171 • *www.pyramidbks.com*

13Moons

YOUR
SOURCE FOR
MAGICAL
TOOLS &
SUPPLIES

THANK YOU
JOHN WATERHOUSE
FOR SUCH AMAZING
PAINTINGS

13MOONS.COM

The Modern Witch's Guide to Magical Aromatherapy

BLACKTHORN'S
Botanical Magic

135
Essential Oil Recipes

The Green Witch's guide to essential oils for spellcraft, ritual & healing

Amy Blackthorn

Amy Blackthorn—the woman behind *Blackthorn's Hoodoo Blends*—offers a complete guide to the use of essential oils in spellcraft and ritual. She takes you on a journey beyond the soothing, healing use of scents to reveal their subtle, hidden powers.

800.423.7087   September 1, 2018
orders@rwwbooks.com   ISBN: 9781578636303
WEISER BOOKS redwheelweiser.com $22.95

AVAILABLE WHEREVER BOOKS AND EBOOKS ARE SOLD

Discover a Mythical,
Mystical Realm of
Books, Incense, Candles,
Gemstone & Symbolic Jewelry,
Herbs, Oils, Crystals, Music,
Cards, Statuary, Tarot, Clothing
and All Things Rare
and Magickal

1211 Hillcrest Street
Orlando, FL 32803
(407) 895-7439
www.AvalonBeyond.com

Wiccan Classes & Events
Psychic Readings

Avalon
All Things Rare and Magickal . . .

The products and services offered above are paid advertisements.

✤MARKETPLACE✤

Blackthorne Grove
of the
Tuatha De Danann

Traditional Witchcraft & Mysteries
Based on Irish Myth,
Legend & Folklore

blackthornegroveri@gmail.com
Northern Rhode Ilsand

Providence Coven

Providence Coven
an Alexandrian Coven
emphasizing coven work,
traditional lore and
ceremonial magick

ProvidenceCoven.org

Introuducing the innaugural edition of
The Witches' Almanac 2019 Wall Calendar

Our readers have told us time and again how much they enjoy the many insights provided in the Moon Calendar in each issue of The Witches' Almanac. We have heeded your advice: the standard Moon phases, channeled actions and an expanded version of the topic featured in the Moon Calendar are now available in a full-size wall calendar.

❧M ARKETPLACE ❧

www.azuregreen.net Jewelry, Amulets, Incense, Oils, Herbs, Candles, Statuary, Gemstones, Ritual Items. Wholesale inquiries welcome.

Voodoo Queen specializing in removal and reversal of evil spells. Be careful of what you wish for before you call me: **678-677-1144**

Starwind Gifts Starwind Gifts New Orleans, LA. Incense, candles, crystals, jewelry, cards, tarot & oracles, herbs, handmade soap, & services. **(504) 595-9627** www.StarwindGifts.com

Twisted Broomstick Potions and powders, charms and tricks! Your inner witch waits at the Twisted Broomstick! www.TwistedBroomstick.com

Mardukite Truth Seeker Press Legendary books and tomes of magick by Joshua Free. Necronomicon Anunnaki Bible, Sorcerer's Handbook, Arcanum, Book of Pheryllt & more! mardukite.com NecroGate.com

The products and services offered above are paid advertisements.

TO: The Witches' Almanac
P.O. Box 1292, Newport, RI 02840-9998

www.TheWitchesAlmanac.com

Name_____

Address_____

City_____ State_____ Zip_____

E-mail_____

WITCHCRAFT being by nature one of the secretive arts, it may not be as easy to find us next year. If you'd like to make sure we know where you are, why don't you send us your name and address? You will certainly hear from us.

ANCIENT ROMAN HOLIDAYS

The glory that was Rome awaits you in Barbara Stacy's classic presentation of a festive year in Pagan times. Here are the gods and goddesses as the Romans conceived them, accompanied by the annual rites performed in their worship. Scholarly, lighthearted – a rare combination.

CELTIC TREE MAGIC

Robert Graves in *The White Goddess* writes of the significance of trees in the old Celtic lore. *Celtic Tree Magic* is an investigation of the sacred trees in the remarkable Beth-Luis-Nion alphabet and their role in folklore, poetry and mysticism.

MOON LORE

As both the largest and the brightest object in the night sky, and the only one to appear in phases, the Moon has been a rich source of myth for as long as there have been mythmakers.

MAGIC SPELLS AND INCANTATIONS

Words have magic power. Their sound, spoken or sung, has ever been a part of mystic ritual. From ancient Egypt to the present, those who practice the art of enchantment have drawn inspiration from a treasury of thoughts and themes passed down through the ages.

LOVE FEASTS

Creating meals to share with the one you love can be a sacred ceremony in itself. With the Witch in mind, culinary adept Christine Fox offers magical menus and recipes for every month in the year.

RANDOM RECOLLECTIONS
II, III, IV

Pages culled from the original (no longer available) issues of *The Witches' Almanac,* published annually throughout the 1970s, are now available in a series of tasteful booklets. A treasure for those who missed us the first time around, keepsakes for those who remember.

A Treasury from past editions...

Perfect for study or casual reading, Witches All *is a collection from* The Witches' Almanac *publications of the past. Arranged by topics, the book, like the popular almanacs, is thought provoking and often spurs me on to a tangent leading to even greater discovery. The information and art in the book – astrological attributes, spells, recipes, history, facts & figures is a great reminder of the history of the Craft, not just in recent years, but in the early days of the Witchcraft Revival in this century: the witch in an historical and cultural perspective.* Ty Bevington, Circle of the Wicker Man, Columbus, Ohio

Absolutely beautiful! I recently ordered Witches All *and I have to say I wasn't disappointed. The artwork and articles are first rate and for a longtime* Witches' Almanac *fan, it is a wonderful addition to my collection.* Witches' Almanac *devotees and newbies alike will love this latest effort. Very worth getting.*

Tarot3, Willits, California

GREEK GODS IN LOVE

Barbara Stacy casts a marvelously original eye on the beloved stories of Greek deities, replete with amorous oddities and escapades. We relish these tales in all their splendor and antic humor, and offer an inspired storyteller's fresh version of the old, old mythical magic.

MAGIC CHARMS FROM A TO Z

A treasury of amulets, talismans, fetishes and other lucky objects compiled by the staff of *The Witches' Almanac*. An invaluable guide for all who respond to the call of mystery and enchantment.

LOVE CHARMS

Love has many forms, many aspects. Ceremonies performed in witchcraft celebrate the joy and the blessings of love. Here is a collection of love charms to use now and ever after.

MAGICAL CREATURES

Mystic tradition grants pride of place to many members of the animal kingdom. Some share our life. Others live wild and free. Still others never lived at all, springing instead from the remarkable power of human imagination.

ORDER FORM

Each timeless edition of *The Witches' Almanac* is unique.
Limited numbers of previous years' editions are available.

Item	Price	Qty.	Total
2019-2020 The Witches' Almanac – Animals: Friends & Familiars	$12.95		
2018-2019 The Witches' Almanac – The Magic of Plants	$12.95		
2017-2018 The Witches' Almanac – Water: Our Primal Source	$12.95		
2016-2017 The Witches' Almanac – Air: the Breath of Life	$12.95		
2015-2016 The Witches' Almanac – Fire:, the Transformer	$12.95		
2014-2015 The Witches' Almanac – Mystic Earth	$12.95		
2013-2014 The Witches' Almanac – Wisdom of the Moon	$11.95		
2012-2013 The Witches' Almanac – Radiance of the Sun	$11.95		
2011-2012 The Witches' Almanac – Stones, Powers of Earth	$11.95		
2010-2011 The Witches' Almanac – Animals Great & Small	$11.95		
2009-2010 The Witches' Almanac – Plants & Healing Herbs	$11.95		
2008-2009 The Witches' Almanac – Divination & Prophecy	$10.95		
2007-2008 The Witches' Almanac – The Element of Water	$9.95		
2003, 2004, 2005, 2006 issues of The Witches' Almanac	$8.95		
1999, 2000, 2001, 2002 issues of The Witches' Almanac	$7.95		
1995, 1996, 1997, 1998 issues of The Witches' Almanac	$6.95		
1993, 1994 issues of The Witches' Almanac	$5.95		
SALE: 13 Almanac back issues (1993–2005) with free book bag and free shipping	$ 75.00		
20 Almanac back issues (1993–2012) with free book bag and free shipping	$100.00		
Dame Fortune's Wheel Tarot: A Pictorial Key	$19.95		
Magic: An Occult Primer	$24.95		
The Witches' Almanac Coloring Book	$12.00		
The Witchcraft of Dame Darrel of York, clothbound, signed and numbered, in slip case	$85.00		
The Witchcraft of Dame Darrel of York, leatherbound, signed and numbered, in slip case	$145.00		
Aradia or The Gospel of the Witches	$16.95		
The Horned Shepherd	$16.95		
The ABC of Magic Charms	$12.95		
The Little Book of Magical Creatures	$12.95		
Greek Gods in Love	$15.95		
Witches All	$13.95		
Ancient Roman Holidays	$6.95		
Celtic Tree Magic	$7.95		
Love Charms	$6.95		
Love Feasts	$6.95		
Magic Charms from A to Z	$12.95		
Magical Creatures	$12.95		
Magic Spells and Incantations	$12.95		
Moon Lore	$7.95		

Random Recollections II, III or IV (circle your choices)	$3.95		
The Rede of the Wiccae – Hardcover	$49.95		
The Rede of the Wiccae – Softcover	$22.95		
Keepers of the Flame	$20.95		
Subtotal			
Tax *(7% sales tax for RI customers)*			
Shipping & Handling *(See shipping rates section)*			
TOTAL			

BRACELETS

Item	Price	QTY.	Total
Agate, Green	$5.95		
Agate, Moss	$5.95		
Agate, Natural	$5.95		
Agate, Red	$5.95		
Jade, White	$5.95		
Jasper, Picture	$5.95		
Jasper, Red	$5.95		
Onyx, Black	$5.95		
Quartz Crystal	$5.95		
Sodalite	$5.95		
Unakite	$5.95		
Subtotal			
Tax (7% for RI Customers)			
Shipping and Handling			
Total			

MISCELLANY

Item	Price	QTY.	Total
Pouch	$3.95		
Matches: 10 small individual boxes	$5.00		
Matches: 1 large box 50 individual boxes	$20.00		

MISCELLANY
Continued

Item	Price	QTY.	Size	Total
Natural/Black Book Bag	$17.95			
Red/Black Book Bag	$17.95			
Hooded Sweatshirt, Blk	$30.00			
Hooded Sweatshirt, Red	$30.00			
L-Sleeve T, Black	$15.00			
L-Sleeve T, Red	$15.00			
S-Sleeve T, Black/W	$15.00			
S-Sleeve T, Black/R	$15.00			
S-Sleeve T, Dk H/R	$15.00			
S-Sleeve T, Dk H/W	$15.00			
S-Sleeve T, Red/B	$15.00			
S-Sleeve T, Ash/R	$15.00			
S-Sleeve T, Purple/W	$15.00			
Postcards – set of 12	$3.00			
Bookmarks – set of 12	$12.00			
Magnets – set of 3	$1.50			
Promo Pack	$7.00			
Subtotal				
Tax (7% for RI Customers)				
Shipping and Handling				
Total				

SHIPPING & HANDLING CHARGES

BOOKS: One book, add $5.95. Each additional book add $1.50.

POUCH: One pouch, $3.95. Each additional pouch add $1.50.

MATCHES: Ten individual boxes, add $3.95.
One large box of fifty, add $6.00.

BOOKBAGS: $5.95 per bookbag. **BRACELETS:** $3.95 per bracelet.

Send a check or money order payable in U. S. funds or credit card details to:

The Witches' Almanac, Ltd., PO Box 1292, Newport, RI 02840-9998

(401) 847-3388 (phone) • (888) 897-3388 (fax)
Email: info@TheWitchesAlmanac.com • www.TheWitchesAlmanac.com